All I Want Is Everything

Also by Daaimah S. Poole

A RICH MAN'S BABY

DIAMOND PLAYGIRLS

EX-GIRL TO THE NEXT GIRL

GOT A MAN

WHAT'S REAL

YO YO LOVE

Published by Dafina Books

All I Want Is Everything

Daaimah S. Poole

KENSINGTON PUBLISHING CORP.
http://www.kensingtonbooks.com

DAFINA BOOKS are published by

Kensington Publishing Corp.
119 West 40th St.
New York, NY 10018

ISBN-13: 978-0-7582-2061-5
ISBN-10: 0-7582-2061-8

First trade paperback printing: September 2007
First mass market printing: August 2009

10 9 8 7 6 5 4 3 2

Printed in the United States of America

ACKNOWLEDGMENTS

Thank you, Allah, for making this and all things possible for me.

Thank you first and foremost to my readers. Thanks for telling your friends and family about my work. I appreciate your e-mails and comments. Special thanks to my readers in Philly, New Jersey, Washington, D.C., Maryland, and New York City.

Many thanks to my boys Hamid and Ahsan Poole for putting up with me always being on the computer. My mother Robin Dandridge and father Auzzie Poole for your love and encouragement. Thanks to all my aunts, uncles, cousins, friends, and stepmother Pulcheria Ricks-Poole for being so supportive.

Karen Thomas, thanks for believing in me. Camille Miller: without you showing "Yo Yo Love" to your mom, where would I be? Tamika Wilson: thanks for every Saturday for months, taking it to the streets with me. Brother Nati and Andy of African World and Book distributors. I thank you guys so much for being there for me. To my author friends: thanks, Shawna Grundy and Miasha. Candice "We Gonna Make It" Dow—thanks for your support and always giving good advice.

My agents, Karen E. Quinones Miller and Liza Dawson: thanks, ladies, for making such a great team.

And many thanks to everyone at Kensington Publishing: Walter Zacharius, Audrey LaFehr, and Jessica McLean.

Thanks again for everyone who has been supportive of my books. I appreciate it so very much. Stay in touch! *www.dspbooks.com*, *Daaimah14@aol.com*, or *www.myspace.com/Dspbooks*

Thanks for the love,
Daaimah

Chapter 1

"Since I could talk I could always remember singing along with my mom's Sade or Anita Baker albums. All I've ever wanted is to be a famous singer. I want the platinum plaques, the adoring fans, the Grammys, the chauffeur-driven limos, the stylist, the world tours. And I want the house, the man, and the life—I want it all. All I want is everything, and somehow, someway I'm going to try to make it!"
Kendra Michelle Thomas

June 2004

As I wiped down the redwood bar, my only thought was that I couldn't wait to go home. It had been a long night of serving drinks and I was ready to go halfway through my shift. The television was tuned to the evening news with the volume down since no one was paying it any attention. I walked past two rows of assorted liquor lining the mirrored wall—everything from big bottles of Absolut, Grand Marnier, Stoli and Alize to a small sixteen-ounce carton of orange juice. There were two video machines at the end of the bar. Three women sat down in front of me. I placed white paper napkins in front of them. One was tall, had big eyes and hair in a ponytail flipped at the end; the other was like 4'11", petite with small features and a short, spiked haircut with blond and brown highlights. The last girl looked like the first two had dragged her out of the house. There were bags under her eyes, her body looked malnourished and her hair was limp, with a headband pushing it back.

"Ladies, what you havin'?" I asked.

"Can I get an apple martini with Grey Goose?" the petite one asked. The second one ordered a Bahama Mama and the other one asked for a glass of merlot.

"Kendra, how you doing?" the ponytail lady asked.

"Okay," I said. I didn't have any idea who she was. I squinted a little, trying to remember.

So she said, "You don't remember me? We went to high school together." She detected I was still having trouble remembering who she was.

"I'm Inez! And do you remember Belinda and Tiffany?"

Belinda looked familiar, just a little older, and Tiffany—I didn't remember her at all. When I looked at Inez again, she did start looking familiar. "We was in home room together. Do you still be with Chantel?"

"No I haven't seen her in years."

"How is your family?"

"My family is doing good."

"That's good to hear," she said as she continued her conversation with her friends. I served them their drinks and then finished straightening up. The group of women flagged me down again and said, "Kendra, can we get another round?"

I made them another round and brought them their

drinks. Inez said, "Thank you," and pulled out her American Express card.

"Y'all running a tab?" I asked.

"Yeah, we can start a tab. Wow, I can't believe we ran into you. You still look the same—all slim. So what are you doing with yourself?"

"Nothing much."

"Well, we're out celebrating. We all had some big things happen. Miss Honey right there got engaged last weekend, and my husband and I just settled on our house in Durham, North Carolina. You want to see a picture?" she asked as she pulled pictures out of her bag. I glanced at the house. It was a big single-family home with lots of windows and a huge lawn.

"That's a nice house," I said. Then she pointed to the other woman and said, "She just graduated from Rutgers' nursing program. That's why she looks all tired. So, yup, I have my house, my husband, and two lovely children. Are you married? Do you have any kids? So what else do you do besides this?" she asked, ambushing me with questions.

"No, actually, I just do this. I'm still with the same guy since high school. No kids, though."

She looked somewhat confused.

"Well, I'm sure you'll get married soon and kids will come. Are you still in school?"

"No, I'm not in school."

She looked at me like she was thinking, and it seemed she was about to ask me something else, but then she changed her mind.

"Do you have an ashtray?" Ms. Tired asked all sluggish.

I gave her one and then I looked at them like "anything else?"

One of my regulars, Lisa, was at the end of the bar

dancing by herself next to the jukebox wearing her Miss Piggy blond wig. She was older, about fifty-five, in shape and was good for trying to hook up with young guys. Another regular named Stacey was at the opposite end of the bar running game. She brought a different man into the bar every weekend. She would get them nice and drunk and be all up in their pockets. She would wink at me and make her latest victim tip me well. When you don't drink you get to see everything. I could sit behind the bar and observe all the action. Men like drinks that are going to take them there immediately, women want to get their buzz one sip at a time. Women get extra giggly when they've been drinking. They will come in classy and cute and leave sloppily drunk.

I still do feel hypocritical at times, because even though I don't drink I still pour the drinks. But it pays the bills—so what the fuck? Just as I turned the channel on the television, a couple walked up to the counter. The woman had big auburn braids going up into a crown, forming a bush at the end. She looked like she should be in a music video waving incense and holding candles. Her guy was the opposite: tall, baldheaded, and mean. Opposites must attract.

"Can I get a shot of Patrón?" a man said. If I didn't know the customer I would always ask the woman what she wanted first and would make sure to place the drinks in front of her. I learned early, a sure way not to get tipped is by flirting with somebody's man, but he ordered first. I started making his drink and then asked his lady, "What are you having?"

She looked me up and down and said, "Give me a minute."

"Kendra, can you make me a Crimson Tide, a Hurricane, a Sex on the Beach, and a Long Island Iced Tea?" Tia asked as she tried to organize all her loose dollars in her black apron.

"A Crimson Tide. I never heard of that. I'll have to look that up. And, Tia, you gonna have to ring your drinks up. I don't want to hear Julius's mouth." I said I wasn't getting yelled at for her.

She walked over to the computer and began typing in her drinks.

"It's not enough liquor in this daiquiri," a woman yelled from the other end of the bar. I told her I would be right there. I poured the man his shot and asked his lady if she was ready yet. She shook her head no. I went to the end of the bar, dumped the daiquiri, and made a fresh one. I don't know why it took her half the drink to realize that there wasn't enough alcohol.

"And, baby, can you make it a little sweeter?" she asked as she winked at me.

I added more strawberries and cherry grenadine mix, doubled the alcohol, reblended it, and poured it in her glass. She sipped it once again and gave me the thumbs-up. Everybody was waited on, so I decided to start cleaning up for the evening. My manager, Julius, came out from the back to see how we were making out for the night. He pulled up his droopy pants and scratched his balding brown dome. The couple left and I started washing the dishes by dipping the glasses in the blue disinfectant. The trio of women flagged me over to them again.

"Another round please, girl? These drinks are good. Keep them coming," she said. They were laughing and joking, and being very loud. Then one turned to me and said, "Kendra remember you was voted most likely to succeed?"

"Yes, I remember."

"So Kendra, what happened?" asked Belinda, the ponytail-wearing woman, a little perplexed.

"What happened to what?" I asked with an attitude.

"You know, like with your life. You are supposed to be

famous. What are you doing bartending? You suppose to be somewhere singing, being rich by now. You was like going to be like the next Mariah Carey."

Her friend stood up and tried to shhh her. "She is drunk. Don't mind her. Damn, two drinks and you trippin'. Shut up, Belinda," Inez said. I acted like I didn't hear what she said and ignored her.

"No, this shit ain't funny," the woman slurred.

"You drunk. Shut up, dumbass," Inez said to her friend.

"You shut up, Inez. I'm not drunk. I know what I'm talking about. I know how much I had to drink," she said as she stopped talking to her and turned her attention back to me.

"Kendra, I am so sad and sorry to see you here. I mean, I can't believe you wasted your voice and all your talent. Like, you was a real good singer, Kendra. I remember you singing at school. You used to sound like Mariah Carey. Like an angel for real. What happened, for real? I'm not being funny. I mean, this is all you did with your life?" she asked again. This time I couldn't even act like I didn't understand or hear what she was talking about.

"Let's go. Your ass is drunk," Inez screamed at her friend as she pulled her away from the bar. The tired girl just shook her head, like she was thinking the same thing.

"Inez, get off of me. Why are you fronting when you just said the same thing when she walked away? I did not. Let's go!"

"I'm not done yet."

"Yes, you are."

"No, I didn't! Get your stuff," she said as she looked to me to see if I believed she was talking about me too!

They went back and forth among each other as I walked away to the other end of the bar. I could still hear them talking—their voices were traveling across the bar.

"Tell your girl to shut up," Inez told the tired one. "Carry your girlfriend out. She always ruining shit."

"I told you to leave her home." Inez helped pull the tall drunk girl out the bar door. As soon as they left I went and removed their glasses.

They tipped me twenty dollars. Any other night I would have been glad someone was being generous, but tonight it felt like they pitied me and thought I needed the extra cash. *Fuck them,* I thought. I was called away again by There's-Not-Enough-Liquor-in-My-Daiquiri. She had found some old granddaddy to sponsor her and her friend's drinks. The old man peeled money out of his wallet, one twenty at a time, and they began ordering.

The rest of the evening was okay. Finally the last customer walked out of the restaurant. I locked the door and counted my register, then my tips. I had made one-fifty for the night—that wasn't bad. I wiped down the counter and turned off the television. I mopped the floor and put each stool on top of the counter. I said goodbye to Julius and the other waitresses. The entire way home I kept thinking about the comment from that girl from high school at every red light. It kept echoing in my head. I don't even remember her name and probably won't see her again, but she just don't know she fucked up my whole night. I thought I had my life together, but not like theirs. Damn, they the same age as me. They only twenty-five. How do they have their shit together already? How are they so on point? God damn. Especially Ms. Two-Kids-Great-Husband-and-Big-House. I bet that other one can get any man she wants, and she is a nurse. I bet she has a big house or condo and just is living the life too! How did my life get so fucked up? How did I end up in this dead-end-ass job? And how did she remember my dreams when I'd forgotten them? I've always wanted to sing. I've been singing since I could remember, and now I don't sing at all.

November 1997

"Sing it, girl, sing it! Like you have some feeling!" I heard my friend Chantel's squeaky voice shout from the first row of the empty school auditorium.

"I believe I can fly, I believe I can touch the sky. Think about it every night and day, spread my wings and fly away. I believe I can soar, I see me running through that open door. I believe I can fly, I believe I can fly, I believe I can fly." I tried to sing, even though I was hoarse from practicing every day. Everyone was listening intently, until a tall, lanky, pimple-faced boy named Terrance walked up to the stage and I heard him say something smart like, "Next."

I stopped singing and said, "What did you say, Terrance?"

"I said 'next.' Get your non-singing ass off the stage."

"Make me get the fuck off the stage," I said as I looked around to see if Mrs. Drake, the music teacher, was anywhere in sight.

"Yo, don't be mad at me 'cause you can't sing and your chest is flat."

"Your mom, bitch," I snapped back.

"You calling my mom a bitch?" He jumped on the stage and acted like he was going to fight me. A few other students intervened and separated us. I was not scared at all. I wish he would have hit me. Other boys were coming up to him saying, "You don't fight girls, man." He was still saying stuff and trying to get to me like a little girl.

"Let 'em go, because the minute he touches me I'm going to bring my brother up here to knock him out."

"Yeah, whatever Dracula. You just need to get that fang fixed and shut up," he said.

"Make me shut up." I jumped in front of everyone and put my finger up to his temple.

"You lucky you a girl," he said, backing away from me.

"No, you lucky," I said as I walked away from his dumb ass. "That's why I hate immature-ass high school boys." I stomped down the stage steps. Chantel met me at the bottom of the steps and said, "Don't worry about him." She was a petite girl with big uncombed curls in her hair and dark chocolate skin. She was very stylish and coordinated, and everything she wore was a designer name.

"Trust me, I'm not," I said, calming myself down. I had shut him right up. He was just trying to get me offstage so him and his friends could do a stupid dance routine.

"Girl, you know you can sing. Last year at the talent show when you hit that high note, people were crying. I saw it with my own eyes. One day you are going to be rich and famous and he's going to be trying to get an autograph."

"You think so?" I laughed as I grabbed my bag off the chair and walked toward the door.

"Definitely. And when you make it big, just don't forget about me."

"I won't forget about you. I'll let you be my backup singer." I laughed.

We walked down the hall to our lockers. I was so excited that our school talent show was coming up—and ours was not an ordinary talent show. It was a big deal. Everybody from all these other schools and people who already graduated would come to see it. People would always come up to me and say, "What you going to sing for the talent show?" or "Let me hear you sing." I had been practicing every single day. I was a senior so it was my last year, and I had to go out with a bang. I was singing R. Kelly's song "I Believe" because it was powerful and I knew I could do it justice. I wanted to sing a song that was in my range. That's how people mess up, singing songs that are too strong for their voices. My music teacher said you always have to make a song your own, and I planned to do just that.

"Walk me to the bathroom," I said to Chantel.

We walked into the bathroom to check my hair. It was black with a part in the middle. My skin was cocoa-brown, I was 5'7", and super slim. My black hair stopped at my jawline. I really think I'm way too skinny. People think being skinny is the best thing. Being skinny is not cool. I don't have any breasts and I've been called everything from Itty-bitty Committee to Piper, but I know I look good, so it doesn't even matter.

"Well, I have to get to work. I'll see you tomorrow," I said as I gathered my belongings and walked out of the bathroom.

"You need a ride?" Chantel asked as we walked through the steel-green double doors and out of the building.

"You driving?" I asked, surprised.

"Yeah, my mom bought me a car," she said, smiling.

"That is so nice. I'm getting a car too!"

"When?" she asked like she didn't believe me.

"Probably in like two months. I have been saving my money and my brother is going to take me to get my license."

"How much you have saved?"

"A couple hundred," I said.

"I don't think you can buy a car for a couple hundred," she said like she knew everything.

"You can. My brother John got his car for cheap. He knows all the places to go. He knows about all that type of stuff."

"Oh, okay," she said, twisting her lips to the side as if she still didn't believe me. I really did have four hundred saved for my car.

Chantel was the kind of person who wanted to be the only one who had. She liked to be the center of attention.

I only hung out with her at school because she is so sometimey. We'd been cool since ninth-grade homeroom. We walked up to her four-door Chevy Celebrity. It was black with burgundy interior. It was nice. She had a peach air freshener hanging from the mirror and red and black dice. I liked it but I didn't let her know. When she asked, I said it was okay. Chantel dropped me off in front of my job. I thanked her and walked into Newman Pharmacy. Instantly, I was depressed. I had been working there for three months and hated every moment of it. It was a family-owned pharmacy. I had the most boring job ever. Our school was in this mentoring program that partnered with businesses in the city. I wanted to work at a radio station, a dance studio, or even a law office. Something fun or interesting. But instead they put me here in a boring-ass pharmacy where the bell rings every time someone enters and old men complain about losing their prescription cards. I help grannies buy Ensure and find the cheapest diapers for new moms. Price-checking deodorant and soap powder is my specialty.

Like I said, it was boring except for every now and then I saw someone from my school. I seen this girl, Carla, from my school buying a pregnancy test. And another time this boy named Simon, who ran track at my school, bought some crab medicine. When he saw me he looked down at the box and said his sister had head lice. I knew he was lying.

The only other good thing about this job is we got three credits for a work roster, so I got out of school at one-thirty. Plus I got paid and had access to all the good magazines. I loved to look through the pages of all the glossy ones. I liked the rap magazines—they told me what was cool—and the *National Enquirer* tabloid types, they were funny—two-headed babies and aliens. I imagined myself one day being on the cover of a hip-hop magazine and being rich and famous.

* * *

Mr. Newman would come out from the back every once in a while and have me call people to tell them their prescriptions were ready. He was about seventy-two with a shaky hand and voice. He was always complaining that big pharmacies were stealing his customers and putting him out of business. I would act like I was listening, but really I wasn't.

After I got off work I caught the 17 bus to City Hall then the 13 trolley home. It was cold outside and the trolley let me off four long blocks from my house. In my neighborhood, people were still outside walking around, standing on the corner in front of the Chinese takeout at seven at night. It had snowed the other day and the snow had turned to ice. I was trying not to slip while walking in the street.

I lived with my mother, two brothers, and two sisters. My sister Alanna was eighteen—we are exactly ten months apart. I'm seventeen and she is eighteen. Her birthday is in February and mine is in December. My brother John is twenty, and my baby sister—her name is Amira, but we call her Bubbles—is ten. My baby brother, Bilal, is nine. My parents divorced about five years ago. My dad keeps in contact, but not that much since he remarried and had another son. We don't even consider that little boy, Jonathan, our brother; at least I don't. The lady, Charlotte, already had three kids and she had a fourth by my dad.

We lived in a big two-story, four-bedroom row home in southwest Philly. My mom had her own room, me and Alanna shared a room, and Bubbles and Bilal shared a room. John got his own because he was the oldest. He was never home; he always stayed with his friend Marcus.

I walked down the street toward my house. I saw all the lights on in my house. I knew my mom was going to go off; she must not be home. Most nights I beat her home. She usually made a stop at the Pearl Lounge on Woodland Avenue and had a drink after work. She always used to drink a beer or two, but when my dad left she started drinking more. I unlocked the door and walked into the house. The warmth greeted me at the door. It was nice and cozy. I rubbed my hands together, took off my coat, and hung it up in the closet. Bubbles's and Bilal's book bags and schoolwork were scattered everywhere.

"It is warm in here. What do you have this heat on?" I asked. Instead of waiting for an answer, I went to check the thermostat. It was up to ninety.

Bubbles came out of the kitchen with a wet stain on her shirt and said, "I thought you were Mommy."

"Bubbles, why y'all got this heat up this high?" I asked.

"It was real cold when we came home from school." Bubbles was short and chunky. She was already in women's size-six pants. She had a little gut, and her breasts were coming in.

"Next time just turn it to seventy. It is baking in here. What are you doing?" I asked as I followed her into the kitchen. I looked around. I smelled food but didn't see any.

"We was hungry. So I was making us something to eat," she said as she tried to clean up the mess she had made. There were crumbles of Oodles of Noodles, water, and frozen hot dogs in a bowl in the microwave. Bilal was sitting at the table there with an empty bowl in front of him, waiting to eat.

"I put it in the microwave like Lana told us. But it's not cooking right."

"You know you not allowed to cook when no one is here."

"I know. Lana is here."

"Where is Alanna?"

"Upstairs," Bilal said.

"Lana here and she wouldn't cook y'all anything?" I asked in disbelief.

"Yeah, she said she tired and have to study for a test," Bilal said.

"Clean up this mess y'all made. Y'all know Mommy's going to go off if she see this. I'll cook y'all something." I reached under the cabinet and grabbed a deep medium-size silver pot. I rinsed it out and then filled it with water. I let the water boil a little and added the pack of noodles and hot dogs. I told them to watch the pot as I ran up the steps to figure out why my sister couldn't feed her brother and sister. I walked down the hall and pushed the door open. I looked in the room and there was prissy-ass Alanna with her hair pushed back with a yellow headband and wearing a yellow sweater. She was sitting on a pink comforter. Her shoes were off and her legs were crossed Indian style. She was talking on the phone while eating a Burger King Whopper. She looked at me as I entered the room, rolled her eyes, and continued with her conversation. I hated sharing a room with Alanna.

"When did you get this food?" I asked, standing over her. She took another bite of her sandwich and ignored me until I asked her again. She looked up at me and told whoever she was talking to that she was going to call them back.

"I bought it before I came in the house," she said as she dipped a fry in ketchup off her plate.

"Really? You bought food and my little brother and sister downstairs are hungry?"

"I told Bubbles to make noodles. I have to study. They ain't my kids."

"You couldn't make them anything to eat?" I asked.

"I didn't feel like it. Mommy should have left them something to eat."

"Oh, really? If you can't make sure they eat, you not going to eat either, bitch," I said as I smacked her burger out of her hand. The salt packets and ketchup splattered on her sweater. She jumped up and tried to swing on me, but I grabbed her by her hair and began punching her in her face. She pulled on my hair and began biting me on my chest. She was trying to scratch and punch me back.

"You fucking bitch, get off me," I yelled.

"No, you get off me," she shouted back.

"No, you get off me," I said as I punched her one good time in the mouth. The kids ran up the steps.

"I think the noodles are ready," Bubbles said.

"Why y'all fighting?" Bilal asked as he turned his head to the side to see who was winning.

She finally let me go. So I let her go.

"Stupid bitch," I murmured.

"Your mother," she said.

"Yours too!" I said as I went downstairs to feed the kids. I started straightening up the living room, and a few minutes later my brother John came in the house. He usually just came past to check his mail. He had moved in with Marcus when my mom said his girlfriend, Nitra, couldn't spend the night.

"Where you been at? I tried to call you at Marcus's house. You never there," I said.

"I be between Nitra's and Marcus's. Nitra's mom don't really want me staying there, but Nitra don't like it too much at Marcus's. We trying to save up for our own place. Where Mommy at?" he asked.

"She didn't get in here yet?" Alanna came from upstairs and walked out the door, slamming it behind her.

"What's wrong with her?"

"Nothing. We was just fighting 'cause she was sittin' up there eating and didn't feed the kids."

"Y'all need to grow up."

"Whatever. She started with me."

"Man, y'all got to cut that dumb mess out."

Bilal ran down the steps and screamed, "John!"

They started play boxing.

"Can I have your room since you're never here?" Bilal asked.

"No, you can't have my room. Man, where I'm going to sleep?"

"What about your PlayStation?"

"You can play with it, but you got to make sure you take care of it. Okay, man," John said as he flipped him upside down and knuckled him in the head. Bilal laughed and kept trying to fight him. He was punching him and kicking. Then he started coughing real hard and gasping for air.

"You know you can't play too rough with him," I said. "Bubbles, go get his asthma medicine." She ran up the steps, then came back down with his inhaler. We sat him down and I pumped once.

"You need to calm down," I scolded him. "John, you shouldn't have got him all worked up." As soon as I said that, Bilal jumped back up and punched John real hard in the stomach.

John bowed over and said, "All right, you won, Bilal. You got me. I'm leaving. I'm out of here," he said playfully.

"Okay, see you," I said as he walked toward the door.

"Tell Mommy to call me."

"I will."

Bubbles and Bilal ate and cleaned the table off. I did the dishes and then began doing my math homework. Math was my worst subject. Most days I would look the answers up in the back of the book and copy off somebody else's before class. I got Cs, and I called them good enoughs. Instead of doing my schoolwork, I wrote songs in class. I didn't need school. All I needed to know was how to add, subtract, and read—so I could read my contracts and count my money when I become a big famous singer. My name was going to be in big, bright lights—KENDRA LIVE IN CONCERT—and it's going to be a banner that goes across that reads SOLD OUT. People are going to be singing along with me to my songs, and I'm going to be on the Grammys accepting my awards. One day that's going to be me. I fell asleep on the sofa with my math book on my lap. My mother came in the house around 1 a.m. smelling like someone had poured a case of beer on her. I guess she was drinking like this to get over my dad, but it didn't seem to be working. When I was about thirteen, my dad just didn't come home, and by the third day my mom sat us all down and said me and your dad are getting a divorce and he is moving out. I could tell then that it wasn't my mother's decision, even though she said it was mutual. He moved in with his sister, Joanie, after he left us. He would come and get Bubbles and Bilal sometimes to take them out. Then he met Charlotte, some young bitch at his job with three kids. My mother said she was a fat, racoon-eye, old-lookin', yellow young girl. From the day he moved in with her he disowned us. My Aunt Joanie started calling and telling my mom what he was doing for his new woman. She was trying to warn my mom, so my mom would never go back to him, but instead she made matters worse and my mom more depressed. So things ain't never been the same. My mom doesn't have any family in Philly. Her family is from Arkansas; she never talks about them. All she told us was that she left home at eighteen, met and married my dad, and never looked back. We try to tell my mom to date, because she still looks good. She is thin and has beautiful mocha brown skin, and she wears her thick chin-length hair in a wrap. But she only meets people who hang out at her spot, the Pearl Lounge, and all the men there are drunk bums.

"What you still doing up?" she asked as she took her coat off.

"I wasn't. I had fell asleep doing my homework," I said.

"The kids ate?"

"Yes."

"Did they do their homework?"

"Yeah, and I had to beat up your daughter this evening," I said as I sat up momentarily.

"What she do?"

"Running her mouth and not feeding your kids."

"I told y'all about fighting. Where she at now?"

"Bruce picked her up."

"I told her she couldn't stay out with him on a school night. I'll talk to her tomorrow," she said as she started going up the steps.

Lana's boyfriend, Bruce, was too old for her. He was twenty-six and in the army. My mom told him to leave her alone or she was going to make trouble for him at his job, but that hadn't stopped him, because Lana was eighteen and legally could date whomever she wanted.

"Night, Mom."

"You staying down here?" she asked.

"No. I'll be up in a little bit. I'm going to finish my homework." I tried a few more problems. I finally gave up. Math was dumb and I was tired.

It was morning by the time a loud knock startled me out of my sleep. I jumped up off the sofa and looked around to see where the noise was coming from. I finally realized it was the door. It probably was Lana; she always forgot her key. *I shouldn't let her in,* I thought. Lucky her, it was time to get up anyway. I peeked out the curtains to make sure it was her and I saw a man with a blue collared shirt and navy blue work pants and hat. He had a work badge hanging around his neck with a big PGW on the front of it. "Yes, can I help you?" I said.

"Are your parents home?"

"Who wants them?" I asked.

"Tell them the Philadelphia Gas Works."

"One moment," I said as I flashed my index finger up and ran upstairs to get my mom. She was stretched out across the bed with her uniform still on from the night before.

"Mom! Mom! Mom, wake up. The gas company is at the door." She shot up and ran downstairs. I followed her. She opened the door while I stood behind her.

"Can I help you?" she asked, trying to act calm.

"Yes, Miss, we're about to dig up the street and shut services off at this address."

"What's going on? Why? I don't understand," she said.

"Miss, we are about to turn your gas off for nonpayment."

"No, there has been a mistake. I paid my bill," she said.

"No mistake, Miss. Here is a copy of the bill. I was going to give you a few minutes if you need to take a shower or do anything before we shut it off."

"No, you can't do this. I have children—it is the middle of the winter," my mom yelled as she read the yellow paper the man had handed her. The man walked away toward a big white truck.

"Please don't do this. I have children. Please! Who's your supervisor? Let me call them," she said as she tried to catch up with him. I saw my neighbor across the street, Ms. Arlene, standing in her door and looking at my mom. She was holding her robe together and had a scarf on her head. She came across the street and asked, "Joanne, is everything okay?"

"Yeah, I'm fine. These people just made a mistake," my mom said, embarrassed.

Ms. Arlene worked at the state representative office. She was the lady everybody in the neighborhood went to if they had an issue.

"Just let me know if you need any help. I might can make some phone calls for you," she said. Ms. Arlene walked over and talked to the man. She came back and said, "He gave me his supervisor's number. Let's call him and see what we can do."

Ms. Arlene came in and coached my mom on what to say to the man's supervisor.

I ran up the steps and awoke Bilal. "Get in the shower. Take a five-minute shower."

I got Bubbles up and she got in just as Bilal jumped out. I could hear my mom on the phone downstairs arguing with the supervisor. Then I heard Ms. Arlene get on the telephone and try to reason with the supervisor. As soon as Bubbles came out, I jumped in. Right in the middle of my warm shower the water turned cold. I rinsed off and came out of the shower. I dried off and began getting dressed. I already figured I would probably have to give my car money to my mom. I put my clothes on and went downstairs. "So what they say?" I asked.

"They said I owe them three thousand dollars and I need to give them at least a third of it to get the service back on. I'm just not going to go to work today. I'll get this mess straightened out. Don't worry," she said.

"Mom, I have four hundred dollars—it's my car money—if you need it," I reluctantly said.

"I probably won't need it, but I'll take it just in case. Okay, I'll give it back to you."

Lana walked in the house. "What are those men doing outside?" she asked.

"They turning the gas off," my mother said.

"For what? Mom, you didn't pay the bill?"

I gave her a glance like, "Shut up."

"Mom, why don't you just call Daddy?" Alanna suggested.

"I tried. His wife said he was at work. Don't worry, I'll figure something out. The gas will be back on by the time y'all come home from school. Just get ready for school and get out of here."

Chapter 2

In the morning I washed up with ice-cold water. It was so chilly in my room that when I yawned, I saw my breath. Without gas we couldn't cook or have heat. It had been like this for three days. My mother bought some space heaters with my four hundred dollars, but they weren't doing anything against the thirty-degree cold weather outside. It didn't seem right that they could turn our gas off, but my mom said by law they could turn off the heat before the first day of winter—December 21—and that was thirty days away. I went to sleep with my clothes on and three blankets over me, and I was still cold. I could feel the cold in my bones and I felt like I was getting sick. At school I couldn't concentrate. I just kept wondering why my mom didn't pay our bill in the first place. It seemed like she made enough money at her job. She worked at a retirement home, and we never had this happen before. We had had our cable get turned off a couple of times until she got paid, and once our phone was even off for a week. But I never in my life been cold before. I think this is just as bad as being hungry.

School was the same bunch of dumb classes, but at least it was warm. I couldn't wait until the end of the day, though, so I could go to practice. That was the only thing that made me happy and kept me going, knowing that the talent show was coming up. When I got onstage I didn't care about anyone saying anything about my teeth or saying I was too skinny. When I sing, no one notices any of that. They only pay attention to my voice. The show was in one week and I couldn't wait to be on that stage and be special and get all the attention.

At practice this girl name Jackie said she was singing Toni Braxton's "Unbreak My Heart." She sounded horrible! Her voice didn't suit the song at all. But she had her heart set on that song and said her mom was getting her a dress made. I told her that was nice, but I wasn't going that far. I was just wearing a blue dress that I had since last summer. We stayed in rehearsal until Mr. Smith, the janitor, told me he was locking up. I practiced my notes over and over again. I was going to sing perfectly and get a standing ovation.

After I left school I walked to the corner and waited for the C bus. It was not coming, so I started walking. I got about three blocks down and saw the bus approaching. I was in the middle of the block, so I ran to the next corner. I thought the bus was going to pass me. The bus driver saw me, opened the door, and let me on. I put a token in and walked to the back of the crowded bus. There was nowhere to sit, but two stops later a lady got off and I sat in her seat. I finally was able to relax until my stop. I laid my head against the window, closed my eyes, and prayed that the heat was back on and everything was back to normal.

From the corner of my block I saw my dad John's car. I

opened the door and hoped that he had taken care of everything.

"Hey, Dad, you got the gas back on?" I asked.

"No, your mom gonna handle that. I just bought y'all a few kerosene heaters to keep it warm in here," he said, pouring something into the heaters.

"Oh? Why didn't you just pay the bill?" I asked.

"Kendra, your mother let the gas get cut off. So she is responsible for getting it back on."

I corrected him and said, "Well, if you would have paid your child support she probably could have paid the bill."

"You don't know what I pay or what I do," he said, stopping and looking up at me.

"I do know what you don't do. I know if you wouldn't have left us, our heat would still be on. I know you care more about Charlotte and her kids than you do about us. I know you don't ever come see us. You worried about that stupid woman. She got you brainwashed," I said as I stood over him with my hands on my hips.

"Kendra, your mouth is so damn smart. You going to end up just like your mother—old, miserable, and alone."

"My mother isn't old, miserable, or alone. You know what? You real stupid, taking care of Charlotte's three kids that ain't yours while you got five here that belong to you."

"Don't mind my business. Stay in a child's place," he said under his breath.

I let him know I heard what he said. "I'm not a child. I'm almost grown. I don't know if you remember, but I'll be eighteen in a month," I shouted.

"Well, I'm glad you almost grown. Don't look for anything from me since you so damn grown."

I wanted to tell my dad, fuck you. But I still had a little respect for him, so I flagged him and said, "Whatever!"

Alanna walked in out of the cold. "Daddy," she screamed as she ran and hugged the man who didn't do anything for us. She treated my dad like a king and he loved her treatment.

"Hey, princess," he said as he gave her a kiss. As mean as Alanna was to everyone else, she adored him. There was something wrong with that girl, but then they say the absent parent gets all the love. I walked out of the living room into the kitchen, opened the refrigerator and pulled out some Hawaiian Punch juice, then sat down and started my homework.

After my dad installed and filled the three kerosene heaters, he walked out of the door like he always did. Usually I would start dinner, but with no gas I had to wait until my mother came home, which she did around five-thirty.

"Daddy was here," I said as she walked through the door.

"What he say?" my mother asked.

"Nothing. He left those kerosene heaters. He got smart with me 'cause I told him he should pay you your child support on time."

"Your dad does the best he can. At least this will give me some more time until I'll be able to get the heat on," she said, a little relieved as she checked out the kerosene heaters.

"You going back out, Mom?" I asked.

"Yeah. Here, order two pizzas. If you need me I'll be down at the Pearl," she said as she handed me a twenty.

I ordered the pizza and fed Bubbles and Bilal when they got home from their after-school program. I had to admit it did feel warmer with the kerosene heaters. I didn't have to walk around with blankets over me, but I still hated my dad. The phone rang. It was Chantel.

"What's up?"

"Kendra, I called to tell you that Dajuan likes you!"

"No, he don't."

"Yes, he do. He told me. You got to get with him. You

know he got a car and he having a party Saturday. He told me to tell you to come. You think he cute, right?"

"Yeah, he is cute, but come on. Ain't he like in the eleventh grade?"

"He really belongs in the twelfth grade, and he goes to night school so he can graduate on time."

"He's cute, but I don't like him like that. I don't have time for dumb boys. And don't he go with Andrea?"

"No, they broke up. Think about what you going to wear Saturday, okay?"

"You going to do my hair?" Bubbles asked, interrupting my conversation.

"Wait a minute. When I get off the phone. Go get the comb and grease and tell Bilal to get ready for bed."

I heard her tell Bilal I said to go to bed and I heard him say, "Man, I'm playing the game."

"You heard what I said, Bilal," I screamed up the steps.

"Man, can't I stay up a little longer?" he yelled back.

"No, 'cause you not gonna want to get up in the morning," I said as I got back on the phone.

"Chantel, I have to go. I'll go to the party on Saturday." I hung up the phone and began to part, grease, and braid Bubble's hair in five cornrows going back. Then I went upstairs to relax and get ready for bed. I put my Walkman on my head and began to sing along with my Mary J. Blige tape. I'd loved her ever since she came out with "Real Love." She was so good, and her voice and lyrics were so deep. I pulled out my song book and began writing. I wrote in my book every time I had a thought. I kept it to the side of my bed. My thoughts were rudely interrupted by Alanna. "Why you always got to be singing? Why don't you shut up sometimes?" she said as she came into our bedroom. I tried to pay her no attention. She was in the room planning her wardrobe for the week like the snob she was.

"Kendra, did you wear my pink and purple striped shirt?"

"No."

"Yes, you did. How come I can't find it?"

"Leave me alone. I don't feel like it," I said as I took my clothes off and got in my bed. I was trying to play it cool because I had worn her shirt and forgotten to wash it and put it back. I hoped me telling her I didn't was convincing enough. I turned my Walkman up higher and closed my eyes.

"I know you wore my shirt. Next time just ask me. I know you want to be like me," she said as she pulled my headphones off of one ear. I put my middle finger up at her and she got in her bed. I heard her call Bruce and say how she loved him so much. She made a kissing noise, then turned the light off and went to sleep. She was so boy crazy.

I liked boys, but they weren't my world. My mom sat me and Lana down when we were twelve and said boys just want one thing and that's a hot and tight place to put their dicks. That was the nastiest thing I'd ever heard, and she turned me off from sex. That same speech ain't do nothing for Lana 'cause I know she giving it up. My sister probably would be pregnant by next summer—at least that's what my mother said, and I agreed. I tried sex twice. Once with this boy named Mookie two years before—I didn't like it— and another time with Dontae at summer school. Everybody I knew was doing it and they liked it. Chantel told me it feels real good, but I don't like no one like that and I don't want to get pregnant and have a bunch of kids. *If my sister gets pregnant maybe I can get my own room,* I thought as I rolled over in my bed and went to sleep.

* * *

The pain in my side let me know that my bladder could not wait until the morning to go to the bathroom. Instead of getting up and going, I yawned and tried to lie on my other side. I didn't feel like walking all the way down the hall to the bathroom. I turned to my side, brought my legs closer to my chest and tried to hold it in and go back to sleep. I still had my Walkman on, and there was a loud commercial on, so I turned it off and placed it to the side of my bed. Then I noticed there was a bright light flickering under the door. I squinted to see exactly what it was. I coughed a little and then sat up. There was a burning smell in the room. I tried to make sense of what I was seeing and smelling. I went up to my door and touched it. It was very hot. I ran over to Lana's bed and screamed, "Lana, get up." I shook her arm and body repeatedly.

"What?" she said as she snatched her arm back and turned to her other side.

"Lana, get up and call 911. I think the house is on fire!"

"What? Leave me alone. Stop playing. I'm asleep."

"Lana!" I screamed again. I opened the door and saw dark yellow and orange flames halfway up the steps. There was black smoke everywhere, but the fire hadn't reached the hallway yet. I closed the door and screamed, "Wake the fuck up, Alanna! It's a fire. Call 911." I snatched her out of the bed. She finally saw how serious I was and got up and searched for the cordless phone.

"It's not working. We going to die," she yelled.

"Be quiet. We not going to die. Yell 'fire' out the window and see if anyone is outside. I have to get the kids."

Me and Alanna were in the front room. I ran into the middle room to check if my mom was home, but her bed was empty. I ran past the steps where the fire was rising rapidly. It was coming up the steps. I could feel the heat on my back and neck. Lana came into the hallway and said the neighbors were calling the police. She then went into the bathroom and grabbed a bucket and threw water down the steps. That made the fire get higher and rise faster up the steps. I ran into the room next to my mother's bedroom. Bubbles was still lying in the bed asleep.

"Bubbles, get up! It's a fire!" I looked all around but didn't see Bilal. "Where is Bilal?"

"I don't know."

I coaxed her past the flames and had Alanna take her into the front room.

"Where you going?" Lana asked.

"I have to find Bilal!" I hoped he wasn't downstairs.

The fire was getting closer to the top of the steps. I was coughing, but I put my T-shirt over my mouth and kept walking toward the back room. There was dark smoke everywhere and I could barely see my own hand in front of me. I extended my arms out to make sure I didn't bump into anything. I reached John's room and found Bilal balled up in John's bed. He had fallen asleep playing the game.

I tried to pick him up, but I was becoming weak and coughing. I almost couldn't breathe. I felt myself losing strength. I couldn't leave him but he felt so heavy. I pulled him out of the bed and began dragging him across the floor. That's when I heard glass break. A few seconds later I saw a figure in a yellow suit coming toward me. He picked me up and pulled me off of Bilal.

I kicked and screamed, "My brother!" I fought him and yelled, "My brother! My brother! My brother! You've got to get my brother!" I continued to yell until I almost passed out.

The man carried me past the flames into the front room and passed me out the window to another firefighter. I unwillingly went down the ladder. All our neighbors were outside looking up. Three fire trucks and two ambulances were there. I could hear the firefighters' radios and their trucks idling. They sat me on a stretcher and put an oxygen mask on my face inside the ambulance. As soon as they sat me down on the stretcher I told them to get off of me and that I had to get my brother.

"Get my brother! Get my brother!" I yelled. They told me to calm down, but I couldn't calm down. I jumped off the stretcher. I ran out and saw Alanna. She was holding Bubbles next to her, and they were looking up at the window. My next-door neighbor, Ms. Arlene, came over to me and said the other firefighters were still in there. I looked up and saw another man coming down the ladder with Bilal. He was carrying him over his shoulders like a rag doll.

"Is he okay?" Ms. Arlene yelled.

The fire fighters pushed everyone out of the way, put him in the ambulance and pulled away. Then they grabbed me, Alanna and Bubbles and asked us if anyone else was in the house. Then they put us in the other ambulance. They said they had to check us out at the hospital. We didn't say anything the entire ride. I think we all were too scared to ask if Bilal was still alive. We would find out in a few minutes when we got to the hospital.

At the hospital they tried to treat me, but I still wanted to know what was going on with Bilal. A nice nurse told us he was alive but unconscious. Lana found out what room he was in, so we asked the same nurse if we could see him. She acted like she didn't hear us but opened the door on the sly. We walked into his room and saw that they had him hooked up to all these machines. Tubes were going up his nose, but at least he was alive. Alanna and Bubbles starting crying. I just wanted to know if he was going to make it and what was wrong with him.

Chapter 3

My mom showed up at the hospital about half an hour after we had arrived. She was crying hysterically and smelled like alcohol. I was so mad at her—she was actually slurring when she spoke. We were just fighting for our lives and she was somewhere having a drink. She tried to fix herself up, though it was so obvious that she was out of it. But we all got up and hugged her, and then we started crying. She walked down the hall with all of us attached to her.

"Where is your brother? Is he okay?" she asked, breaking away from our group hug.

"They won't tell us anything. They were waiting on you," Alanna said.

My mother went up to one of the nurses coming out of Bilal's room. "Hello, ma'am, I am Bilal Thomas's mother. What's wrong with him?"

The nurse looked at us. Then she walked my mother into the room. The nurse came out and then brought a group of doctors back with her. Bubbles asked the group of doctors, "What's wrong with my brother?"

One of the doctors stopped, kneeled down, and said, "Your brother's going to be okay. We're just checking him out, making sure he is one hundred percent before he leaves." He touched Bubbles on her cheek, smiled at us and walked away.

My mother came out of the room and told us that he had smoke inhalation and they had to monitor him because his asthma could be affected, but he was not going to die. I went and walked to the bathroom. I felt a little better knowing Bilal was going to be okay. When I came back I saw Bubbles talking to the nurse who had been talking to my mom. I kept coughing. When she saw me she smiled and offered me a ginger ale. She then pulled me to the side.

"So how are you feeling?" she asked.

"Good."

"I was talking to your little sister and she said your mother is never home and she leaves them home by themselves."

"That's not true. My mom be working all the time. When she's not home, I'm there. I'm seventeen and my other sister is eighteen."

"She wasn't home when the fire started, right?"

"No. She stepped out for a moment."

"Do you know where she went?" she asked, frowning.

"No." I knew better than to say the bar.

"Okay, thanks for speaking with me." She went back to the nurses' station and jotted something down. Then my mother came out of the room and asked her for a blanket. The nurse gave her an attitude and said she would bring one in there shortly. We all sat in chairs around Bilal's bed.

It was two in the morning, and Alanna had called Bruce and he came to the hospital. Moments later she announced that she was leaving and for us to call her later. I was starting to get sleepy too. Bubbles was already balled up in the chair next to my mom. I went and got another soda. I couldn't wait to go home. Then it occurred to me that we might not have a house to go home to.

"Excuse me, do you have a phone I can use?" I asked one of the nurses.

"Yes, it's over there on the wall. Dial nine and then one to get an outside line." I called my dad's house. Charlotte answered the phone.

"Let me speak to my dad," I demanded.

"Do you know what time it is?" she asked.

"Yeah, it is an emergency," I said, sighing.

"John, the phone."

My dad picked up the phone and said, "Hello?"

"Dad."

"What's wrong?"

"Our house caught on fire."

"What? Are you okay?"

"Yeah. Bilal is in the hospital and I don't know how bad the house is yet."

"Is he okay?"

"I don't know yet."

I told him what hospital we were at and he said that he was on his way. After I called him I called Marcus's house for John. Marcus said that John wasn't there. I told him what happened and he said he was going to try to reach him, I didn't have Nitra's number on me.

I took a deep breath and went back into Bilal's room and sat next to my mother. I closed the door and then the curtain. There was a light knock on the door. The nurse came in the room, asking if were we okay and if we needed anything else. My mother told her we were fine. A few moments later she came back in with a tall brown woman, with a short, black spiked haircut, and wearing a blue trench coat. She introduced her as Ms. Norton and said that she needed to speak with our mother.

"Why don't you come with me and bring your sister?" the nurse said. I awoke Bubbles and figured out that the nurse had called the Department of Health Services on my mother. She sat us in a room a few doors down the hall from Bilal. I heard my mother down the hall cussing.

"Don't be asking me no questions about my children. Bitch, get the fuck out of my face!" Then I heard a door slam. I jumped up to see what was going on and the nurse sternly told me to sit down. I looked at her like she was crazy. She stepped out of the room and I followed. Then I heard someone say, "Call security." I ran down to Bilal's room and saw they were pulling my mom out of the room.

I screamed, "Get off my mom," and then I swung on one of the guards. Someone grabbed me, and I started biting and kicking. I saw them dragging my mother down the hall. They finally pulled me back in the same room with Bubbles. I tried to get out.

"Where are y'all taking my mom? Yo! Y'all better let me out of here. Yo, let me out," I screamed. "Where is my mother?" I ran toward the door, and the guard grabbed me.

"Get off me! Get off me!" The guard finally let me go and then the woman with a blue trench coat came up to me and said, "Settle down. Your mother is fine. We just need to speak with her."

"Well, I want to make sure she is fine," I said, looking around for my mom.

"No, actually you can't. Listen, you and your younger sister are going to stay the night with a foster family until we can get things settled." I looked over at the woman as she stared me directly in my face.

"No, I can't do that. My mother really needs me," I said.

"She'll be okay," the woman said.

"Okay, I'll say goodbye to her, then."

"I'll walk you," she said. I guess she knew I was about to leave.

I went back and forth with the woman, then she told me she could send me to the Youth Study Center if I couldn't cooperate with her. She said that they just took my mom downstairs to calm her down. She finally let me talk to my mom, who said, "Don't give them any problems."

Ms. Norton put us in her silver four-door Honda Accord and slammed the door. She eyed me from the rearview mirror the entire ride. We drove for a while, then pulled up in front of a big old house in North Philly. She introduced me and Bubbles to a foster mom named Ms. Waters. She was an older lady, about sixty with silver hair that showed through her burgundy dye job.

It was five in the morning. The sun was rising and we were just getting in. Ms. Norton introduced us and then Ms. Waters asked us if we was hungry. We told her no and she walked Bubbles and me upstairs to our room. Inside were two dark wood-frame beds and a tall, narrow dresser with an old-fashioned silver alarm clock on the top.

I said thank you as Ms. Norton pulled me to the side and whispered in my ear, "If you think about running I'm going to have you arrested and sent to the Youth Study Center." I didn't even respond to her. I was so tired, and I just wanted to go to sleep and figure everything out when I awoke.

Bubbles looked at me after they left us alone in the room and asked, "How long you think we going to have to stay here?"

"I don't know, not going to be that long," I said as I gave her a hug. We settled into our beds, and before I knew it we were both asleep.

* * *

The next thing I knew Ms. Waters was knocking on the door saying, "It's time to eat."

It was twelve-thirty in the afternoon. I got up and looked around, trying to place where I was. At first I thought I had dreamed what had happened the night before. It seemed unreal. As soon as I realized I hadn't been dreaming, I thought about my mom.

"We're not hungry," I shouted out.

"I'm hungry," Bubbles said as she got up, walked past me and opened the door.

"Okay, I'll be right down," I said.

A few minutes later I went down the steps and joined the other three kids. There was this slightly retarded boy named Dennis and a teenage girl named Tianna. She wore a large black T-shirt with no bra on, and her hair was braided to the back. Then there was Charles, a short boy with big, thick glasses looking like he was out of it. They all were eating sandwiches.

Later on Ms. Waters took Bubbles and me to Kmart. She bought us underwear and horrible clothes. The jeans she picked out for me were fake paper-thin jeans that looked like back-in-the-day stretch pants with a tapered leg at the ankle.

That evening she came into my room, gave me a token and said that I needed to come straight home from school or she was going to call Ms. Norton.

I called Chantel to ask her to bring me something else to wear. She picked up in three rings.

"Chantel, it's Kendra."

"Why didn't you come to school today? You missed practice. You know the talent show is in a couple of days."

"I had a fire at my house."

"Oh my God! Are you okay?"

"Yeah, I'm fine. Can you do me a favor?"

"What?"

"Can you bring something to wear?"

"My clothes are going to be too big for you," she said.

"Just bring something you think might fit me and meet me in the second-floor bathroom before advisory."

Chantel met me in the bathroom with some blue jeans and a white shirt with a red star on the front. I went in the stall, took my clothes off and put on the things she'd brought me. I stuffed my other clothes in my book bag. When I came out the bathroom stall, I checked myself out in the mirror. Chantel handed me another bag. "These some other clothes you might can fit into."

"Okay, thanks," I said.

"So what happened? Where are you staying?" she asked.

"It is a long story. I don't want to talk about it."

"So are you going to still be in the talent show?"

"No, I can't go."

"What about Dajuan's party?"

"No."

"You should go to Dajuan's party. It's going to be good. And I can come and pick you up."

"I'm not going anywhere. Don't you understand? I don't know where my mother is and my little brother is in the hospital." She was so damn dumb and she was making me mad. I walked out of the bathroom. She followed and said she was sorry. I ignored her.

"You're not coming to class either?" she yelled down the hall as she followed me.

"I have to make some calls and check on my family."

She finally stopped following me and began walking in the opposite direction toward class. I went into the school nurse's office and asked her if I could I use the phone. She was busy taking a boy's temperature but said yes and pointed to the phone in her inner office. I closed her door a little and called my dad's house.

"Charlotte, my dad there?"

"No, your dad's not here. He's at work."

"Do he know we in foster care? Why didn't he come up to the hospital?"

"Yeah, he knows. He thought you were lying, so he didn't come to the hospital. He been talking to some woman, I think her name is Ms. Norton. She said he got to go to court and go before a judge and bring in all this paperwork, and they got to come and inspect the house."

"So why he didn't go talk to the judge?"

"'Cause your dad can't be doing all that, missing days from work. He don't have no sick days left."

"Well, can you tell my dad I called?"

"Sure, mm-hmm, I'll tell him," she said. I couldn't believe my dad didn't even check to make sure we were all right. He is so fucked up and Charlotte is just as dumb. Next I called Alanna. She said that Bilal was getting out of the hospital and that our mother was staying at Aunt Joanie's house. She also gave me John's number at Nitra's house.

"Did Mommy tell you how long we were going to have to stay there?" I asked Alanna.

"No, she told me they said she was under investigation for child neglect and child endangerment."

"Oh," I said.

"How is the lady's house y'all staying at?"

"It is okay. She's an old lady. Alanna, give Mommy and John our number."

I didn't know what else to do. I wanted to see my old house, but it was more important to go to class. Ms. Norton said she was going to be checking up on me, and I remembered she was going to lock me up if I thought about cutting classes.

If I had somewhere else to go I would. I would never go back with Ms. Waters. I hated it there already and I wanted to go home. But I had to make sure Bubbles was okay. After school I stopped past my job. Mr. Newman was working the register when I walked in the door.

"What are you doing here?" He looked me over and said, "What's going on with you? Why didn't you call me to tell me you quit?"

"I didn't quit," I said as I explained to him what happened.

"Well, can you work today?"

"I have to ask my foster mom, because they said if I don't come straight home I was going to jail."

"Where are your parents? What kind of parents do you have?" he asked.

There was no explaining to the old man. So I just stayed until three and then I told him I had to go. That was enough time for him to catch up on his prescriptions. He then told me he would hold my job for two days and then he would have to hire someone else.

Ms. Waters didn't like anyone on her phone. She said she only had one line and nobody was going to be tying it up. I went in the kitchen and asked permission to use her phone. She said I had five minutes. I dialed Ms. Norton.

"Hi, Ms. Norton," I said.

"Who is this and how can I help you?" she said, all mean.

"It is Kendra Thomas. I forgot to tell you that I have a job and I would like to keep it."

"I have to call your job and confirm your hours with your manager." I gave her all the information and she said she would call me back.

Ms. Waters was a church fanatic. She kept Bibles in every room except for the bathroom. She didn't allow any television in her house until after dinner and then it was only for an hour or two. I just stayed in the room and listened to the radio. Bubbles was adjusting just fine. She liked playing with Dennis, that slow boy, because he made her laugh. The other boy, Charles, didn't talk to anyone. He just stood in the corner and kicked the wall. When he wasn't kicking the wall he was ripping pillows apart.

I had finished my homework and was tired of being in that room, so I walked downstairs to get some water. I sat down at the table. The girl Tianna said, "What's up?"

I said, "Nothing."

"Where y'all from?" she asked.

"Southwest Philly."

"Why y'all here?" she asked.

"I had a fire in my house. And you?"

"My mom had an overdose."

"How old are you?" I asked.

"Sixteen."

I told her I was seventeen and she said Dennis was her little brother. Then she took a blunt out of her pocket and offered me some weed.

"I'm good. Ain't she going to smell that?"

"That lady can't smell, and she go to bed like clockwork every night by nine. I sneak back out every night," she said as she emptied the blunt out onto the table.

"How long you been here?" I asked.

"Six months."

"Why so long?"

"My mom didn't get herself together yet. I actually just came back here. I was at the Youth Study Center for two months 'cause I missed curfew two days in a row."

After talking to her I knew there was no way I was staying here for six months. Plus I would be eighteen in a month. They would have made Alanna come too if they knew she was still in school, even though she was eighteen.

Bilal finally came home. He acted normal, but he was on all this medication. Ms. Waters said he couldn't sleep in our room, but I didn't care what she said. I layed my little brother next to me, and Bubbles was on the other side. With Bilal with us I felt a little better.

I spoke to John and he said that my mom was working with the social worker to get us home. I missed the talent show but I didn't even care. I'd failed three tests in the two weeks since everything had happened. It was only December, and as soon as I got back home I could make those grades up. Nobody at school knew what was going on and I liked it like that. I was still normal there. I called my mom. She was still staying at my Aunt Joanie's.

"Y'all okay?" Aunt Joanie asked.

"Yes."

"Where they got y'all at?"

"Some lady house named Ms. Waters. She's nice, though. I just called to tell my mom that we were okay and don't forget to go to family court." My Aunt Joanie said she would give my mom the message. After I called my mom I called John again.

"John, I don't have any clothes. My friend let me wear her sister's stuff and the lady have me wearing these messed up clothes. You think we can go see if we can get anything out of the house?"

"Kendra, there is nothing in that house," John said.

"Let's at least go try and see."

"I'll come and get you from school tomorrow. Wait on the Thirteenth Street side." The main reason I wanted to go back to the house was to see if I could get clothes and see if there was anything we could use now.

We went to my old house and saw that they'd put a big padlock on the front door and an orange sticker that read NO TRESPASSING. It wasn't as bad as I'd thought—it was worse.

The building structure looked sturdy from the outside, but you could see the imprint on the wall where the flames left their mark. Our neighbors were watching us as we looked at our house. I wished they'd go in their own houses. *Nobody wants to be looked at,* I thought.

"Let's go around back," John said. "Maybe we can get in that way. Matter of fact, let's wait until it gets dark. Nobody won't see us. I can get Marcus and he can help us. You want to get something to eat?"

"I don't care."

We went and ate at Taco Bell. I ordered a Nacho Bell Grande and he had four soft tacos. I carried the food to the table and sat down. John made sure we had napkins.

"Are you okay with that lady?"

"I'm fine, and Bilal and Bubbles seem like they're having fun. There are a bunch of kids there and she has games. And she has been taking them somewhere every other day. You talked to Mommy?"

"Yeah, she supposed to go to a custody hearing tomorrow."

After we ate we went to go pick up his friend Marcus. I had only met Marcus a few times before. He would come around, say hi and keep it moving.

"Who's that?" Marcus asked when he got in the car.

"Man, that's Kendra, my little sister. Don't be looking at her."

"Come on, man, I'm not. She just look different. She grew up. Man, I'm twenty-two."

"Exactly! She's only seventeen. What tools did you bring?" he asked.

"I brought this lock cutter my pop had and this sledgehammer."

"That should work."

We parked around the corner from my old house.

"Stay in the car," John told me.

"No, I'm coming with you." We walked to the end of

the block and came down the alley. A neighbor's dog was barking at us but we just ignored it. John climbed the gate and Marcus pushed me over it, then climbed over himself. They took out the sledgehammer and John hit the door twice hard at the lock, and the door popped open. There was no electricity but we'd brought a flashlight to look around. Everything in the kitchen was how we'd left it. Cereal was still on top of the refrigerator and dishes were still in the sink. Just about everything was ruined—there was black soot everywhere. I grabbed trash bags out of the drawer and went to the basement to see if any clothes might be salvageable. Marcus followed me. Everything was still wet from the water the firemen sprayed all through the house. Some of the clothes had already started to mildew, and everything else had a heavy smoke smell, but I managed to find a few things I thought might be okay after they were laundered.

"Come upstairs," John yelled.

Everything in the living room was destroyed. The steps were just about gone. John took a few things out of his room that weren't damaged.

The whole ordeal of coming back to the house that I'd lived in my entire life and seeing it basically gone was so devastating that I got depressed. After we left we went to the Laundromat and washed the clothes.

Chapter 4

Ms. Waters was starting to get on my nerves. I had been in her house for two weeks and hated every moment of it. She made us do chores. I had to clean the kitchen and bathroom. Bilal's job was watering the plants and putting the toys back. And Bubbles had to vacuum.

"So what time you get out of school? Do you have to work today?" she asked.

When the fuck I get out, I mumbled under my breath. *Don't try to clock me,* I thought. I wished I could go home. But right then, even if they didn't make us stay there, where else could I go? Right then there was no home, my mother didn't have any family, Aunt Joanie said she didn't have any room, and my dad had not tried to come for us.

My mom showed up late to the court hearing, so it got rescheduled for the following week. I hadn't really been talking to her. Every time I called Aunt Joanie she said that Mom wasn't there. Ms. Norton hadn't really been riding me as much as she did in the beginning. She only checked on us once a week. Alanna was going on with her regular life. The fire hadn't affected her at all. She was just happy that she got to live with her boyfriend. John met me after school almost every day and had been checking up on us.

School was going okay. My grades had come up a little and I had been trying to just make it through. I called my aunt's house to see if my mom was there.

"Hi, Aunt Joanie. Is my mom there?"

"Hey, baby, you okay? You don't sound so good."

"Yes, I'm okay. Where my mom at?"

"Um, she is not here. Your mother need to get herself together. You know she lost her job. I'm sorry, but I put her out."

"Why you do that?" I screamed.

"Kendra, your mother has lost her house, her kids, her job and she still wants to drink, and I just think that there has to be some intervention."

"So you just put her out?" I screamed.

"Yes, well, I offered her to go to counseling and she was like she hadn't been drinking, but she smelled like an old drunk man. I'm sorry, Kendra. She needs a reality check. My brother told me not to even let her in and I went against him. I'm still here for you and the children. How are they?"

"Bubbles and Bilal and me are still with our foster mom, and Alanna is with her boyfriend. Your brother hasn't even checked on us," I said, not bothering to hide the disgust in my voice. "Aunt Joanie, I have to go. Can you give my mom this number if she comes back?"

"Okay, you take care of yourself."

I hadn't called my dad in a couple of weeks, but I was going to try him one last time.

"Daddy, do you think you can get us?" I blurted out as soon as I heard his voice.

"No! You know Charlotte ain't going for all three of y'all," he said with an attitude.

"I can stay with Aunt Joanie. Can you just take Bubbles and Bilal?"

"I can't do it. I would have to take off of work, and anyway y'all be all right. Y'all fine where y'all at."

I couldn't believe my dad. I wasn't going to beg him. I just hung up on him.

I went to Ms. Waters's house and thankfully she wasn't home yet, so I had a moment to breathe. I sat on the sofa and watched television. I figured if she came in and questioned my television watching, I'd tell her I already finished my homework. A little while later the phone rang. It was probably one of Ms. Waters's church members. She wanted us to answer the phone "Praise the Lord," but I just answered, "Hello?"

"Kendra?"

"Mom!"

"Yes, how are you. How are the kids? I've been worried sick about you."

"Mom, are you okay? Aunt Joanie said you not staying with her."

"Yeah, Joanie kicked me out, so I've been staying at the shelter."

"A shelter? Oh my God."

"Kendra, it is not that bad."

"Where are you now?"

"I'm at a phone booth on Market Street, downtown."

"Stay right there. I'm going to meet you." As soon as I said that Ms. Waters came walking in the door with a big white fur hat on and a black wool coat.

"And where are you going?" she said as she noticed me putting on my coat.

"I'm going to meet up with my friend Chantel at the mall."

"Well, you know curfew is at nine."

"I know. Did you need me to pick you up anything?" I asked.

"No, just make sure you here by curfew."

"Yes, ma'am."

I went outside and was trying to figure the best way to hurry up and get downtown. The bus wasn't coming, so I started walking. The wind was just about picking me up. I walked four blocks to the subway. I was supposed to meet my mom at City Hall at the big four-story sculpture that everyone called the Clothes Pin. As soon as I saw my mom I gave her a long hug and started crying. I hadn't seen her since the hospital. She looked like she had been beat down. Her eyes had dark rings around them and she looked like she'd lost about fifteen pounds—her clothes were hanging off her slightly. She carried two filled white plastic grocery bags with faded red "Thank You's."

"Mom, are you okay?"

"Yeah, I'm fine. Y'all deserve better. Y'all good kids. I just feel like I really messed up this time," she said as she shook her head and wiped away tears.

"Mom, it's okay. We are going to get through this," I said as I comforted her and we began walking. I took her bags from her.

"I know we will. But you know, Kendra, it's just one thing after the other. How is that lady? Is she nice? Is she treating my babies good?"

"She's nice." I could look at my mom and see that she needed some serious rest. She needed to relax, take a shower and get her head together. The only place I could think of going was Alanna's house. She and Bruce lived in an apartment on Lions Road in Northeast Philly, and I knew he wouldn't be there because he was working.

"Mommy, let's go to Lana's house." We had to catch the El, the aboveground train, and then the 3 bus. It took us about an hour and a half to get there. I knocked on the door.

"Who is it?" Alanna said.

"It's me and Mommy."

"What are y'all doing here?" she asked as she opened the door. She invited us in and we all had a seat.

"Mommy, you want something to drink? You look a mess," Alanna said. My mother stood up, looked in the mirror and patted her hair down. I walked Alanna into her kitchen. "Alanna, why would you tell Mommy she looks bad?"

"Because she does. You don't look that great yourself. What time is your curfew?" she asked.

"Nine."

"It's like seven. You better get home," she said, looking at her watch. I pulled her to the side and whispered, "Look at Mommy. She was crying and I couldn't leave her. She needs to rest and get herself together."

"So, what, you just going to show up at my door? What am I supposed to do?"

"Mommy, you okay?" she yelled to my mother, who was still sitting in the living room.

"Yes. I'm fine," my mother answered.

"See? She's okay."

"No, she is not! She needs a bath and she needs to get some rest. Can she stay here? Auntie Joanie kicked her out. It is cold outside, and I don't want Mommy out there by herself. You know she has been staying at a shelter."

"Bruce will flip if he comes home and he sees her here. Y'all cannot mess up my situation."

"Alanna, but she don't have anywhere to go," I said stressing how important this was.

"Mommy put herself in this predicament and she is going to pull everybody around her down with her. If you know what's good for you you'll get your butt to that lady's house before your curfew."

Alanna walked back in the living room. "Mom, you know Kendra needs to go back home, so y'all better get out of here," Alanna said as she handed her a glass of juice.

"Alanna, please don't do this," I begged.

"Look, I don't have anything to do with it. You have to go." I wanted to fight her. I wanted to pull her hair out. How could she be so evil to her own mother? I tried one last time to reason with her before we walked out the door. "Can Mommy please stay here with you?"

"No, she can't stay here. She don't want anything with her life."

My mother drank the rest of her juice, then hugged Alanna and followed me out the door. I didn't say anything to my mom as we left her building.

"There's something wrong with that child," my mother said as we walked toward the bus stop. I nodded but didn't say anything, I was too mad. I didn't have a plan, but I knew we should go back downtown where we had met. That would give me at least an hour to get my thoughts together.

As we exited the El I figured that I would go home, call my Aunt Joanie and beg her to let my mom come back. It was so cold out and the city streets were becoming empty. The only people out were homeless men and people waiting at the bus stop trying to get home. I had to start going home—and I only had about half an hour to make it. I tried to leave my mother but I couldn't. I gave her a hug and she just broke down crying. Tears began flowing down her face.

"I don't know what I'm going to do. Please don't leave me. You all I got," my mother cried as she clung to me.

"Mommy, I'm not going to leave you alone. I don't know where we going to go, but I promise I won't leave you."

"You can go with me to the shelter."

I didn't want to go with her, but there weren't really any other options.

"I'll stay with you at the shelter," I said.

We went to the Salvation Army at Broad and Fairmount Street. It was a big two-story building, six houses long. When we arrived an older black woman sitting at a desk asked me to fill out all these forms. "This my next to oldest daughter," my mother proudly told the lady. The woman asked my mom to sign me in and asked if I was under eighteen.

"Yes," my mother said as she gave me a long glance. "She's going to stay with me."

The first thing I noticed when I walked in was that it was loud and crowded. I followed my mom to a lady who was giving out blankets and pillows. From there we went and found two cots next to each other. There was a girl next to me who looked like she was my age with two kids. Her baby was crying loud. Her face was chubby and like she had seen it all and been through hell. I looked around, and there were cots everywhere. I didn't know people had it so bad. There was an elderly white woman with matted hair and five shopping bags setting up her bed. My mother said people steal and told me to take my shoes off and put them under me. I felt so uncomfortable. We didn't belong here.

I could not close my eyes. This place was not home and it did not feel safe. This old lady kept coughing like she had a piece of something stuck in her throat. It was awful. It was a hacking cough that made my ears hurt. I couldn't sleep. I looked over at my mother as she slept innocently. I felt so sorry for her. She was raising five kids on her own and the world was attacking her at every angle. I wish we had some family. My mother didn't deserve this. This was what she got for trying to be a strong woman. This was my dad's fault. I hate him.

I put my jacket over my head and closed my eyes. I tried to come up with some ideas, something to get us out of this situation.

* * *

"Come on. It's time to go. You can't sleep past seven-thirty in the shelter," my mother said, waking me up as she was shaking me. I took my coat off my head, got up and went to the bathroom. I washed my face, and I wanted to take a long, hot shower, but I didn't like the way the bathroom looked. So I just washed a little in the sink.

"You have money on you?" my mother asked me when we got outside.

"A few dollars," I said.

"Let's go get some breakfast."

We headed to the McDonald's at Broad and Arch, one block from where we met the night before. It was in the middle of downtown. People were on their way to work. There were women speed walking in nice suits and sneakers, and men with briefcases walking to their offices. In the middle of the street a police officer was directing traffic. We walked into McDonald's and my mother ordered coffee and a bacon and egg sandwich. I didn't have an appetite. All I could think about was how fucked up we were and that Ms. Waters probably called Ms. Norton on me and I was going to get sent away. My mom got her food and we located a seat in the back.

As soon as my mother sat down I looked her directly in her eyes and said, "Mom, we have to do something. Lana is not going to let us stay with her. And we need a house. We need our own space." I wanted to choose my next couple of words carefully. "Mom you can't stay at the shelter, and you have to get yourself together."

"I know. I know," she said, nodding.

"So the first thing is, Mom, you have to get some help."

"You're right. I was thinking about that. Where could I go? Who could help us out of this mess?"

"What about Ms. Arlene? I know she can help us. Let's go down to her office."

"I don't know where exactly the office is."

I suggested we call information, so I cleared the table, put her trash in the can, and stepped back out into the cold. The library was the only place that was safe and warm where we could stay all day. They would have the Yellow Pages and I could find my mom help.

When we got there I looked in the Yellow Pages for state representative Alonzo Parker's office. Ms. Arlene picked up the phone.

"Ms. Arlene, this is Kendra from across the street."

"How you doing, baby? Are you okay?" she asked.

"Yes, I'm fine. I was calling to ask if you knew where my mom could get help."

She put me on hold, then came back to the telephone and said, "Call this number and she should be able to get help. As soon as she get clean she can get grants and stuff for housing. She has to go into rehab first, though." Ms. Arlene told me not to worry about insurance or any of that and that Horizon House would set her up with everything. She said my mom would have to talk to an intake counselor.

The Horizon House was a regular-looking building on a residential block. The only thing that made it appear different was that it had a heavy metal door and an intercom system at the front door and no window. My mother pushed the bell. She didn't seem a bit nervous about coming. She knew it was time.

An older thin black man with a bald head came to the door.

"May I help you?"

"I'm here to get some information about getting some help," my mother said.

"Okay, come on in, have a seat. I'm Mr. Matthews."

We walked in and found ourselves in a waiting room outside a small office. He went to a filing cabinet and pulled out some forms. He asked my mother for identification and he made copies of it. He asked her what kind of treatment she was looking for. My mother looked at me, then at the ground, and said, "I need help with my drinking."

She filled out the forms and then she whispered, "I'm going to put down that you're my next of kin." She handed her paperwork back to the man and then he asked her to come with him. She followed him through a narrow room into a little office. I looked around. The phone was ringing and there were posters and flyers over the desk about substance abuse. A big sign read REBUILD, RENEW, REWARD, RECLAIM YOUR LIFE.

I picked up a few of the flyers and began reading them. The man, Mr. Matthews, opened the office door and waved his hand for me to follow him. He brought me in the room, sat me down and said, "Your mother wanted you to be present. She'll be entering our program today."

"Today?" I asked as I looked over at my mother.

"We don't send people away when they are ready. We are funded by the state and private donations, so don't worry about insurance. Our program lasts for sixty days. She's gonna need seven days' worth of clothes. She is not allowed any products that contain alcohol. No mouthwash and no rubbing alcohol. There is a seven-day blackout. Once she is in she cannot talk or have visitors for seven days. After those seven days she can have visitors on Sundays from one to four."

"You ready 'cause once you walk through the doors you here," Mr. Matthews asked my mother.

"Mom"—I looked at her—"you going to do this?"

"Yes. I'm ready."

I gave her a hug and told Mr. Matthews to give me a list. I told him would be back. I had only forty dollars and that wasn't enough to buy what she needed. I had to call John to take me to get her clothes and the rest of her supplies.

"Mommy checked herself into counseling, but she needs some stuff."

"Like what?" John asked.

"She need a—" Before I could complete my sentence I was interrupted by a recording requesting me to put another thirty-five cents in the pay phone. I dug in my pockets but I didn't have any more change.

"Just meet me at Aunt Joanie's." I heard him say okay, and then I was disconnected.

I caught the bus to my aunt's house. She lived in a small apartment in Logan. She was a crossing guard and home every day by four. I rang her bell and she came to the window. She said she would be right down. She buzzed me in and I walked up one flight of steps to her apartment. She was sitting on her plum-colored sofa watching *Oprah*. She smiled at me, then pushed a few green and plum pillows to the side so I could have a seat. She took her remote and turned the volume down. I could hear the sizzling of hot oil and smelled chicken frying. The aroma smelled extra good because I was hungry. I hadn't eaten all day.

"Your chicken smells good," I said, hoping she'd offer me some.

"You want something to eat?" she asked.

"If you have enough," I said.

She said that there was more than enough and she had peas, white rice and gravy to go along with it. She began making me a plate and asked, "What are you doing in these parts?"

"I'm meeting John here. My mom went into rehab this afternoon."

"That is so good. Oh, I'm so happy. Thank you! She needed it. I've been praying for her."

"We have to get the rest of her supplies, though."

"What does she need?"

"Toiletries, underwear and seven days' worth of clothes.

The man at the place said just get her a bunch of sweat suits. So John is going to take me to get her stuff."

"This is so wonderful."

"It is," I said as I took a long sigh. "Only thing, while I was out with her I didn't check in last night at my foster mom's house and if I go back she might have already called the social worker and she is going to send me away."

"They will understand you were with your mother. You want me to call?"

"No, they won't care. I'll figure something out."

I ate my food and John picked me up. We went to Forman Mills, this discount store, and got my mother the things she needed. During the ride I began to tell John about how Lana did us the other night.

"You know Lana wouldn't let me and Mommy stay at her house."

"Lana got problems. If you want you can come stay with me and Marcus. You're almost eighteen."

"His dad won't mind?" I asked.

"No, he don't care and they have an extra room."

"Where his mom at?"

"His mom died when he was younger."

"Dag, that is a shame, but I don't know. I don't want to be around a strange man."

"No, his dad stays downstairs. He lost both of his legs because he got diabetes and don't be taking care of his self. His bed and bathroom are set up downstairs. Mr. Skip don't do anything but sip on something and smoke a cigarette every day."

"I'll check it out."

"No, I'm telling you . . . long as you buy Mr. Skip some cigarettes, he is good."

"I have to think about it. Right now I'll just try to see if I can go back to that house so I can keep an eye on the kids."

John then suggested I call first to see what she said. If she was talking crazy, he said, I just wouldn't go back.

"You have some change?" I asked him. John gave me the change and I got out of the car. I dialed the number and took deep breaths as the phone rang and rang. Thank God, Bubbles picked up the phone.

"Bubbles, where is Ms. Waters?"

"Kendra, you is in big trouble. Ms. Waters said she is going to tell Ms. Norton you didn't come home last night."

"Do you know if she told her yet?" I asked.

"No, but I think she called her at her job."

"Put her on the phone." Bubbles gave Ms. Waters the phone.

"Hello, praise the Lord."

"Hi, Ms. Waters, I am so sorry I didn't call you. I totally forgot. I stayed over my friend house and accidentally fell asleep, then we went straight to school. I didn't want to be late."

"Well, you know we got rules in the house. You can't be breaking these rules. Just come on home and we will discuss it when you get here."

I didn't know if I could trust her. She might call Ms. Norton, but I didn't think she was going to. I got back in the car and closed the door.

"What she say?" John asked.

"She said she didn't tell the social worker yet and I should just go on back to her house."

"You know, just tell her you were so sorry and it will never happen again."

I took John's advice. I came in and told Ms. Waters I was so sorry, and she said it was okay, just come and eat. Her house wasn't home, but it felt so good to have somewhere clean to rest. I went upstairs to wash and change my clothes and Bubbles and Bilal ran into the room, gave me a hug and asked where I'd been.

"I'll tell y'all later. Go eat."

After dinner they both came into my room. "Listen," I told them, "I was with Mommy."

"Is she okay?" Bilal asked.

"Yes, but listen. She is going to get us out of here, but it's going to take some time. I need y'all to just do whatever Ms. Waters says to do. Mommy is in treatment for her drinking problem, and once she is out she can get a house, and we're going to move."

After a while I realized that Ms. Waters's was not that bad. I went to school like I was supposed to, then to work, and then I came in on time and was very sweet to her. I brought her the *Philadelphia Daily News* and *TV Guide* from the pharmacy. She trusted me so much, she even let me take the children out.

I asked Ms. Waters if I could take the kids to the movies. She said it was okay, but instead of going to the movies I took them to the rehab center to see my mother. She was in recovery only a week, but already she looked better. The children were excited to see her. They sat on her and just clung to her. As she hugged them back she told me, "Listen, I got all this info from this woman in here. She said they're taking applications for these low-income houses over in Camden starting tomorrow. You go over there and just act like me. Just put down my old job information. You know what to do."

We were there visiting my mom for a while, but I didn't want to stay too long and have Ms. Waters get suspicious.

As we left I made the children promise that they wouldn't tell where we had gone.

The next morning I got up extra early and took the bus from downtown Philly to Camden in New Jersey, across the bridge from Philly. I wore glasses so I could appear to be older. The office opened at eight, but I was there by seven-thirty and I was glad because by the time the lady opened the door a little before eight, there were thirty people behind me. She handed me a clipboard and said, "Fill this out," without looking at me twice. After I'd finished filling out the two-page application the woman looked it over and said, "We give first preference to New Jersey residents."

"That's fine," I said. "How long before I know if I've been approved?"

"In about a month or two. You'll need a first month and last month security deposit."

"How much is that?" I asked.

"That's fifteen hundred dollars."

"Okay." I thanked the woman and began thinking about how I was going to get the money up. I knew I could ask Mr. Newman to give me more hours. Maybe I could come in on Saturdays and Sundays and maybe stay all the way until closing.

I was back across the bridge and in school just before advisory ended. I walked into the classroom and immediately I felt everybody smiling and looking at me. I don't know why, but I put my head on the desk. Then I heard our teacher, Mrs. Edmonds, say, "Excuse me, Kendra, can you come to the front of the classroom?"

I lifted my head off of my desk and walked up to the front of the classroom. I assumed she wanted me to take the attendance sheet down to the office. She said, "Stand right here," then she pulled out this manila envelope and said, "Kendra, on behalf of your advisory class and James T. Pattison High School, here is six hundred eighty-two dollars and twenty-nine cents. We know about your family's tragedy, and we want you to know we are your extended family and we are here for you." She handed me the big heavy envelope. It was slightly open and I saw piles of dollar bills. Then she hugged me and everybody started clapping.

I quietly said, "Thank you," and walked to the back of the class. I looked around the room and I was about to cry, but I couldn't. I was so mad at Chantel. She was the only one that knew. Why would she tell my business? The gesture was nice, but I'm not feeling everybody feeling sorry for me. I put my head on my desk again and tried not to cry, but I couldn't hold back my tears. I didn't want people to know I didn't have any clothes, that I was living with Ms. Waters, that my mom had lost everything. I wanted to keep that to myself. The bell rang for first period. I could hear everybody collecting their stuff and walking out of the classroom. As they walked past me they began trying to hug me and pat me on my back. I didn't lift my head because I was so ashamed. My head was buried in my arms. All these burdens on my shoulders were coming out all at once.

"Leave her alone and go to class," Mrs. Edmonds yelled. After everybody was gone she came with a box of tissues and then Chantel walked me to the bathroom, where I dried my eyes.

"I'm sorry. I didn't know that it would upset you," Chantel said.

"No, it's just like . . . I didn't want anybody in my business. I know you were trying to help. I just feel so bad now . . . like I don't want anyone feeling sorry for me."

"So what are you going to do?"

"I don't feel like facing anyone. I'm going home."

"You sure? You want me to go with you?"

"I'll be all right. I'll try to call you later." I placed the money-filled envelope in my book bag. I didn't want to go to class; I didn't want everybody looking at me. Plus I don't like everyone asking me about my family—about how my mom was doing and all that other bullshit. I went to work early and asked Mr. Newman if he could give me more hours during the week and maybe weekend and until closing.

"I know your family had a tragedy but I can't give you any more hours. You have to go to school. I wish I could help, but I can't," he said.

"All right, thanks," I said. He didn't understand, my family needed money now and if he didn't give me more hours I wouldn't be working here.

The next day I went downtown and walked around, looking for a job. I went into a clothing store. A girl about my age was folding jeans. I saw a lady behind the register and I asked her if they were hiring.

"Yeah. What kind of hours can you work?" the lady asked.

"Whatever hours you need after one p.m."

"Are you still in school?"

"Yes."

"How old are you?"

"I'm seventeen. I'll be eighteen in a few weeks."

"You have to be eighteen to work here."

I thanked her and walked out of the store. I filled out another application at this restaurant called Holmes. I told them I was eighteen and they hired me on the spot. They were going to give me forty hours a week, so I quit the pharmacy. I was the hostess, so all I had to do was get a white shirt and black pants. I seated people and if it got really busy, I would clean the tables and help the waitresses carry food to the tables.

I stopped going to school. I didn't care about prom, graduating, or any of that. I could always go to night school when all this was over and get my diploma. I just wanted my mom to have somewhere to come home to when she got out and I was going to make sure she was all right. Bubbles and Bilal were doing okay at Ms. Waters's, but they needed their own space too. They not used to having to ask permission to do everything—even to get something to eat or use the telephone. I just wanted my family back in the same house.

"Ms. Norton called and said that she would be over," Ms. Waters said as I came in the house one evening. I knew what that was about. My job at Holmes was working out, but I hadn't been to school in two weeks. She probably was going to try to come and get me and ask why I wasn't going to school. I wasn't going to allow her to send me anywhere. I had money and I had a job and things to do, and I wasn't going to sit there and wait for her to come. I was out. I packed my things. My mom would be home in a few weeks and Bilal and Bubbles would be okay until then. In a few weeks Ms. Norton wouldn't be able to do anything to me. I could just stay with John's friend Marcus.

I rode with John to Marcus's house. Just like John had said, Mr. Skip was sitting downstairs in his chair smoking a cigarette. He didn't have his legs from the knees down.

"Mr. Skip, this my sister. Can she stay here for a couple of weeks until my mom get herself together?"

"Huh? She going to pay me rent?"

"Yeah. How much you want, Mr. Skip?"

"She know how to cook?" he asked.

"No, Mr. Skip."

"I was only joking. Just tell her I smoke Newports and I like Johnnie Walker Red."

"She can get you your cigarettes, but she is not old enough to get any liquor."

"How you doing?" I said, looking down at his missing legs.

"Make yourself comfortable. The boys will help you out."

"I'll stay here with you the first couple of nights to get you situated," John told me. "I'll tell Nitra to come over here."

Marcus came in the door. "My dad said it was cool, right?"

"Yeah."

"All right, well, I'm going back out. I'm going to the movies with that girl Nikki."

"See you, man."

John took me to the middle room, right next to the bathroom. The paint was peeling off the wall and the sheets on the bed were dingy. But I could clean it up. And it was better than Ms. Waters's house because I could do whatever I wanted and go to work without being sent away. I took my clothes out and began to unpack.

"You know me and Mommy are trying to get money together for a house over in Jersey. I filled out this application for her to get this house. The only thing is you have to be ready to move in. They just want you to have your fifteen hundred down: I got six hundred so far."

"By the time Mommy out and y'all ready, I'll try to help as much as I can, but Nitra pregnant."

"Oh my God!" I said.

"Yeah. We ain't really ready, but we happy. We just have to get our place before she tell her mom and start showing. You know her mom is going to kick her out." John helped me get settled in, then he left.

I walked into the bathroom and you could tell that only men lived there. The seat was up and a yellow circle stained the inside of the toilet. The only thing that was left from a roll of tissue was the spine. I walked to the corner store and bought myself some chicken noodle soup, cleanser, bleach and dish detergent so I could clean the kitchen and try to clean the room I was staying in, and some cigarettes for Mr. Skip. I handed him his cigarettes when I came in the house, then I disinfected everything, washed my sheets by hand and let them air dry.

I had been staying at Marcus's house for four days. I knew by now Ms. Waters hadn't had any choice but to call Ms. Norton. But I'd be damned if they sent me to some Youth Study Center. All I had to do was wait to turn eighteen, and when my mom got out we'd have to go down there and get everything settled so I wouldn't have a warrant.

I took a shower and sat on the bed. I called and checked on Bubbles.

"Ms. Norton keep asking me where you are."

"Tell her you don't know. Bilal okay?"

"He was fighting Dennis."

"For what?"

"They were fighting over a truck."

"Who you on the phone with, gal?" I heard Ms. Waters say in the background.

"Get off the phone. I'll call y'all tomorrow."

I heard Marcus come up the steps and go to the bathroom, then walk down the hall to his bedroom and begin blasting his music. He played that music all night. I just put my head under the pillow and went to sleep. Somehow he still managed to get up and go to work in the morning. He worked at UPS lifting boxes.

The next day John and Nitra came to the house to take me to get something to eat.

"Hey Nitra."

She was always so happy. She said, "Heeeey Kendra, you okay?"

"I'm all right."

"Well, if you need someone to talk to just call me."

"I will." She smiled at me. She was a cute girl; she had been following my brother since they met working at a summer camp two years ago. She had a chubby face but was petite. Her eyes were hazel which made them pop out against her walnut skin. Nitra wore her hair up in a ponytail all the time with hoop earrings.

John hadn't been there in a few days. I heard some noises, and I looked down the steps and saw Marcus coming in. I went back in the room and turned on the radio. Seconds later there was a knock on my door.

"You good?" Marcus asked as he opened the door and walked in. I turned the radio down to see what he wanted.

"Yeah, I'm fine."

"All right. I was just checking on you."

"Thanks, I'm okay."

"If you need anything just ask me."

I turned the radio back up and started getting my work clothes ready for the next day. I went to take a shower before I went to bed and I realized there was no soap.

"Marcus, is there any soap?" I asked as I peeked my head out of the door.

"Yeah, hold up."

I stuck out my arm to reach for it. Instead he opened the door. I ran into the shower and screamed, "Marcus, get out of here!" I didn't like Marcus like that, so he'd better stop playing with me.

"Kendra, nobody's looking at you. I'm a grown man. I seen a naked woman before," he said as he pulled the shower curtain back and handed me the soap as I tried to cover my private areas. Marcus made me feel very uncomfortable. He wasn't supposed to be walking in the bathroom on nobody.

I awoke to a light wet feeling going on between the inside of my legs. I looked down and saw Marcus. He was licking me up and down. I hadn't been kissed there yet. I wanted to protest, but I kind of liked it. Girls had told me it would feel so good I wouldn't be able to speak, and now I was lying there speechless. His hands were gently stroking my breasts. I'd had sex before but nobody had ever done that to me. I didn't know what to do. I sat up a little and he pushed my head and body back down. It felt good, and instead of stopping him I opened my legs wider and brought my hips up higher to connect with lips, tongue and face. Marcus knew what he was doing, so I was wet soon. My legs shook, and I was jerking. I grabbed his head and pulled it closer into my body and then everything in me exploded.

He then got on top of me and put his bare, smooth thickness inside of me. I wasn't sure if I wanted to go there with him, but if I said no he might tell his dad not to let me stay there. He moved his hips around side to side like he was trying to hit something. It felt so good. I kissed his neck. He held on to me tightly and then he took it out and stroked himself until he released. He kissed me on the forehead and then picked his boxers off the ground, walked out of the room and shut the door. After he left the room I felt differently about Marcus. I thought I might be starting to like him.

The next night Marcus came in again. I started to look at him differently. Marcus made me feel like a woman every time we did it I would always wrap the covers around my body. He would pull them off and tell me I was beautiful. He taught me everything about love and sex.

Chapter 5

"Kendra, are you fucking Marcus?" John yelled at me over the phone

"No, why you ask that?" I stuttered.

"Because he keeps talking about you and asking me what if questions."

"No. I don't deal with him like that," I lied to John.

"Kendra, if I find out he messing with you I'm going to beat your ass, then I'm going to kill him," John yelled over the phone. I had denied it, but I was with Marcus now. At first I didn't like him coming in the room in the middle of the night, but he was nice to me and had grown on me. I was really starting to get feelings for him. He had been comforting me and reassuring me that everything was going to be all right with my family. He met me at my job so I didn't have to ride the bus alone. He bought me my weekly pass to get on the bus, food and clothes. I had been able to save up my money for the house.

Marcus always paid for everything. For my eighteenth birthday he bought me a pair of sneakers, balloons and a teddy bear. Me, him, Nitra and John went to Pizza Hut and to the movies to see *Titanic*. I really liked Marcus, but I didn't want to get pregnant. I asked Nitra what to do and she took me to the clinic with her. I got an examination and got on the pill.

My mom had been in rehab for sixty days. When she walked out the doors, she looked so pretty! Her eyes were bright and wide open, her skin was glowing and she had her hair braided back into two French twists. I wished everyone could see her. She had even gained back her weight and then some. I told her I had the money for the house and then we took her to Old Country Buffet because she said she wanted some real food. She piled all this food on her plate.

"You gonna eat all that food?" I asked.

"Yeah, that food was awful in there. I couldn't wait to get me some real food. I can't wait to just be back in my own house with my own things. So I'm about to be a grandmama at thirty-eight, I heard."

"I didn't know John told you."

"He also told me you and Marcus are sneaking around."

"He told you that?" I said, shocked.

"Marcus is a little older than you. I don't like that," my mother said.

"Mom, he's real nice," I said, taking up for him.

"Y'all sleeping together."

"No."

"Oh, Lord. Yes you are. Y'all grown. All I can say is make sure you love him and he loves you equally. 'Cause I'm going to tell you something, I don't recommend that young love, Kendra. One day you young and the next thing you turn around, sit back and are married with a bunch of babies and then all your dreams and hopes are gone."

"Mom, he is good to me. I really love him."

"Kendra, I really loved your dad too! As a matter of fact I loved him too much. I loved him more than I love y'all and myself. I didn't know any better 'cause I was lost for so many years drinking. When me and your dad broke up I just lost it. It's like when he left I didn't know what to do. I didn't know how to go on. How to make it. I had five kids and I thought life was over. Who's gonna want a woman with five kids? But I shouldn't have did that. When I stopped drinking the first week, that's when I realized life goes on, and one person can't stop you from living. Kendra, everything looks different to me now. And I just don't ever want you to get stuck."

"I promise I won't get stuck." It felt so good having my real mom back. Now all we had to do was get Bubbles and Bilal home, get a place and life would be perfect.

My mom went to the housing office and told them her situation and they gave her the first house available. It was only three bedrooms but that was better than nothing. I went and got a cashier's check for fifteen hundred dollars and they gave us the keys two days later.

"We're home. We have our own space again. We have a home," she said as she opened the door with the key. I followed her in as she looked around our new house. The entire house was painted white with blue industrial carpet all throughout. The sun was shining bright. There was a master bedroom but there weren't any curtains.

The first night me and my mom slept on the floor. It didn't matter though. The only thing that mattered was that we had a home.

* * *

My mom got up early and went and filled out job applications. She wanted to have a job by the time she went back to family court. I waited for the Rent-a-Center to deliver our furniture and for the phone man to come. They both took all day.

My mom came home. "I filled out applications everywhere—somebody is going to call me."

"They will, Mom."

"Pass me the phone. I'm going to call your sister to see if she wants to come home. You too! You don't have to live with that boy," my mother said.

"I know," I said.

My mother began to search in her bag for Alanna's number. She found it and called Alanna and then said she was going to cry. "Your sister got married and is moving on base with Bruce to California." *Damn,* I thought. A little tear formed in my mom's eye, then she said, "Kendra, thank you for being my rock, for being strong. I really appreciate it."

"You're welcome."

"We just got to go get Bub and Bilal back and everything will be fine again," she said, reassuring herself.

My mother was able to regain custody of the kids after we went to court. Ms. Norton had gotten promoted, so we had this new social worker who didn't love her job as much as Ms. Norton had. She took the order on me out of the system. They came and inspected our house and verified my mom was working a job. Our family was back together and I felt so thankful.

Chapter 6

June 2004

On the ride home from the bar I was still evaluating my life. *Why those bitches had to come up in my job and talk shit about me?* I thought as tears began to flow down my face. *My life is okay—I'm doing all right. Yeah, I don't have a big house, but I'm happy. I have my family, and I have my health. With all that happened to me I'm doing good.* I tried to make myself feel good about my accomplishments, but the truth was seeping in slowly. I hadn't done shit with my life in the last seven years. I couldn't think of one thing besides helping my family. My life had been on pause, I was stuck in neutral. I have done nothing with my life. I never went back to school, I don't own a home and my car is a dirty white rusted 1992 two-door Corolla. I always told myself I would go back and get my GED and take some classes, but I never did. Every time I filled out the application, something would happen. The only thing I do is spend time with my family, making sure they are all right, and go to work.

Really, besides work I don't have a life. Me and Marcus still together, but he turned into an old man, too. All he do is go to work, come home, grab a beer and watch television. We still stay with his dad because he doesn't want to leave him alone or put him in a nursing home. I do help my mom with her bills and I buy Bubbles and Bilal clothes and sneaks. I take them out and do things with them as much as I can. My mother works at Pathmark, but she still don't make enough to take care of three people. Plus she spends up all her money. My mom has traded her drinking in for gambling. Yup, out with one bad habit, in with another one. She is a professional lottery ticket buyer and slot machine puller now. She buys two hundred Powerball tickets and goes to casinos and horse races. She was betting on everything and wasting every dollar she had, but at least she doesn't drink. My little sister, Bubbles, is in the eleventh grade. She is doing good. She thinned out and lost her baby weight. She has a job at McDonald's. Bilal's in the tenth grade, and he plays basketball. John and Nitra got married and have three children, and then there is Alanna.

Well, Alanna is still the same evil person, only now she is a bitter, angry, fat, twice-divorced woman. Once she hit twenty-three, Bruce left her for an eighteen-year-old. He found somebody young and dumb like she had been. She comes around the family more but still keeps her distance. She lives in Bakersfield, California. She has a daughter, Ayanna, and a son, Anwar. However, she is such a mess of a mom that her kids live with Bruce.

Her second husband, Ernie, that only lasted three months because she found out he was gay. But we all knew that the moment she brought him around the family. We told her but she didn't listen.

I haven't talked to my dad in years—whenever he calls I pass the phone to Bubbles or Bilal. I never forgave him for not coming to get us. If my mother didn't get herself together we would have been stuck in the system.

I tried to shake off that girl's comments. I was home

now and I would never see that bitch again. I walked in and Mr. Skip was still on the sofa. Everything was basically the same in the house. He was lying in the bed watching television. His walker was sitting next to the bed. He had prosthetic legs that he almost never used.

"Mr. Skip, you want something to drink?" He looked away from the television and at me.

"Yes, can you get me something? My nurse warmed up that food you made me. It was good."

"You want some more?" I asked as I checked the mail.

"If you could, please."

I walked in the kitchen and made Mr. Skip another plate of macaroni, greens, and ribs. I gave him his warm plate of food. Mr. Skip in the last two years hadn't been able to get out of bed at all. He has a nurse come every day and then he was home for a few hours by himself until I got in.

I walked into our room and took my clothes off. I looked around our bedroom. It was a damn mess. We had piles of junk everywhere. Marcus's shoes and boots lined one wall and mine lined the other. There was a stack of magazines in the corner. We had this old yellowed bed frame with gold trim. One of our dressers was missing a handle. The bottom drawer was just an empty space where a drawer should have been. We needed to get a new bedroom set. I bet you those bitches have master bedrooms with big beds and big closets, and look at how I'm living.

I walked around the room and tried to straighten things up, but it was just no use. I was living in a dump. I felt another tear coming. I looked around again. I should be doing way better than this. Instantly I felt like my eyes had just opened up and I could see clearly.

I walked into the bathroom and turned the shower on. The bathroom looked awful. It wasn't dirty, because I cleaned it up every other day. It was just old-looking. The old double silver faucet was dripping nonstop—it had been broken for a while. The "c" and "o" on the word *cold* were missing. The floor had tiles missing, and there was a hole in the wall where the toilet tissue holder used to be. I was beginning to give myself a headache. I looked in the medicine cabinet, popped two Advils and then took a quick glance in the mirror at myself. I noticed puffiness beginning to form under my eyes. I needed to stop crying and worrying. It is what it is. I got in the warm shower and let today's bullshit roll off me. I closed my eyes and just exhaled. I took a long shower, then walked out of the bathroom. Marcus had come in from work and already laid out on the bed. I gave him a kiss on the lips.

"I didn't even hear you come in," I said as I dried off.

"Yeah, I'm tired. My body hurt. All this overtime is killing me," he said.

I slipped on the nightgown and lay next to him. I began stroking his hair and closed my eyes.

"How was your day?" I asked.

"It was good. What about yours?"

"It was kind of messed up."

"Why? What happened?" he asked.

"Nothing. I don't want to talk about it. Did you get a chance to pay the cell phone bill?"

"No, not yet," he said.

"You know they are going to turn our phones off," I said sighing.

"You don't have the money?" he asked.

"No. I paid last month."

"You might have to take care of it again, okay? My overtime should be on this check, but I'm not sure. So are you going to tell me what's bothering you?"

"Nothing is bothering me."

"Yes it is, baby. Tell me. I can see it in your face. What's on your mind?" I sat on my side and said, "Baby, these women I went to school with came into my job today."

"Okay, so what happened?"

"Well, they asked me what was I doing with my life."

"Okay," he said like he was waiting for me to tell him what else had happened.

"That's it. One of them got drunk and she was just talking shit. She was really loud, saying, 'Oh my God, Kendra, you used to be a good singer. Now all you do is this.' "

"How could you allow someone to come into your job and make you feel bad? You should have said, 'Bitch, what the fuck do you do?'" he said as he stood up. I knew he could see how badly it had affected me.

"I couldn't say that because they all had their shit together. Like one was a nurse, the other just bought a house in North Carolina and the other was engaged." I saw the dumb look Marcus was giving me.

"So? They still don't have anything on you," he said.

Obviously he wasn't getting it, so I said, "Just forget it, Marcus."

"You shouldn't be upset. It is really not that big of a deal."

"Don't tell me I shouldn't be upset. You don't know how that shit felt, having a bitch you hardly remember tell you basically your life ain't shit," I snapped as I stood up.

"Baby, listen. I'm not telling you how to feel. I just don't see why you are so upset," he said, standing up, easing me back on the bed.

"Get off me, Marcus. Get off me, Marcus!" I said as I tried to stand up. "It hurt, baby, to have them look at me like I'm nothing. It hurt because maybe they are right. Maybe I'm not living the life I'm supposed to be living. Baby, I feel like I'm supposed to be doing something else with my life." I felt tears rush down my cheeks.

"Like what?"

"Like something. Why didn't I ever think to get a real job? Huh?"

"You have a real job."

"No, I don't. You can't retire from being a bartender. Why didn't I go to school or something?"

"You are doing good," Marcus said.

"No, I'm not. I mean look around. I should have more. I'm twenty-five years old. In five years I'll be thirty and what the fuck do I have? We should have more. We need to buy a house."

Marcus stood up and began walking around the room and said, "Yo, what's wrong with what we have? We doing good. I mean, we both working and we have cars. You know my dad is going to leave us this house. And then we'll get a loan against it, fix it up, do some remodeling and live a good life."

"Marcus, I'm not sitting around waiting for your father to die so we can own a home."

"Okay, we can get a house before that."

I didn't say anything for a moment.

"What is it that you think you might want to do?" he asked.

"I don't know," I said angrily as I turned over and went to sleep.

The next morning, I shook the day before off. My mother called and said, "Don't forget your nephew's party is today."

"Mom, this my only day off. I'm tired, and I don't feel like dealing with any kids."

"I don't care. Don't stand my grandbaby up on his birthday. I better see you there. You know John and Nitra will be so upset if you aren't. We have to go to Toys "R" Us and pick something up."

"I'll see what I can do." I forgot that I had to go to my

damn four-year-old nephew's birthday party. John and Nitra have three kids. The first is my nephew Montae—he was about to be seven—and my niece Laila was a month old and Damir was turning four today.

Marcus and I arrived just as they were opening gifts. Nitra and John had made a nice home for themselves. They lived in a spacious row home in the Overbrook section of Philly, on a block lined with trees and small lawns. The theme for the party was Power Rangers. Nitra had Power Ranger everything everywhere. She had transformed her house into a Power Ranger station. Nitra was always good at that motherly stuff. She was still carrying a little bit of her baby weight, but she looked great.

"Marcus, John's upstairs putting that game together. You should probably help him," she suggested, and Marcus went up the steps.

"Come on in the kitchen and get yourself something to eat," she said, pulling me by the arm.

We walked past the children running all around the party. The birthday boy—his name was Damir, but his nickname was Boy Boy—ran into the kitchen behind us.

"Hi, Aunt Kendra! Look what I can do!" He tried to flex his little-bitty muscle. I told him that was nice and took a seat. Then he began dancing, doing side flips and moving his feet real fast like he was a chicken running in place. We all began laughing. It was so funny because he was bony and couldn't dance, but in his little mind he was doing good.

"You doin' it, Boy Boy. It's your birthday. Get down," Nitra said, encouraging him. Then he ran out of the kitchen.

"You need any help?" I asked.

"Yeah, I do. All these kids' parents just dropped their kids off. I don't understand people. When my kids go to parties, I stay there with them. Kendra, I just need help with putting the food out," she said as she took a tray of chicken out of the refrigerator.

* * *

I helped Nitra pass out the hot dogs and cleaned up all the half-finished soda cans. Then it was time to sing "Happy Birthday." I scooped out ice cream and passed out cake. I was tired. That's why I didn't want to come in the first place, because I knew I would wind up doing work. Boy Boy ran in the kitchen and tapped my leg and asked, "It's my birthday. What did you buy me?"

"You'll see when you open up your gifts," I said.

"We can open them now," Nitra said as she gathered all the kids into the living room. John came down the steps with a camera and this huge Power Ranger game he was putting together. He gave me a kiss on the cheek.

Boy Boy sat in the living room with all the other kids and began opening his gifts. He tore through the layers of wrapping paper. He was upset because all his gifts so far were clothes.

"More stupid clothes," he said as he threw the outfit I bought him on the floor.

"Boy Boy, don't do that," Nitra scolded him.

"Look in the other bag. Uncle Marcus got you something else," Marcus said.

"A truck! Thank you, Uncle Marcus!"

"You're welcome," Marcus said as he palmed his head and shook it slightly. My mom and Bubbles came through the door with more toys.

"How you get here?" Nitra asked.

"We caught the bus," my mom said.

"Mom, why y'all catch the bus? We would have came and got you."

"I know but I was trying to wait on Bilal to come home. Then he didn't come, and we didn't want to miss the party, so we left. He's somewhere playing with his friends."

"I'll make you a plate, Ms. Joanne," Nitra said as she got up.

"Nitra, make that plate to go. I have to get out of here soon. My bus to the casino leaves at five. Can somebody give me a ride to the bus depot?" my mom asked.

"We were about to leave anyway," I said. "I have to go to work tomorrow and I'm tired." I had fulfilled my auntie obligation.

We dropped my mom off at the bus station. "Give me a lucky number," she said as she got out of the car.

"Ten, twelve, a hundred, two, and five. Mom, why does it matter? You're not going to win," I said. I was damn tired of her gambling.

"Don't say that. You don't know that," she said, irritated with me.

"All you doing is wasting your time and your money."

"Whatever. This is how I like to spend my money and one day I am going to win, and when I do, don't come and ask me for any money."

"I won't."

After we dropped her off we went and grabbed something to eat, then went home and watched *CSI Miami*. I eventually nodded off.

Marcus awoke me by whispering in my ear, "You ready to have a baby, Kendra?"

I pretended to be asleep. My eyes were shut.

I didn't say anything. I was hoping he would just go to sleep if I didn't answer him.

"Kendra, you not ready to be my wife and have my baby?"

"Not now. I'm sleeping," I whispered.

"Wake up. We've been together for all these years. I think it is time to start our family."

"I don't know what I want to do with my life yet. And

I definitely don't want to bring anybody into the world when I don't know what I want to do with myself. We still have so much to do with ourselves like get somewhere nice to live first."

"Kendra, you know I'm going to get you a house and make you my wife and then we going to have a baby. Now say yes."

"I'm not saying yes, I still want to wait. I want to get another job or go to school or something," I said as I turned around to him.

"I said we going to get married. You going to let me put a baby in there," he said, grabbing me around my waist. "I want you to stop taking your pills."

"No I'm not going to do that, not right now." I was becoming more and more irritated.

"No? You don't want to have my baby?"

"Marcus, leave me alone. I'm going back to sleep," I said as I clutched my pillow and turned my back to him. I knew what had happened to him. He saw John and Nitra and now he felt like he wanted to have a family too. But I wasn't feeling that right now. I had to do something else with my life.

I was back at work. It was kind of slow. It was so ironic, I worked in a place that my mom can't even walk in, but whatever. I sat there looking around. How did I stay in this place for all these years? It wasn't exactly a dump, but I knew I could do so much more with my life. Like some people are just so smart they just know they are supposed to go to school without anyone telling them. And after college they are supposed to be able to get a good job and go to work every day. Maybe I didn't care back then, but I sure did now. My daydreaming was interrupted with, "Kendra, give me a whiskey sour." It was one of my regulars.

"How you doing, Mike?" I asked as I put a napkin in front of him.

"Not so good. I can't go home—might as well stay here," he said, hunching his shoulder.

"Why? What happened?" I asked.

"My woman left me. Messed up right," Mike said, shaking his head.

"Why she leave you?" I asked placing his whiskey sour in front of him.

"'Cause she found out about my wife." He laughed. He threw back that drink and said, "Can you give me one more?"

I poured him another. I then sat and did a crossword puzzle.

"Kendra, one more," he said, calling me over. Then he said, "As a matter of fact make it a double." He was up to four drinks. I sat down and then he waved me back over to him.

"Kendra, I got to tell you something."

"What you got to tell me, Mike?" I asked.

"Kendra, you know you got to believe in something. Well, I believe I'm gonna have another drink," he said as he fell off the stool laughing.

I looked over the bar, and there he was on the floor with his head bashed in with blood pouring from it. He pulled himself up, said he was okay and staggered to the bathroom. He came back five minutes later and said, "Pretty lady, I'm going to need one more for the road."

"No, that's it, Mike."

"Bitch! Give me another drink," he demanded. I wasn't about to argue with his drunk ass, so I called Julius from the back. He came out and I said, "Tell him that's it."

"Sorry, pal, no more tonight."

"Fuck it. I'll get a drink from somewhere else," he said as he fell one more time before walking out the door. "Isn't that something—he wants to cuss us out for trying to save his life," Julius said. I was beginning to hate my job and my life. I started getting a headache.

I went home and just lay in the bed. I felt sad for no reason. I was still thinking about my life. What could I do and what could I do fast that would make up for the years I didn't do anything with my life? The only thing I was ever interested in or good at in my life was singing. Singing was what made people pay attention to me. It was what made me special. I had forgotten how to be special. I remembered people coming up to me asking me to sing. I was missing my passion. I didn't even remember why I stopped singing. I just did.

When Marcus came home, I asked, "Do you remember me wanting to be a singer?"

"Yeah, you used to say you sung when you was little. Why?"

"I was thinking about how happy singing used to make me feel."

"Okay, so what are you saying?" he said, taking off his uniform at the edge of the bed.

"What do you think about me singing again? Like really trying to make a living at it?"

He looked at me like I was dumb and said, "Realistically, how are you going to be a singer, baby? You know how many people can sing, Kendra? And you sing great, but what, are you going to go audition for *American Idol*? I mean, be for real. Be serious. You're twenty-five. That's something you should have tried to do when you was a teenager, like at seventeen or eighteen."

"You're right," I reluctantly admitted.

"No, listen, I support whatever you want to do. I'm behind you one hundred percent. I just think you can find something to go back to school for. And I support that, but being a singer . . . it's not realistic."

"So you don't think I could be a singer?" I asked him.

"You can be a singer, but to make a living off of it—I don't know, babe. You're good, but it might be other singers that are better."

Marcus was trying to be supportive, but then again he wasn't. He was saying, "Yeah, I believe in you, but I don't think you will make it." I looked up at the ceiling for an answer and all I saw was chipped paint. Why was I asking Marcus about moving on when he was still sleeping in the bedroom he grew up in? And the trifling thing was that I was lying next to him.

Chapter 7

I had a dream last night. In my dream I was at the old house I grew up in. Everything was still in the same place like right before the fire and I opened the closet door. When the door opened I saw light, so I kept moving forward and then I found another bedroom. I didn't realize my mom's house was that big. There was another bathroom and another living room. It was almost another apartment. It didn't look like anyone lived here. I exited the room and then I awoke and called my mother.

"Mom, you have your dream book?" I asked.

"Why, what you dream about?"

"I dreamed that there were extra rooms in the house." My mom said, "Hold up," as she found her book.

"More rooms? Yeah. Room means 532. I'm going to play that today. It says here that finding rooms in your dream means that you have room to grow and unfulfilled dreams. You don't have any unfulfilled dreams do you?"

"I kind of do, Mom. I was talking to Marcus about trying to sing again. He said he thinks I'm too old. What do you think about me trying to sing at twenty-five? I'm too old, right?"

"You're never too old. If that's your dream, you need to follow it. The way I look at it is, you're going to be twenty-six next year, if you try to make it happen or not. So I think you should do it." My mom was always honest with me.

"Okay, but do you think I could make it?" I asked her again.

"Kendra, um, I think you can. But it ain't going to be easy."

"You right. But it is at least worth a try. Right?" As soon as I hung up with her I decided that I was going to look into singing again. I haven't sung in years. The most I ever sang nowadays was in my car at a red light and in the shower. After everything happened, with the fire and us being homeless for a while, I just didn't want to be bothered anymore. I didn't think about writing a song or lyrics but now I felt like I wanted to sing—and what could it hurt if I try?

I went to Borders and spent eighty-seven dollars on books about songwriting and breaking into the music industry. The first page I read was about defining your musical goals. I knew exactly what I wanted to do, and that was be a singer.

I needed three songs for my demo tape. The book said you should have at least two original songs and maybe one cover song (you singing someone else's song). At work I had all these tunes start coming to me. Like I was just thinking of beats and I just started humming them, and lyrics started coming back to me. Every time I got an idea I wrote it down, and by the end of the night I had all these little napkins with songs on them. I wrote this one song about not giving up on love.

* * *

I looked online at work and found a studio that only charged twenty-five dollars an hour to record. It was run by a young white guy named Sam, whom I spoke to on the phone. He said he had all-new equipment and he made beats, or he could give me some instrumentals. I was going there on Thursday evening. I was so excited. I took off from work, and didn't even tell Marcus. I wanted to surprise him. Actually, I think I really didn't want him to talk me out of it.

I took the address out of my bag and found the block. It was a small, narrow side street. I parked the car, then got out and rang the bell. A young redheaded guy came to the door.

"I'm looking for Sam."

"He's upstairs," he said as he opened the door. We ran up about four flights of steps. The studio was a little room with a bunch of equipment, and keyboards with a small laptop computer. I was very disappointed and I was questioning his professionalism. The studio really looked like someone's bedroom.

"Kendra, I'm Sam. Hi," he said, as the guy I'd talked to over the telephone stood up and shook my hand.

"You don't have a booth?" I asked, looking around for more in the room.

"Oh. Yeah. See, you don't really need a booth to achieve good sound quality," he said as he began to show me his system.

"Your neighbors don't mind?"

"No, 'cause the girl next door is a sculptor and the guy upstairs has a band. Everybody works different hours and makes noise and is artistic, so we all mesh perfectly.

"I'm going to play some of the beats, and you can tell me what you think." He played ten tracks, but none of them was a fit for what I had written. I settled for an instrumental.

I recorded all the songs straight through for the most part. I paid him his seventy-five dollars and he made me copies of the CDs. As I was leaving Sam said, "You're good. You should really come down to North by Northwest on Thursday Nights. It's open mic."

"Where at?"

"On Germantown Avenue. You have to get there early to sign up."

I thanked Sam and left. I walked to my car, inserted the CD and played it the whole way home. I was so excited. I sounded good.

I walked in and gave Marcus a hug and said, "Listen to this. I have something I want you to hear." I put my CD in the stereo and played it.

"It's nice. Who is that singing?"

"That's me, baby."

"Really? Oh, you sound pretty good!" he said. "I would buy it. How did you get it made?" he asked.

"I went to the studio."

"You did? You didn't even tell me," he said, scratching his head.

"I wanted to suprise you."

"It sounds just as good, if not better, than anything I hear on the radio now."

Chapter 8

Now that I had a demo, I didn't know how to get it in the right people's hands. Nitra was listening to the radio and heard that Andre Scott, this popular R&B singer, was in town to promote his new CD. She said he was having a fan appreciation record release party.

"Kendra, you have to go. I will make John go with you." Nitra was right. I went home and changed my clothes to go.

The meet-and-greet line was around the corner. There was no way we was getting in. He had so many fans. They had pictures of him and magazine covers. I thought about jumping the line, but people who were in line were mean, mugging like "I dare you to bust." I didn't feel like getting into anything with anyone. So I walked up to the doorman and said, "How you doing." I was trying to flirt, but it wasn't really working. "I am a singer and trying to get in here."

The big bouncer turned to me and said, "Yeah, only

way you not standing in this line is if you got something to put in my hand."

"Okay, I can do that," I smiled.

"How many people with you?" he said, looking around to see if anyone would notice what was going on.

"Just one."

"Okay, just give me thirty." I pulled out thirty dollars, folded it very small and gave it to him.

Once inside I saw the line for Andre Scott's meet-and-greet. His fans were very serious about meeting him, and they would scream every time he answered a question and were taking pictures on their cell phones. The lights were just flashing, and he knew how to handle it. He seemed genuine. People were running up asking for pictures and autographs. I didn't want to come across as one of those people, but how do you approach a celebrity without seeming like a fan? They get that every day—*listen to my CD, I'm the next big thing.* I couldn't get anywhere near him.

John went to the restroom, then came back and said, "The man at the door that let us in told me that he heard that Andre Scott was going over to Tragos after this. Let's go there and then you can walk right up to him and give him your CD and he'll probably actually listen to it."

I agreed and we left and drove to the other club. We sat at the bar for two hours, but it was worth every minute when Andre Scott came through the door. Nobody in the mostly white crowd had any idea who he was. He was with two guys and three girls. They walked over to a table and had a seat.

John nudged me in the ribs. "This is much better now. You can walk right up to him, have a conversation and not seem like a groupie." This was my opportunity to go over to him. This was my chance. He and his security were trying to get to the bathroom. I walked up behind him. I was about to tap him on the shoulder but then I got scared, and instead of handing him my CD I walked back over to John and had a seat.

"I can't walk up to a stranger. I can't," I said nervously.

"Yo, how about if he sign you? You didn't come out here tonight just to see him."

"You're right, you're right." With that thought on my mind, as soon as I saw him walk out of the bathroom and sit down at his table, I walked over. His little entourage was looking at me like *what the fuck do you want?* I took a deep breath and said, "Hi. How you doing? I just wanted to tell you I really like your music, and I was wondering if I can give you my CD. I'm a singer."

He looked over at his crew. They giggled a little, then he said, "Okay, sweetie. What's your name?"

"Kendra."

"Okay, Kendra, I'll make sure to give it to my manager."

I got a few steps away and I heard him say, "Throw that shit away. Man, I'm so sick of people giving me their damn demo."

I felt so stupid. I'd had to get the courage to walk over to him and then he was an asshole.

"What did he say?" John asked.

"Nothing. Come on. He took the CD and then when I walked away, I heard him say throw it in the trash. If you don't walk up to people, how do you get on?" I asked myself out loud and walked toward the door mad—mad that we had waited for that asshole and he was so rude.

"Don't worry about him. Everybody is not an asshole like him. Fuck him," John said, catching up to me as I walked down the street upset.

"I know, but what makes me so mad is that these people know at one point they were trying to get on and somebody gave them a hand, but now they act like 'I got the key to the door and I'm not letting anyone else in.'"

Already I could see this was not going to be easy at all. Nobody takes you seriously until you are on their level. *Fuck him*, I thought. I swear when I get big I will never forget how it feels to be small.

Chapter 9

I was at my first open mic at North by Northwest. It was a really nice restaurant bar. There were spoken-word artists, poets and singers. Little triangle lights hung from the ceiling above each booth. There was big storefront windows and beautiful floors. The stage was squared a few feet off the ground. A brick wall was the backdrop.

I got onstage and told the crowd I was a little nervous. It was the first time I had sung in front of someone in so many years. It felt so natural, though. I closed my eyes and just began to sing. I sang Anita Baker's "Angel." People were feeling it. I thought I did okay but I was scared and next week I would be better.

My mom and Marcus came out with me the following week. I felt more confident.

"How y'all doin' tonight? My name is Kendra Michelle and I'm about to sing a song for you. Who out there has been through something or is going through something?"

I waited for the audience to respond and then I said,

"Well, so have I. Let me tell you about my life." The drum started going *boom tap boom tap*. I closed my eyes.

"My life my life in the sunshine when you think of my life la di dod di da. Life is what you make it." My eyes were closed and I opened them a little to see the crowd's reaction. They were paying attention and grooving with me. Somebody from the front of the club yelled, "Sing it, girl!"

I got through the song without crying. When I got offstage everybody applauded.

As I walked toward my seat, a man with a bald head and a medium-size frame with a goatee and thinned-out mustache approached me.

"How you doing? I'm Tony Staton," he said as he put his hand out for me to shake. I left him hanging like, *I don't know you.*

"I caught the end of your set. Your performance was great."

"Thank you."

"Do you have a manager?"

"No."

"Well, I would like to talk to you about management."

"Okay, what other artists do you represent?" I asked. I took him a little off guard with that question.

"I represent a girl group that just signed to Columbia Records, and I handle a few other artists who are in the process of being signed. I had another boy group, but as soon as I got them a deal they got another manager. But that's another story. Take my card and when you get some time, give me a call. I can get you shows up and down the east coast where record execs are going to be."

"Thanks. I'll call you," I said as I walked over to the table where Marcus and my mom were sitting. Marcus gave me two dozen red roses. "You were great," he whispered.

We sat, ate dinner and then left the club.

As we left the club, these girls yelled, "You are so talented, girl, you make me want to go get a Mary J. Blige CD. You was good."

"Thanks," I said. When I was on the stage I felt so big.

"Look, you have fans already," Marcus said as he held my hand and we walked to the parking lot. The same gushing girls were getting in a big white Cadillac Escalade as I entered my little Toyota Corolla. They smiled and waved again. *I think I do need a manager. I'm tired of this stage of the game already.*

The next morning I found that man Tony's number. I dialed him up.

"Hi, Tony. This is Kendra."

"Yes, Kendra. It's good to hear from you. So when can we can meet up in person?"

"Can you meet me today?"

"Sure. What time?"

"We can meet in Center City at the London Grille at six."

I hung up the telephone and started to get dressed. I heard so many horror stories about people being taken advantage of. I had to make sure Tony was real. I was going to have Marcus go with me—he just didn't know it yet. When he pulled up, I didn't let him get fully out of the car before I said, "Baby, you have to go with me to meet this man. I need to meet that manager, the one I told you about. He wants to meet downtown in an hour to discuss managing me."

"Do I have enough time to take a shower?"

"A quick one," I said as I gave him a kiss on the cheek.

On the ride over Marcus and I already agreed that we were going to let Tony talk and see what he had to say. He came and had a seat at our table. He looked a little different in bright light. His mustache was coming in salt and pepper, and he had a big bald head. He was wearing a black sweater and blue slacks.

"I think you are very talented. I haven't heard a singer blow like that in a long time. If I were your manager I would get you doing some shows first, then eventually get you signed to a record deal."

"And how does all that work? How much do you get paid?" Marcus asked.

"I get fifteen percent of all her shows."

"And what about if she get signed? I don't want her getting jerked."

"I wouldn't allow her to sign anything that I didn't believe in. And I know plenty of entertainment lawyers. I would definitely make sure she has her business right. We would sign a management contract that's good for two years, but for any reason at any time you want to terminate me you can." Tony kept talking on and on about how I was talented but that was only going to take me half of the way. I needed somebody to let me be an artist and let them handle my business. He went to the bathroom, and when he left the table I asked, "Do you think he selling me dreams, Marcus?"

"No, he seems legit." I was relieved that Marcus had come with me, because I wouldn't have been able to make this decision on my own.

Chapter 10

We were on our way to Washington, D.C., but we were stuck right in traffic on Interstate 295. On a Friday afternoon it wasn't even moving at all. Tony had booked me for a show in D.C. and we were running late. I was so upset.

"Tony, I am so sorry. We are lost," I said over the phone. I was mad at myself for not allowing enough time. When I had checked for directions, it said two and half hours. I'd thought three hours and I would be good. I couldn't breathe.

"You okay for time. I'll just let one of the other groups go in front of you," he said reassuringly.

I didn't want to be late for my first show. My mom and Marcus were driving down with me for support. I was so excited to be having a big show in D.C. This was a great opportunity. I looked at the address Tony had written for the club. We were on the right block, but I didn't see the spot until Marcus pointed to a house and said that's it.

"That's not the club!" I said as Marcus pulled over in front of some rinky-dink neighborhood bar.

"Yes, it is, Kendra. Look at the address." I didn't even want to go inside it looked so bad.

Tony talked all that stuff about who he used to manage, and here he had me in Northeast Washington, D.C., in some dive. I was performing on the second floor. I was so irritated. If it wasn't for my mom and Marcus being with me, I would have left.

Tony walked up to us and said hi. I pulled him to the side and gave it to him.

"Tony, I brought my family down here and I'm telling them I have this big show in Washington, D.C., and you should have just told me it was not a real place."

"Kendra, I've been doing this for ten years. I know what I'm doing. You just have to trust me. A lot of people can sing. What makes you different? What's going to make you stand out from the rest? We've got to develop you some more. We are going to get to the big clubs and meet with the labels. But what sense does it make if you are not ready?"

"I think I'm ready."

"No, this is what you have do to get ready. You have to get rid of your stage fright and get your presentation tight. Why am I going to put you in front of somebody when you still forget your lyrics sometimes? I have relationships at labels, and I don't want to lose my credibility, you know. The question is, will you get yourself ready? Will you work harder and better than the artist they saw the day before, and the next artist they'll see the day after?"

I just nodded my head as he kept running his mouth.

"I understand all that, but why do you have me at this small-ass place? How is this going to help my singing?"

"It's going to help you, because a real artist will get onstage and give a great performance for six people and sing like they are singing for six million. You sing because you enjoy it, not because you think you're about to get paid. Don't forget that," he said.

I thought about what he was saying and decided to follow his lead. Face it—he had more knowledge of this business than I did.

My next show was in New York City at a place called the Sugar Bar. This husband-and-wife singing group from the '80s, Ashford and Simpson, owned the club. It was small but it was packed to capacity, and it had a different vibe. For some reason I was so nervous—maybe because I knew there could be somebody in the audience who could change my life. Or it could have been because everyone who was on the stage was really good, except for this one guy. He was on the stage singing Al Green's "Let's Stay Together," ruining the song. His voice kept cracking and he kept saying that he was sorry but he wasn't feeling well. *Don't make any excuses,* I thought. Then the girl who went on before me sang "Over the Rainbow." She didn't know the words and tried to compensate by oversinging and yelling. She almost blew my eardrum out. She wasn't that good but the crowd still respectfully clapped. Then they called me up to the stage. I took the microphone.

"How y'all doin'? I'm from Philly. My name is Kendra Michelle, and I'm going to sing a little Stevie Wonder." I took the microphone out of the holder.

I was singing Stevie Wonder's "Ribbon in the Sky." The band began to play the music. "Speed it up," I said to the band so they could pick up the beat. I was a little nervous and I missed my cue.

"Bring it around again," I instructed the band—the bass, loud guitar, drums, electronic keyboard. The beat began, and I started swaying. I took the mic out of the stand and began to sing. I looked out into the audience and I was nervous for about two seconds. Then I closed my eyes and sang. The crowd was really into it. As soon as I left the stage, people started asking if I had a CD for sale or a website. I was flattered, but I felt unprepared. I told the guy who asked, I was working on it. We stayed around for a little while then we left to go home. On the drive back Tony said he talked with a couple of people about me.

I got home about one in the morning. I could tell that Marcus was getting a little fed up with all my late nights singing but it wasn't like I was just partying—I was basically working. When I came in the door he looked at the alarm clock and then at me.

"I told you my show was in New York. Right?"

"I understand, baby. I just miss you being in the bed with me. How was your show?"

"It was good. Tony did get business cards from some A&Rs from a few different labels. He's going to make some calls in the morning."

"That's good but I miss you. I need to feel you come and get in bed with your man."

I took my clothes off and fell into Marcus's arms.

Over the next few months Tony had me singing everywhere—talent shows, karaoke nights, and even at birthday parties and weddings. I was tired but it kept me motivated. So far he was doing a good job. Tony got me an interview with a local weekly alternative newspaper and I met the journalist at a café on South Street. I told her about all the shows I had coming up and about my music. *Philadelphia Weekly* did a big article on me, and when I went to work some of my customers brought the article in and asked me what I was doing still working there.

Chapter 11

Tony followed up with this guy he'd met at the Sugar Bar who was an A&R for Sony Music. He was already coming to Philadelphia, and he wanted me and Tony to meet him at his suite at the Loews Hotel. I told everyone at my job, my mom, Marcus, my brother and Nitra, and everyone was so hyped. My mom was so excited she wanted to take off from work. I told her not to though.

"You're going to be a star. Forget this job. You're about to be a star," my mom said.

"Mom, please go to work. It is not that serious."

"Okay, I'll go, but call me as soon as you finish to let me know how you made out." I promised her I would.

His name was Eric Dawson. He was in his early thirties with almond skin and light freckles. He was very tall and intimidating. His suite had a big sofa and a big window. He was sitting on the sofa.

"How you doing?" he said.

"Hi."

"So how long have you been singing?"

"Since I can remember," I said.

"Let me hear what you have."

I sang my heart out for him for three minutes of Alicia Keys's "I Keep on Fallin'."

"What do you think?" I asked Tony once we got in the hallway.

"He said you need some work. I told you, Kendra, he said he would be in touch. I'll call him on Monday but I have to be honest with you, it does not seem promising."

I had met with four A&Rs each time but nobody was interested. I didn't know why, because I knew I could sing. I always looked nice. It was just something crazy. They already had an idea of what they wanted and I wasn't it. Tony was reading the frustration in my face, because each time we had a meeting and didn't get a response, I was losing confidence in myself.

"Kendra, I'm going to keep it a hundred percent. We have to clean up your look. Like right now they can't tell who you are. You a cute girl but you need some jazzing up."

I looked at Tony like, *excuse me, look at yourself in the mirror.* "What's wrong with me? I look nice."

"Okay, you look nice, but the last two guys kind of said the same thing—that we had to get your image together. Next time I want you to wear your hair down and basically come looking like you are a star, 'cause you are. No more jeans, and wear some makeup. Look like a grown-ass woman. As a matter of fact, we are going to buy you a few dresses and I'm going to have my wife, Liz, go shopping with you."

Chapter 12

Tony was able to get me a meeting at Touchlight Music Group, a midsized label in New York City. Tony's wife, Liz, gave me a total makeover. She was a makeup artist at M.A.C. and did makeup for weddings and photo shoots. She taught me how to do my makeup and had my skin looking flawless. She also told me to be "on" twenty-four hours a day. That meant as soon as I awoke in the morning I should do my hair and get dressed, even if I was just doing nothing in the house all day. I had to act like a star like there were cameras following me. And so far it was working. Marcus thought I was acting a little crazy because I was actually keeping up with the beauty regime. As soon as I awoke I glammed it up and discovered it made me feel good too. He thought I looked good, but he hated all the extra time I was beginning to spend in the bathroom. I had to work some of that confidence today.

I couldn't decide what I was going to wear. It was between a green wrap dress or a short black halter dress. My hair was the only thing I didn't have to worry about. I had already gone to the hairdresser and was wearing a chic long, flowing weave with a part in the middle. I was going to be a star, I said as I looked at myself in the mirror.

My attitude now was, "You are going to sign me." I had to get on now. I can really sing, I look good and I write my own songs.

I decided to wear the black dress with black and white knee boots. I had big gold bangles on and glossy peach lipstick. This meeting was so important because the A&R, Thomas, had actually seen me before at the Sugar Bar and personally requested that I come to his office.

We walked into Touchlight Music Group's doors at eleven in the morning. The receptionist was a very pretty Latina. She was wearing a short red-brown skirt, nude stockings and black high heels. Tony told her we were there to see Thomas Reid, and she said that he would be out momentarily and to have a seat. We sat down and I began taking everything in. I was really at a record label. It could really happen—all my dreams could come true. That would be so good. If I could be a signed artist my life would change dramatically. Gold and platinum records decorated the walls. I turned around and looked at Tony like, *do you see this?* He just nodded like, *I know.* The tables were filled with postcards and huge illuminated wall posters of album covers. The office was so busy with people walking in and out.

"You okay over there?" Tony asked as he patted my arm.

"Yeah, I'm cool. Just thinking," I said as I snapped out of it and looked over the office. After what seemed like an eternity the receptionist finally said, "You can come with me." We both followed her down a long hallway.

The receptionist showed us into a meeting room with a view of the Manhattan skyline—big office buildings in every direction. We sat at a long pine table. There was a container of pencils and paper and a half-finished water bottle. Thomas came in. He was short and had a low haircut with a slightly pushed-back hairline. He was speaking to someone through his Bluetooth headset and typing on his BlackBerry. Tony got up and shook his hand. He said hello to me and sat down. But once he was seated, another phone started ringing. He took that phone out of his pocket, then he looked down at the screen and said, "Sorry. Excuse me, I have to take this call." He appeared to be very busy.

When he walked out of the room Tony whispered, "This is your chance. You have to be great."

His little comment made me scared. I knew what was at stake; I didn't need him to remind me. I closed my eyes and took a deep breath. When I opened my eyes Thomas was entering the room again. "Okay, sorry about that." He sat down, glanced at his notes, then looked up at me and said, "Ms. Kendra, I enjoyed your performance at the Sugar Bar."

"Thank you," I said smiling.

"Well, you can begin when you are ready."

I stood up and placed my hands on my waist and began to sing Alicia Keys's "If I Ain't Got You."

As soon I began he interrupted me and said, "Sing something else." I could tell he was trying to make me nervous.

"Okay, okay." I was nervous, but this was my chance. I had to sing. I had to prove to him that I was the one. I began to sing "Make It Happen" by Mariah Carey. I started off slow and then when I got to the end of the song I hit the high note and then brought it back down. "If you believe in yourself make it happen."

When I stopped, he looked at me and said, "Very good," and then he stood in the doorway.

I attempted to look at Tony to see what was going on as

Thomas called two other people into the conference room. Was he happy? Was he sad? Was this a good sign that he was bringing other people in the room? It had to be a good sign, right? They both sat down. It was an older white guy with a gray suit and brown hair and a young black woman with big glasses and naturally bushy hair pulled back with a headband.

"Kendra, I want you to sing that song you just sang and do something else by Mariah Carey."

I sang "Make It Happen" again and then "Dream Lover." I looked over at Tony for guidance. I couldn't read his face. After I finished I just stood there and waited. Then they started asking me questions.

"How old are you?" the woman asked.

"Twenty-five," I said quickly, waiting for the next question. They looked over at Thomas and made expressions to him that I couldn't determine if they were good or bad.

Shortly afterward they thanked us for coming in and said they would be in touch. I couldn't tell how things had gone. But I know I felt lonely when Tony put me on the Greyhound bus home, even though he told me I did very well. He was staying in town for other meetings. He had some other business to take care of and he would call me. I rode home on the bus feeling defeated. If I was any good they would have signed me on the spot, I thought.

As I passed through the Lincoln Tunnel I felt like my dreams of being a singer were just that—dreams.

After a few days went by I knew they weren't going to sign me. I gave up hope of them ever calling me. Tony told me labels generally sign on the spot or within a week if they really think they have something because they don't want anyone else to take their find. So life for me went back to normal. I was so glad I hadn't told Marcus or my family. I didn't want them to be disappointed again. People who love you hurt when you hurt. The last time a record label didn't call me back, my mom called me crying, telling me I was going to make it and to just believe in God. She said I was special and for me not to forget it.

I had been at this for a couple of months now and I was ready to give up. I mean, I didn't know this shit was this hard! I don't know how long you're supposed to keep your dream alive without finally giving up and getting a real job. I don't know. Maybe I'll just do something else. Only thing was I didn't know what that something was. I didn't know what I wanted to do with my life. But I did know I had to get up out of this restaurant. I was tired of my drunk patrons and the waitresses' little attitudes. The waitresses were always taking down the wrong drink order and blaming it on me when I made their drink wrong.

Tonight it was the same tired shit and I was not in a good mood. This new waitress Adrian spilled her drinks and I had to make them over. Who told her dumb ass to try to carry all those drinks at once? I started wiping down the counter but all of a sudden heard my phone ringing. I looked in my bag. It was Tony calling me, but he could go to hell too! I sent him to voicemail several times. I just didn't feel like dealing with anyone, but he kept calling, so I answered.

"Yeah, Tony?" I said.

"Where are you at?" he asked.

"At work."

"Okay, so I heard back from Touchlight."

"You did? What did they say?" I asked, suddenly all excited.

"Kendra, they are going to sign you for a two-album deal."

"What? Oh my God! Are you serious?" I started screaming.

"Kendra, yes. You have a deal."

"No, stop playing. Why you lying, Tony?"

"I just got off the phone with Thomas Reid. You know

it doesn't happen this fast. Most people be out here for years before they even get someone to listen them, but you got a damn good manager."

"You are good! Thank you." I laughed.

"Congratulations. I'll call you tomorrow and tell you all the particulars."

I contained my excitement and just sat down, ignoring the customers trying to order drinks. My eyes started filling with tears. I kept silently thanking God. I called my mom. As soon as she picked up, I screamed, "Mom, they're going to sign me."

"Kendra, I knew you were going to do it!" she shouted into the phone. Then I heard her yell to someone, "Your sister got a record deal!"

"Thanks, Mom. I'm going to call you back. I have to call Marcus."

Adrian ran up to me. She and the other waitresses had seen me crying and thought something had happened.

"What's wrong?" she asked.

"Nothing. I'm okay," I said as I wiped away my tears. I was crying, but they were tears of joy. "My agent just called me and told me that I'm getting signed to a record deal."

"I didn't even know you sang."

"Yup."

I told one person and the news spread around the bar fast. Everybody started coming up to me congratulating me. Julius came over to me and said, "So I guess you leaving us."

"Yeah, I think so." I laughed.

I called home and told Marcus to come to the bar and that I had some good news for him. When Marcus walked into the bar my eyes were still a little puffy from crying.

"What's going on, babe?"

"Tony just called me—I'm getting signed."

He gave me a hug and said he knew it was going to happen for me. I told him all about the meeting and explained why I hadn't told him. He was excited but wanted to make sure my paperwork was right. He called a guy at his job who knew an entertainment lawyer.

Chapter 13

Touchlight signed me for a two-album deal with a $100,000 living allowance and a $250,000 recording budget. The first thing on my list was to buy a new car for myself, and a new house for my mom. She had been renting the same house for all these years. It was okay, but she deserved a nicer neighborhood to live in. I want my mom to have a lawn and a back deck to go out to and just sit.

"Can you believe that they are paying me all this money just to sing?" I said as I waved an $80,000 check at John. I had just received my advance, less the lawyer and manager fees.

"You deserve it," John said as he drove me to Wachovia bank. I went inside the bank and cashed my check. Which took an hour for them to verify a check drawn on their own bank.

Coming out of the bank John asked, "So what're you going to buy first?"

"I don't know."

"You need a new car."

"A new car," I said, repeating him.

"Yeah, you are about to be famous."

"What kind of car do you want?" John asked.

I had no idea. I never ever thought I would be able to afford a new car. I just wanted something brand new that didn't break down, with front headlights that worked, and a nice stereo. We rode past the Acura and Honda dealerships and drove up to a Mercedes-Benz dealership.

"You think I should get a Benz?" I asked, raising my eyebrows.

"Why wouldn't you?"

"I don't know. I never seen myself in a Benz."

A Mercedes-Benz was for rich people, not for people like me. I thought that way but didn't feel that way. He parked the car. I followed him. I tried to hold in my excitement and walk off the lot, but John was right—I deserved a Benz. Why not?

There were so many rows of nice shiny new cars. We started walking past multiple rows of cars, then I came to a silver CLK 500. It was perfect, and I wanted it. It was a convertible coupe with double oval-shaped headlights.

"You like this one?" I asked, standing in front of the car, eyeing it.

"Yeah it's real nice."

"You like the black one or the silver one?" I asked as I noticed a black one right next to it.

"I like the black," John said as he walked up and looked inside the window. A salesman approached us with brown slicked-back hair, tan khakis and a blue shirt that read DONNELLY MERCEDES.

"What's going on, guys? I'm Adam. Would you like to test drive this?"

"Yeah, she wants to see it," John said.

"I'm just going to need to see your license and I'll get those keys for you."

I handed him my license and Adam went into the building to retrieve the keys. I peered through the window and saw the inside of the car. It had a gray leather interior that looked so soft, and there was brown wood trim on the console.

Adam came back with the key and gave it to me. I got in and inserted the key in the ignition and the whole console lit up with a bright white glow.

Adam got in the back and John got in the passenger seat. I adjusted the rearview mirror and turned the radio on to see how good it sounded, then I put my foot on the gas. Immediately I could just imagine myself riding down the street. I went two blocks and I knew I wanted to take it home. After my test drive I handed Adam the keys and walked around the car once more. It was nice. Adam walked away, allowing me and John to talk.

"I didn't even look at the price. How much is this?"

John said, "It don't even matter how much the sticker price is. As long as your monthly payment is less than a thousand, you'll be good."

"So how much should I put down?" I asked.

"Let me take care of everything. I'm going to talk them down for you," John said as Adam approached us again and asked us if we'd come to a decision. In the middle of all this, Tony called and asked what I was doing.

"Nothing," I said. I didn't want to tell him I was out spending money already. He had told me to not make any big purchases until my album came out and I was able to go on tour. All I could say was "uh-huh" to everything he was saying to me.

"I want you to start thinking about your album. Make a list of dream producers and artists you want to work with."

"Uh-huh," I said again.

"Work on your songs that you were writing too. I already started booking your studio time."

"Uh-huh," I said.

"What are you doing? Do you want me to call you

back?" Tony asked. I guess it was obvious that I was trying to talk to him and John at the same time.

"Yeah, I'm busy. I'll call you back, Tony."

I didn't have much credit, but somehow the credit specialist at the dealership said I would be able to drive away with the car today. All he needed was to verify my income. I had to go home and get my contract. I also had to stop and get a certified cashier's check. I put ten thousand dollars down and after hours of back and forth, I drove my first brand-new car off the lot.

I opened the sunroof up and put the air conditioner on. John was following behind me. *This is the life,* I thought. I was letting my arm hang out the window and dip in and out of the wave of wind. John called me on my cell phone. "So where you want to go next?"

"I don't know. I think I want to stop and get Mommy something and surprise her."

We went into the Cherry Hill Mall. I bought me a watch and a little pair of diamond stud earrings. John picked out a simple ESQ Swiss watch for Marcus for me. He wasn't into all that, but I was sure he would like it. We went to the Coach store, and I bought my mom a Coach bag and put five hundred dollars in it.

We left the mall and went to my mother's house. I called her to come to the door. Bubbles and Bilal were sitting outside. They began jumping up and down and going off when they saw me pull up.

"Oh my God, this car is so decent. Can you take me to school? People are not going to believe this," Bilal said.

My mother came out. "Oh, this is nice," she said, looking at the car.

I handed her the bag I'd bought her. "Mom, look inside." She opened the bag and saw the money. She thanked me and said, "Thanks, Kendra, but I can't take this."

"Yes, you can, Mom."

"Come on, y'all. Let's go to dinner and I'll take y'all to the mall," I said.

"I know just what I am going to get too!" my mom said as she fanned herself with the money I'd just given her. They all piled in my car.

We arrived at the Springfield Mall. My mom ran into Macy's and got a dress she said she had been looking at for weeks. While we waited for her I gave Bubbles and Bilal two hundred dollars.

"Here! Y'all got thirty minutes. Go get whatever you want."

Thirty minutes later Bubbles said, "I don't see anything." She was walking around bagless.

"You couldn't find anything in this mall, Bubbles?" I asked.

"No, I didn't see anything."

Bilal came back with Aeropostale, Foot Locker, and Lids bags. He was not playing. Bubbles just wanted to hold on to her money.

We went to Outback Steakhouse for dinner. We laughed and joked over bread and salads waiting for our meals to come. I ordered lobster tails and a big lime margarita.

Marcus called me. I had forgotten about him all day. He didn't even know I had my check or that I'd bought my car. I didn't want to tell him I was out to dinner. He would be upset that I forgot about him.

"Hey, baby," I answered, covering the phone trying to hide the noise.

"Where are you? What are you doing?" he asked.

"I'm on my way there. I got a surprise for you."

"What?"

"You'll see. I'll be right there."

We were in the middle of dinner and John playfully got

up, raised his glass and said, “To my sister. I am so proud of you. You had a dream and followed it. You’re really doing it.”

“No, we are doing it,” I corrected him, laughing.

Bubbles said as she stood up, “It’s my turn. I have something to say, okay? Kendra, I’m real proud of you. I want you to go platinum so you can buy me a car like yours. But until then can I have your old car?”

We all laughed. Bubbles was silly. I felt so good having all my family around. And I was able to do for them.

“Yeah, you can have it,” I said as we finished our meal.

When the check came I didn’t even look at it, just paid and signed. We were all completely full. Everybody thanked me as we headed back to the car. I looked down at my phone. Marcus had called me six times.

I hadn’t even heard my phone ring. He was calling nonstop. I picked up the phone.

“Hello?”

“Where are you?”

“I’m on my way.”

“You said that like two hours ago.”

“No, sorry, babe. I got caught up. I’ll be right there.”

“What are you doing, Kendra?”

“Nothing, babe. I’ll be right there.”

I dropped my family off and went to go meet Marcus. I could not wait to show him the car. When I pulled in front of the door, Marcus was sitting on the steps looking like he was wondering who was in the car. I rolled down the window and once he saw it was me he shook his head, then got up off the steps and walked in the house. I parked and ran in the house behind him.

“What’s wrong with you? Come look at my new car,” I said, catching up with him.

“You bought that car?” Marcus asked, shaking his head.

“Yes,” I said.

"Why didn't you take me with you?"

"You were at work, so I just took John," I said.

"So you spending your money up like you're crazy. I thought Tony told you not to do that."

"I needed a car."

"You had a car, Kendra."

"A Corolla. I'm giving that thing to Bubbles."

"Why didn't you call me when your check came or tell me before you went out and bought a car? A Mercedes-Benz at that. I don't believe you!"

I stepped in front of him and said, "What else am I supposed to drive? I'm about to be a star. Stars have images." I laughed and gave him a hug.

He didn't laugh. Then I remembered the watch I'd bought him. I pulled it out.

"I bought me something, but I also bought you something," I said as I put the watch on his wrist.

He barely looked at it. "Kendra, what's this? I don't need this. No, please stop spending money like you crazy, okay?"

"Yes, but I thought you would like it. I got caught up with my mom."

"And when I call you, answer your phone. All right?"

"I will. Now you want to look at our car?" I asked as I dangled the keys.

"Yes, I'll look at it."

As we went out to the car I explained that the payments were only nine hundred a month including insurance. It was like a sparkling toy. I got in the passenger seat and let him drive. He loved the car as much as I did. When we pulled up to the light I gave him a kiss and sang softly in his ear.

I'd been looking at houses for three weeks. I could not find anything in south Jersey for less than $300,000 to

$500,000. I thought I would be able to get something nice for $200,000, maybe even $100,000, but I hadn't seen anything. I'd been looking in every county in New Jersey. I had this new home guide and a real estate agent named Tina. She was always friendly and cheerful.

I'd seen houses I wished I could afford for $800,000, with super-lengthy driveways. I'd have to upgrade to that type of house—maybe next album. Right now I just wanted a house that my family could feel comfortable in. I wanted a four-bedroom house. I'd already estimated that whatever I bought, my payments were probably going to be at least $2,500 a month. Plus I had to pay homeowners' insurance and property taxes. It was a lot, but as long as I was doing shows and I had a deal, we would be okay. I just wanted my family to have somewhere nice to live. My mom deserved it.

John was with me as I walked around the latest house Tina was showing us. She tried to have us follow her, but we were giving ourselves the tour. The house was located in a development called Waverly Estates in Burlington County. The house sat on the end of the block and was surrounded by green grass and beautiful flowers. It was a decade-old single-family home with a mixture of brick and aluminum siding. "This is really nice," I said as I took off my sunglasses to get a better view. "Why are they selling it?"

"Well, their children are grown and they don't need anything this big anymore."

There were two windows in every room, double closets, a balcony and a man-made lake was in back of the house. There was a deck and a garden with all types of flowers. Downstairs there was a finished basement. I could see having a big flat-screen television on the wall and a big fish tank along the other wall. I went back upstairs and started envisioning where I would put everything.

"Mommy can have this room," I said as I walked into the master bedroom, John following behind me.

"No, you should take the master room. It's your house. You'll need this big closet for all of your clothes and shoes."

"Okay, you're right, and Marcus will be here too! His stuff can go over there."

"Marcus is not going to stay in this house with Mommy and the kids," John said.

"Yes, he will when he sees how beautiful it is. And this is just the beginning. When I start making money from touring I'm going to get another house for me and him.

"Well, Mommy can have this room," I said as I pointed to the second-biggest room. "I'm going to buy it," I said, admiring my possible new home.

Tina heard the word "buy" and came running in the room.

"You want to put an offer in?" she asked.

I made an offer on the house and it was accepted. I was all ready to go to settlement. I had to use stated income and get a no-document loan because my credit was so new, plus I hadn't been signed that long, so the interest on my loan was going to be higher, but I didn't care. I had a house. I had to put $30,000 down. That withdrawal was going to hurt my bank account. I'd checked my account balance. I had already spent about ten thousand on my down payment on my car and five thousand on miscellaneous things like gifts for my family and me and Marcus. My money was going fast, and I was still going to have to buy furniture for the house. But I told myself I was going to do one thing at a time, I couldn't do everything just yet. Plus, that house was so beautiful I would sleep on the floor until I was able to buy furniture. But I was about to be a homeowner.

I was in the middle of getting dressed. I was about to

leave the house and go to settlement when Marcus began asking me why was I buying my mother a house.

"Are you sure you want to buy a house? I mean, you just bought a car. She already has a house."

I wished he would stop counting my money. I resented him asking me why I was helping my family out.

"You can move in too," I assured him.

"You know I can't leave my dad. It's like everything that you have been doing has been about your family. You act like I'm not your family," Marcus complained. He was obviously upset.

I went up to him, hugged him and said, "Baby, you are my family, but I needed somewhere for my mom to live, and I told you we can live there. And plus I'm going to be in New York and we're going to have to get another place eventually, okay."

"Yeah, but it just seems like you're moving too fast for me, you are doing too much," he said.

I looked Marcus in the eye and said, "This is the way I want to spend my money."

After that he didn't say anything.

Tony informed me that the label said I had to pull out my extra tooth. I knew it was going to hurt. I hated the dentist—that's why I never went. They always want to poke and drill shit. He also suggested I enhance my cleavage.

I walked into the doctor's office. I didn't want plastic surgery. The thought of having something foreign in my body made me cringe. I mean, yeah, I have been getting teased about my breasts—or lack thereof—all my life. But implants seemed like the ultimate fakeness. I felt like all I needed was some blue contacts and a long blond weave and then I could hang out with Pamela Anderson. I didn't want to be fake, but if it was going to help my career, then I had to do it.

"Okay, how does this help my career again?" I asked Tony. He had to explain this to me as we waited for my consultation exam.

"The men who are going to buy your songs are going to judge you by your appearance, not your singing ability."

"I don't care about men buying my albums. I want my songs to be about women overcoming. My songs are for women. I want to be like Alicia Keys and Mary J. Blige."

"Well, we want men sales, too," Tony insisted. "They'll be the ones who will say, 'She is so hot—I have to buy her album.'"

"She is so hot," I repeated, imitating him.

He laughed.

My name was called and the doctor came into the room and introduced himself. I told him I wanted believable breasts. He told me I was an A cup and he was going to bring me up to a C cup.

"Do you have any questions?" he asked.

"Yes. How long will I be out of commission?"

"Each person varies, because I have had patients who take weeks to recover and others who start feeling better in a few days." He sat down on his rolling stool and said, "What we have to do now is determine the size you're going to be." He showed me the saline breast versus the silicone breast. I decided on the saline because they seemed the safest to me.

The day of the surgery Marcus took off work and drove me to the hospital. I didn't tell my mom—she could yell at me after it was done. I was already scared and didn't need anyone screaming at me too. I was feeling very anxious and wanted to get it over with. As I dressed I double checked my list. I couldn't bring any shirts that went over my head. I had to go buy all these loose-fitting sweat shirts that zipped up. I needed pillows for the car ride home. They said I would probably be hungry and want water and crackers.

We arrived to pre-op. They gave me the anesthesia, and I didn't remember anything else.

I awoke so groggy, I just wanted to go back to sleep. Then I looked around and immediately I wanted to sit up. They had me wrapped tight in ACE Bandages, and underneath that was white gauze laid directly over my incisions. Every time I moved any part of my body I could feel the pain. They put me in a wheelchair and Marcus drove me home.

The next day I awoke to pain so great I wondered, "Why did I do that dumb shit?" I couldn't sleep on my stomach, I was feeling out of it from all the medicine and I couldn't take a bath. Marcus gave me a sponge bath and had to change my bandages. He didn't mind. But I felt a little helpless.

"Baby, I need my medicine and I need help going to the bathroom. Please." Marcus was taking his time, moving slowly. I moved one leg at a time and tiptoed into the bathroom. I just wanted to sleep the pain off. Marcus got in the bed with me and tried to comfort me. I felt his every movement when he breathed.

"Marcus, please get out of the bed. Every time you move I can feel it."

The next morning I felt so much better. I saw the tanks in front of me on my chest. When I went to the doctor for my post-op visit three days after the surgery, the surgeon assured me that my breasts would not remain that big. I did not believe him.

Two weeks later, my breasts were still huge. They went down a little, but they were now the first things you saw on me. I stood in the mirror and felt them—they were not jiggly. They seemed like big cantaloupes attached to my body. I felt like a freak show. I couldn't even go to the post office without a man being extra nice and trying to open the door or whistle at me. The dirty old men were the ones who really made me sick. So I started to wear two sports bras just to look normal to hold the puppies down.

But I didn't have time to have regrets—what was done was done. I had to move to New York to my new apartment the label was paying for. Marcus didn't want me to leave, but he understood after we had a long talk about what was best for my career. He was going to come up every weekend to visit.

Tony and his wife, Liz, moved me in. I just brought my clothes and pictures. The apartment was already furnished and not that big, but nice. I had a doorman and a nice lobby. There were two big windows with white drapes, and a plain bed with cream-colored sheets and a comforter.

"This place is small. I thought a record label would give her something better than this," Liz said.

"This is very good for New York City. Manhattan apartments are so expensive. You know how much it costs to live here? It is good they even gave her this. They want her close to the studio. This is all you need, Kendra. You being up here is about getting that album done."

Chapter 14

Tony and I were waiting in the conference room. We were about to have our first marketing meeting with the label about my image. Tony said they would develop my name and style. I didn't really want them to put any name on what I do, because once they put me in box I wouldn't be able to climb out of it. I really didn't want to be R&B, pop, or neo-soul. I just wanted to be a good singer.

"I wonder if my breasts and my teeth being fixed are enough for them," I joked as I grabbed a piece of honeydew melon off a fruit tray on the table.

"No, you look great," Tony said.

"So I didn't look great before?" I playfully asked.

"No, you always looked great." He saw I was being silly and kept reading text messages on his phone.

"Looking good," Thomas said as he entered the room and pointed in my direction. Maya and the others followed him inside.

"Hi, Kendra. I'm Maya Gomez, and I'm in the Publicity Ad Image Department. You are a cute girl. It is so nice to finally meet you in person. I've heard a lot about you."

I smiled and thanked her and she sat down. I couldn't tell if Maya was black or Hispanic. She was pretty, about forty-something with a medium cropped bob. She was wearing a blue suit, black glasses and big white pearls. Everyone around the room stood up and introduced themselves. I didn't remember anyone's name, but I smiled and said hello.

Maya started the meeting.

"So Kendra we love you. Thomas has told us great things about you. And this meeting is basically to get us all acquainted, and decide on your style, brand, and the direction of your project."

"What have you come up with so far?" Tony asked.

"We've decided on the look we want for you. You're going to be the modern-day Toni Braxton. We want you to sing ballads but be able to tear up a club with a hip-hop inspired track. Have you thought of a name?" she asked.

"No, not really," I said.

"In our sales meeting we came up with a few ideas." She stood up like she was proud of herself and she had just made a great scientific discovery.

"Kendra, we think your name should be Siren. You're hot, you're young, and you are on fire. We are going to dye your hair red, and this will be your signature look. This will make you stand out in the crowd." She revealed a digital picture of me with red hair. Then she continued on.

"When a fan picks up a magazine and sees the red they will go straight to the article with you in it. They are going to know Siren. She is on fire."

"I'm not feeling that," I said as I looked around the room to see if anyone would disagree. "Like I would prefer to just go by my name, Kendra."

Another guy introduced himself as Charles. He had on a light blue dress shirt and a brown tie. He was short with long-trimmed sideburns and a funny block haircut. He was sitting at the other end of the table and asked me my middle name. "Kendra is way too common," he said.

"Well, I don't like Siren," I said.

Tony stepped in and said, "Her stage name now is Kendra Michelle, and people know her by that name."

"I like it, so you will be Kendra Michelle," Maya said.

We discussed my look and style. They agreed that I would be a straight-up R&B singer with a touch of neo-soul, and I would not be dying my hair red.

Today was going to be my first day in the studio. Tony had just called to tell me he was on his way to take me. Tony had moved to New York last weekend. He found a place in Brooklyn. He couldn't keep going up and down the turnpike every day. It was getting too expensive. He was more excited than me. His plan was to get my career off the ground and get more artists. I could tell that he felt validated by me getting signed. He said Liz was not happy because he'd uprooted her and moved her to New York.

"You ready, Kendra?"

We rode down Eleventh Avenue. There was traffic everywhere. Yellow cabs owned the streets. Tony almost crashed three times. The cab drivers would not let anyone in front of them. They kept braking hard and jumping into the next lane, almost making us hit them.

We arrived at the studio exactly at six. Tony looked down at his directions and the address.

"You have to go to the fifth floor. Ask for Brian Edwards."

"I'll just wait for you," I said.

"No, look, don't be late. First impressions are everything. Go up. I'm going to park, and I'll meet you upstairs."

I went up to the fifth floor and found that there were five recording studios. I walked into studio C and saw two men sitting at the boards. One was a real 3X type of guy—not fat, but not far from it. He was big like a big teddy. He had these long dreads, a light beard and brown skin. He might even have been cute if he cut that hair and lost a little weight. When I walked into the studio he said, "You must be Kendra Michelle. What's up? My name is Beazie." He extended his hand for me to shake.

"Nice to meet you, Beazie."

"No, it's pronounced like 'be easy.' Brian Edwards—nice to meet you," he said, laughing.

"Oh, I'm sorry."

"Don't be sorry, be careful. It's cool. This is Davis, my engineer."

Davis came over and said hello.

Beazie invited me to have a seat so we could plan the album. We waited for Tony to come up, and when he did he came in, shook Beazie's hand, caught his breath, and took a seat. Beazie began talking about the direction of my album.

"Thomas wants at least twenty songs. Out of those twenty we are going to pick about fourteen songs to go on the album. He wants you to have an equal number of up tempos, ballads, and club songs. Your project is scheduled for the second quarter. They want you out by next spring, so we have about three months to get this done. I don't want to take the entire three months. So when I call you into the studio I need you to get here and be ready to work."

"Okay, I will. And here are the songs I wrote." I tried to hand him the notebook, but he ignored my outstretched hand.

"We'll get to them. Listen to these songs and tell me

which one you like," he said as he began playing tracks. He played an array of six beats—some slow, some fast.

"I like tracks two and six. Tony, which do you like?"

"Can you play three and five over again?" Tony asked.

Beazie played them again. Listening to five again, it sounded really good. The drum was loud and I could hear a sped-up guitar in it. There was someone else already singing the songs on the next two tracks he played. He told me to just sing like the girl already on there. It was called "What's It Going to Be." It had a real nice groove to it.

"You ready?" Beazie asked.

"Yes."

"Go on in the booth."

I walked in the booth and it was just what I'd expected—big and roomy. This was a far cry from the so-called studio where I had first recorded my demos.

I could see Beazie and the other guys through the glass. I picked up the headphones and looked down at the lyrics. I wanted to get the melody right. I started singing it over again in my head.

Beazie came across the speaker and said, "Let me know when you ready."

"Play the song one more time."

The music started playing, and I was still trying to catch the feel of the song. I put my head up and he began playing the track. He started it again and I began to sing, "It's time for you to make up your mind. What's it going to be? Who you gonna see? Who you going to make ya ladee?" I sang.

The music went off, and Beazie came across the speaker again.

"That was good, but give me a little more energy."

I said a little prayer and looked down at the lyrics. Then I signaled him to start the music again. This time he didn't stop me. I got to the hook and stopped looking at the song, and ad-libbed a little through the entire song without stopping.

"Okay, baby Whitney. How something so strong come out of that skinny body?" he yelled. "That's what I'm talking about, one-takes."

Tony gave me a thumbs up like I was doing a good job. I started feeling more relaxed. I had impressed Beazie.

I was done for the day. Beazie said I was damn near perfect. After spending six hours recording I was tired as hell. When we left the studio Tony was still on the telephone talking to Thomas, who said for him to tell me to get some sleep and he would talk to me in the morning. Tony dropped me off at my door. The doorman opened the door and I went up to my apartment.

I was happy to be in my new place. I turned on the living room light, then walked into my bedroom and fell onto my white sheets. I shut my eyes and began to relax. I got about one minute of sleep and then I heard my phone ringing. I looked down at my phone screen. It was Tony calling me.

"Yeah, Tony?" I said.

"You have an interview set up tomorrow and a photo shoot."

"Already? With who?"

"Yeah, this is not a game. They are trying to do your web site and get this ball rolling. The interview is with Online Music Gallery. Get some rest and I'll be there at seven to come and get you."

Since I was up I took my clothes out for the next day and checked my messages. Marcus was in there twice. I dialed him.

"Marcus, baby, I miss you," I said, whining.

"I miss you too! I'll be there this weekend. How is everything going so far?" he asked. "You okay baby? I miss you girl."

"It's going good so far. I went into the studio today."

"How was it?"

"Everything was just coming natural to me in the studio. The producer said I was perfect. Baby, I am so happy I did this. I love it! And I have my first interview and photo shoot tomorrow."

"Yeah, that's good, Kendra. You deserve all this."

"Marcus, I can't wait to see you. How was your day at work?"

"It was okay. It's just so strange coming home and you not being here. But other than that it's the same shit. I just wanted to talk to you, baby. I'm going straight to the train station after work. Expect me about nine."

"All right, baby. I love you."

"I love you too! Good luck tomorrow."

I awoke, dressed, and took a cab over to the photo shoot. I thumbed through the new *XXL* magazine on the ride over. It took about fifteen minutes to get there.

For the photo shoot I had to meet the stylist, Angie. She was a black girl with short, green, fuzzy hair. She had piercings going up and down her ear and a small dolphin earring in her nose.

"Hiya," she said as she looked me over. "So you know your measurements?"

"No. I wear like a two." She pulled out this bohemian red and orange beaded scarflike maternity-looking dress.

"How you feeling this?" she said.

I looked down at the clothes and said, "I'm not."

"Okay," she said, curling up her lips.

Then she pulled out a short black dress with pink rhinestones on it. She held it up to me and I took one look at it and said, "This dress is too short and it is going to make my legs look extra skinny."

"No, it's not. Once you try it on, you will see."

I tried the dress on. It wasn't that bad. She then walked me over to a table with rows of shoes on it. There were stiletto pumps, clogs, wedges and sandals. Out of all the shoes I could choose from she wants to pick yellow pumps to go with a pink and black dress. I put the outfit on. I looked like Rainbow Brite. This was not a good look. "Uhm this does not match."

"No, this look is good for what we are going for. One thing you will learn about fashion is that everything doesn't have to match. And you make the style and the trends, you don't follow them."

I looked at her, then looked at myself one more time in the mirror. *If she says so,* I thought. I knew I was new and I didn't know everything, but I did I know looked a hot damn mess.

She then sent me to hair and makeup. Okay, so now I was thinking at least my hair would compensate for my horrible outfit.

"Hi, I'm Paul," said a thin man with short twisties. His bottom lip was pierced, and he wore black square-framed glasses. His jeans were extra tight and he had on a Rolling Stones T-shirt with a big red tongue sticking out on it.

"Hi, honey," he said as he gave me a cheek-to-cheek kiss, tapped the salon chair and said, "Sit." He made small talk with me as he then held different foundations up to the light. He was trying to find the perfect brown to match my skin tone. He selected one and put the others back. His makeup case was filled with M.A.C., Bobbi Brown and Urban Decay makeup. He pulled out tweezers and began to arch my eyebrows. It hurt every time he took a piece of hair from my brow. He then put on white powder. He must have seen the horror in my eyes, because he said, "Baby, this is the cover."

He began dusting his makeup applicator into the container and applying it to my face. I was staring in the mirror. The big bulbs going all around the mirror were shining so bright, making me hot. Then he turned me away from the mirror. He was dabbing layers of makeup on my face. After the one-hour makeup session, the layers of makeup made me feel like my face was turning to stone. After he was done he turned me around in the chair and said, "Voilà."

The first thing I noticed was my overarched, colored-in eyebrows. The second thing I noticed was my ghostlike appearance.

"I don't wear my makeup this heavy," I said.

"This is for the camera. It will look good once you get in front of the camera. Trust me." He put thick black eyelashes on me and took the liquid mascara to extend the corner of my eyes.

Right in the middle of all this a woman named Monica Hudson came up and introduced herself as the journalist from Online Music Gallery. She sat down with her tape recorder and began to ask me questions about my life. I had to remember my stage age, which was twenty-two. The label had pushed my age back. I didn't think it made a difference, but they said it did. I knew the people who went to school with me would be thinking, "How is she only twenty-two?" The reporter pulled up a chair right beside me.

"I'm going to ask you questions. Then I'm going to just flow around," she said as she settled in. "What do you want people to know about you?"

"I don't know. I'm a good singer. I have a great voice."

"So who inspires you?" Monica asked.

"Growing up I loved Mariah Carey and Mary J. Blige."

"Okay, what makes you different than the next person? Why will people enjoy your music?"

"I think people will enjoy my music because I'm real. I'm coming from the heart with my voice, with my struggle. I'm just different than what is going on right now."

She kept the questions coming. I answered them as fast as I could. My phone kept ringing. Tony was calling.

"I'm sorry. This is my manager. I have to take this," I said.

"No problem," she said, adding notes.

"Tony, I will call you back," I said as I turned the phone off. It was so hard trying to talk to the interviewer, answer my cell phone, and make sure they weren't about to mess my hair up. The journalist, Monica Hudson, gave me a look like, *Are you ready finally?*

I was ready until they brought over different wigs for me. I had to say something before they put that monstrosity on my head.

"I don't like blond hair on dark skin," I said as I looked at the Barbie-blond bouncy wig.

"You're brown, honey. You can do blond or red," he said like, *Listen, bitch, I know what I'm talking about.*

"How are you going to make my hair blend in?" I questioned.

"I got this," he said as he looked at me, waiting to get my approval. I wasn't about to let them slap straight blond weave into my in-need-of-a-perm dark brown hair. Hell, no. I was going to take up for myself.

"I am not wearing this. It is bad enough with my makeup making me look like Michael Jackson, and that I have a clown outfit on, but the blond hair—I'm not feeling it," I yelled. "No," I said, looking at him in the mirror.

"Calm down, feisty mama. Okay, let's compromise. How about this wig?" he said, pulling out a straight brown wig that was slightly flipped at the ends.

I made a face.

"Look, if you don't wear that we don't have anything else for you. You know what? Somebody talk to this girl.

I don't have time," he said, walking away from me frustrated. The woman who had styled me came up and said, "Babe, come here. Listen, you are getting a bad rep already. How long have you wanted to be a singer?"

"All my life," I said.

"If that's true, let me ask you this—before you got your deal, if somebody could have come up to you and said I'm going to make you a star but you have to trust me, would you have jumped at the opportunity?"

"Probably."

"Well, now you have to act like it. Your job is to sing and theirs is to make you look beautiful. Okay, sweetie? Don't be a temperamental diva."

"I wasn't trying to be a diva. I just know what looks good on me. And I don't want to lose who I am in the process."

"You won't. The end result will be great. Trust me."

I felt like a baby, but damn, they had me looking crazy. My hair and outfit looked like someone was playing a practical joke on me. I came back and finished the interview without crying. I pushed the tears back up and took long breaths. For the photo shoot there was a big white drop as a background. There were cameras everywhere. I just tried to smile.

"Look at the camera," the photographer said, adding that I looked good. *Stop lying, bitch,* I thought. He guided me through my poses and movements. I felt so ugly because of my outfit, makeup and hair.

After the shoot was over I could feel the pimples rising from all the gook. I went in the bathroom and washed all the makeup off my face. This shit was starting to get on my nerves. They wanted too much, and I hadn't even finished a fucking album yet. I was feeling lonely and homesick, but this was my dream and if this was what it took then I had to do it.

Chapter 15

So far making the album had been fun and challenging. I hadn't realized how much work would go into it. I'd been working with so many up-and-coming producers. Thomas brought in people he said were hungry and who were going to make my project hot. All I did was work. It sounds crazy but at least with a normal job you get Saturday and Sunday off. Most producers are nocturnal and don't sleep.

Beazie, Thomas and Tony kept me in the studio, and the studio was open twenty-four hours a day, so I got no days off. At least Marcus was coming up for the weekend. I needed to see my man and get some relief from the past week. I was so happy to see him I ran up and hugged and kissed him.

"You miss me?" he asked.

"Yes, I do. They got me doing everything up here in the studio every day," I said as I held on to him.

He was looking around at everything. I was so happy to have him with me.

"This is a nice place," he said as he pulled back the

drapes. He took a little tour around the place. I hugged him again.

"You miss me like that?" he joked as he kissed me. "I missed you too!" He let his lips touch mine.

"I mean, I like it. It's just a lot harder than what I expected," I confessed.

I was about to get to complaining, but the truth was that I was lucky to have the opportunity.

"What were you about to say?" he asked.

"Nothing. I just want to spend some time with you." I'd missed my man so much. I pushed him into the chair. He sat back while I unzipped his pants and I kissed all over the lower region of his stomach. His pubic hair brushed against my face. I pulled his firmness through the slit in his boxers. It was smooth and pulsating. I let his body disappear into my mouth. I totally consumed it with every suck of my jaw. He let out a little moan. He was almost at his peak when I began stroking the slippery tip of him against my breasts. I then straddled his body, allowing my body to engulf him. I squeezed tightly and moved in a round motion. Marcus took control and sat me on the chair. He positioned his body into mine. His pants were still on and I could feel his pants tapping my legs and thighs. He lifted his shirt and then let out an incredible shriek. The rest of the night we did nothing but enjoy each other's company. My man reminded me why I loved him so much and would never leave him.

Marcus went with me to the studio the next day. I wanted him to see what I was doing. Beazie greeted me with a hug. "Hey, Miss! You ready?"

I saw the way Marcus looked at Beazie when he gave me a hug. He didn't understand that's what you do. So I instantly said, "I want to introduce you to my man. This is Marcus."

Beazie came over, shook Marcus's hand and said, "You should be proud of your lady. She is doing great." Marcus smiled and had a seat.

"Kendra, we need to go over a few things before Corey gets here."

I had heard a lot about the producer and songwriter Corey Washington, also known as Core. He had a lot of hits with R&B and pop artists. He was a really good producer and everybody was saying I was lucky to have him working on my project. The only reason he was even working on the project was that he was Thomas's frat brother.

Beazie handed me the lyrics and I started reviewing them. I was going through the lyrics: *Can I love you? Can I stop holding back the way I feel? Can I give you all of me? Can I love you exclusively, just you and me? Tell me how it's going to be.* He played the track and I was trying to get the harmony down.

We were just waiting for Corey, but he hadn't arrived yet. It was very boring for Marcus but he was being good about it. Beazie ordered some soul food platters and added it to the session bill while we waited for Corey to come through. He was already two hours late.

Corey finally walked into the studio like he wasn't late. He had on faded blue jeans, a black blazer and a teal button-down shirt. He had two diamonds in both his ears. They were square yellow and blue. I was so excited he was working on my project, it didn't even matter that he was late. He had his million-dollar smile on. His style was so different. His nails were short and manicured and his skin was brown and clear, not a bump or imperfection anywhere. He was well groomed. He had a girl with him and she was dressed like a copycat video girl—brown skin, hazel contacts and a brownish-blond weave hanging to the middle of her back.

"Hey, y'all. Sorry I'm late. I'm Corey, and this is my

lady, Aisha," he said as he hurriedly started setting up his equipment. He pulled out a laptop and hooked it up.

I said hi to his girlfriend. Marcus looked at me like I forgot to introduce him. I introduced him to them and then the girlfriend went and had a seat next to Marcus.

"Did you get a chance to look over the song?" Corey asked.

"Yeah, I already gave her the lyrics. She has been looking them over," Beazie said.

I went into the booth and waited for the music to start. I looked down at the lyrics and the track began to play. It was a light, mellow ballad, and I began to sing.

Shortly after starting Corey came across the speaker and interrupted me, saying, "One moment." Then he walked out of the studio.

I came out of the booth and asked, "What's going on?"

Marcus said, "His girl was starting to get restless. He said he be right back. You were great, though."

I thanked him, got a drink of water and waited for them to come back into the studio. We could hear them out in the hallway cussing and fussing about something.

She was saying, "You said we wasn't going to spend all day in here. I'm tired. Well, tell me one thing. Are you almost finished?" she asked rudely.

He told her no and then she said, "Well, I'm leaving. Meet me at home." His girlfriend was tripping. She was very unprofessional. He came back into the room alone and we continued the session.

After the studio Marcus went to the apartment and relaxed. I wanted to go to dinner but Marcus said he was tired.

The next morning I made him pancakes, sausage and eggs. He awoke to breakfast in bed. He thanked me and I said, "I wish you didn't have to leave me," as I bear hugged him.

"I know. I don't want to leave you, but I have to go to work."

"You coming next weekend?"

"Yes, I'll be here every weekend, and the weekends I don't come here you have to come home."

"It will be all right. Let me get dressed so I can make the train."

"Baby, just drive. Won't you take the car home? Then you can leave later."

"Why?"

"Because I'm not driving it and I have to keep paying for parking."

Marcus took my car home. I knew driving that nice car around would make him feel good and he wouldn't be sweating me as hard. I was off to get a manicure and pedicure. Sundays had become my unofficial "me" days. Tony called me right before I went out the door. He was calling to tell me that my first interview was posted online. I jumped out of the bed and—instead of leaving—got on the computer.

The title was "Diva in the Making."

Kendra Michelle may be the next R&B princess, and I caught up with her as she argued with her stylist about her hair and makeup. She said that her voice was one to be reckoned with and that she would give Mariah Carey a run for her money. Will she be like other R&B legends or is she another wannabe? . . . I think she is the real deal. Makeup aside, she is someone to watch . . .

I was speechless. "I mean, she took my words and totally flipped them. She dissed me and complimented me in the same article," I said to Tony.

"It's a good article. Things like this happen before going to media training. Once you go to media training you'll know what not to say during an interview. Go to

Touchlight music homepage and see your pictures. They look great," Tony said.

The Touchlight website had my bio and picture online. Seeing that made my entire mood change. Even though I wasn't really feeling the style, I looked great.

The next day the studio was crowded when I arrived. There was a rapper named Eliminate finishing up his recording. All his people were being loud and smoking weed. They also had a pole dancer in their studio; they said it was for inspiration. But all the guys in the studio were always respectful to me. Beazie made sure of it. It was like a miniature party. It was loud and they were playing the music that Eliminate had just recorded. In the middle of all of that, I picked up my phone without looking at the screen.

"Where you at?" Marcus asked.

"I'm in the studio. I'll call you when I get out of here," I said.

"What time is that going to be?" he asked.

"I don't know."

"Why can't you talk to me now?" he questioned.

"Baby, give me until about eleven. I have to get back to what I was doing."

"It don't sound like you're working! It sounds like a big party, like there's a bunch of niggas in there with you. What, you don't want to talk to me?"

"No," I said, lying. He wouldn't understand that I was just one of the boys and nobody was thinking about me. He was tripping on me for no reason. I didn't have time for this. "I'm laying down my vocals again. I'm almost done. I will call you when I get out of here." Beazie and Davis were laughing and being extra loud. I was trying to cover the telephone and muffle the sound but he still heard them.

"Man, that's bullshit," he said. "Who are those niggas? I hear them in the background."

"You ready? Baby, come on. We ain't got all night," Beazie yelled.

"I have to lay down my vocals one more time. Baby, I love you but I have to go."

I put my phone in my bag and instantly it began to ring again. Marcus was calling right back.

"You hanging up on me now, baby?"

"No, Marcus, as soon as I leave here I will call you."

I was singing and singing. My throat was becoming hoarse, but Beazie said I had to get it right. He kept me in the studio all night.

I called Marcus as soon as I got home and he didn't pick up. So I left him a message.

"Marcus, it is six in the morning. I just got in. I was working all night long. Have a good day. I'm going to turn my ringer off. I don't want anyone to wake me. Call me at your lunch. Love you." I disconnected the call. I knew he would be mad, but just like he had to go to work, so did I.

Chapter 16

My next photo shoot went so well. I got to wear this diamond bracelet and diamond necklace, with this slit silver shirt. I had just come back from a photo shoot. I was tired and ready to take a nap when I heard a knock on my door. I opened it and my mother said, "Surprise."

"What are doing here?" I asked as my mother, Bilal, and Bubbles came walking in my apartment.

"We just wanted to come and see you. Where are you going looking all stylish?"

"Nowhere. I just came back from a photo shoot," I said as I yawned.

"Oh you look tired. We wanted you to go out with us."

"I'm too tired, but I'll give y'all some money to go out with."

"We wanted to spend some time with you," my mother said, disappointed. Bilal and Bubbles came and were hugging me. Bilal just came and just leaned on me. "What, y'all missed me or something?" I said as I hugged them back.

"Yeah I miss you. I need someone to rescue me from our neighborhood," Bilal said.

"What are you talking about."

"He hates the kids in the neighborhood. He said one of them called him a real black boy," my mother said.

"Those kids get on my nerves. They act too suburban. I wish I was back in my old neighborhood."

"No you don't," I said shaking my head.

"Kendra, I want to know can you get me a new car for my graduation?" Bubbles asked.

"No."

"Your sister can't afford to buy you a car, Amira. Plus you don't deserve one. You know she barely graduating and she have to go to a summer program just so they will let her in."

"You have to get your college grades up Bub. Oh let me show you the pictures I took today," I said, showing my mother.

My mom put her glasses on and said, "You look beautiful, but why do they have you looking all light skin?" I did look four shades lighter than I actually was.

"I don't know. It probably was the flash from the camera."

"No, they probably trying to make you look light skin. They do it all the time."

"That's not it. Here take this. Have fun and I'm going to get some rest," I said as I gave my mom three hundred out of my hand bag to take the kids shopping and they left.

"You must be Kendra Michelle," said the short, forty-something, dark-haired, green-eyed white man who stood in front of me when I walked out of the elevator at the studio.

"Thomas has said so many great things about you. I just wanted to come in and see for myself what all the hype was about," he said.

"Thank you," I said, smiling and playing it off as best as I could. I had no idea who I was talking to.

"You are a gorgeous young woman," he added.

"Thank you," I said again.

Beazie introduced us and said, "This is the vice president of Touchlight Records, Peter Sutton."

"Nice to meet you, Mr. Sutton," I said.

"It is my pleasure. Call me Peter. I would love to have you sing at my party next week. If you're available, come. I'll send an invitation over to you."

I thanked him again, and as soon as he left Beazie said, "How nice is that? The vice president is coming to the studio just to see you. He don't come to the studio for everyone. You the next big thing. You're Thomas's little gem and Peter wants you to sing at his party."

"You think so?" I asked, blushing.

"Definitely. The whole label is talking about you."

He made me smile again. I was excited that everyone was interested and believed in me. I opened the studio door, and in the first hallway I saw all these people. It was crowded. Beazie came up behind me.

"Who are all these people?" I asked.

"They're here with Tashay."

"Who is Tashay?"

"This other singer they just signed. They all about to leave, though. Kendra, this is Tashay."

I said, "Hello."

She said, "What's up? You Kendra right?"

She did not look like a singer, but more like a stripper. Her waist was a size four but her ass belonged on a woman wearing a tight size sixteen pants. Her pants were literally hugging every curve. Her weave was straight and black and covering her eyes, so she had to give a seductive squint to see. Standing next to her I looked like a boy with boobs.

"Yeah, how you doing? Nice to meet you. I heard all about you. Well, let us get out your way. Come on, y'all. It's time to go," Tashay announced to her squad, and they all jumped up and began following her out the door. I had counted about seven people with her. Davis's eyes followed her as she sashayed down the hall. She was gone, but her presence was still being felt in the room.

"That's a star right there," Davis said loudly, clapping, being silly.

Beazie told me all about Tashay, how she was a video girl and she was in *King* magazine. Her boyfriend played ball for the Detroit Pistons and his industry connects got her a deal.

"What's up, Core?" Beazie said as Corey walked into the room. They shook hands. "You just missed Tashay."

"Oh? The chick they just signed from Detroit?"

"Yo, dude, she is so major. Her body is sick," Davis said.

They spent a few more minutes harking over her and how fly she was.

"I'm supposed to be doing some work on her project," Corey said.

"Well, man, don't bring your girl when she come. 'Cause your lady is going to be like, 'hell, no.' She would be at every session getting on your nerves," Davis said.

"Man, I'm good. I love my lady," Corey said. Then he turned his attention to me. "What's good, Miss Kendra? You ready?" he asked as he came in and began to set everything up. His laptop was very small and silver. He played a beat with a girl singing on it and without. I listened and nodded my head to the beat. The song was called "Tell Me Why." It was a love ballad.

"You like? Listen, with me nothing is set in stone. I'm open to comments and criticism."

With him saying that, I was able to open up.

"I like the track but I'm not really feeling the lyrics," I said as I looked down at them.

"What would you have it say instead of 'let me go there'?"

"I would maybe say 'let me love you,'" I said.

"Yeah, that sounds good."

We started rewriting the song and talking about my music industry experience so far. I told him it was not exactly what I'd thought it was going to be, how everybody I'd met was about chasing checks and phony.

"Let me hurry up and get in the booth before your girlfriend come," I said playfully.

"She is not coming today."

"You sure you won't be leaving early?"

"No interruption this time. I'm sorry about the last time. My chick wants me to take her out all the time for her stuff but can't sit still a minute when I need to work. She is never satisfied. I'm even paying for her to go to fashion design school. She wants to start her own fashion line and she wants me to fund it and gets mad at me when I'm working."

"Wow! Aren't you the good boyfriend," I said.

"At times. I just try to make her happy. We've been together two years and she still learning. She only twenty-two, she'll mature eventually."

"That's real nice," I said.

"What about your boyfriend? What does he do? He live in the city?" he asked.

"No, we from Philly. He work for UPS."

Corey started laughing. "UPS wow."

"What's so funny?" I asked, not finding anything amusing.

"Nothing, I just thought of that song 'Nigga, Please, You Work for UPS,' or what Biggie said, 'Don't get mad, UPS is hiring.' I can't believe your dude just got a regular job. How can he afford to take care of you?" he asked.

"I take care of myself," I said, feeling a little intimidated. I know Corey was getting money and all that, but he still didn't have the right to laugh at anyone if they didn't make as much money as he did. I was done talking personal with him. He was an asshole.

I quickly changed and said, "So are we going to get back to the song?"

"Yeah, the song. Okay, so we are going to change the hook?" Corey started laughing again. Now I was getting annoyed.

"What's so damn funny?" I asked.

"Nothing. I just like that you with dude and he got a regular job. You must really love him."

"I do."

He could see in my face that I wasn't appreciating his disrespect. He turned to me and said, "That is so good you with your man for him."

"Well, we been together through everything for just about seven years."

"Damn, how old are you?"

"Twenty-five."

"So he trust you out here by yourself?"

"Yeah, why wouldn't he? So far I'm just in the studio or home on the phone with him. Soon as I finish my album, I'm going home, so we will be okay."

"I don't know. I wouldn't trust my beautiful woman alone in another city."

He was being smart, but his one little comment made me smile. Corey was a nice-looking guy and he had money. He had been producing songs for the last three years, he had made hundreds of thousands, and he was trying to get his own label. Him saying I was beautiful was a major compliment to little ol' me. After he said that, it was hard to work on the song. After the session I thought about what he had said about staying with Marcus no matter what. But that's what I was supposed to do. It didn't matter that I made more money than him—he was still my baby. He had my back and I would never leave him.

The blaring cell phone ring awoke me.

I sat up and searched and searched for it, and finally found it under the bed cover. I snapped it open and said, "Hello?"

"Kendra, you haven't called me in two days," Marcus yelled from the other end of the phone. I sat up and tried to get my thoughts together. I looked over at the time. It was eleven thirty-two.

"Marcus, I have been so busy. I'm really trying to handle all these things at once. I'm in the studio every day, trying to choose songs, getting no rest and a bunch of other shit. Leave the studio at four back in by noon."

"There is no excuse, Kendra. You need to call me to let me know what's going on with you. You haven't even called your mom. She calling me like, 'Is Kendra okay? Have you talked to her?' And I'm like, 'Miss Joanne, I haven't heard from her.' How come I didn't talk to my woman in a couple of days?"

"Baby, it is not like that at all. I just been real busy."

"Tell me what it is like, then," he said.

I got out of the bed and turned on the shower so I could get dressed. I was trying to listen to him but he was acting like it was the end of the damn world. He was whining like a baby. I wasn't really for it.

"You sitting back, neglecting me and shit."

"I'm working around other people's schedules. If they say, 'come meet me at this time,' I have to go and get it done. Like right now I have to get out of here."

"Here we go again. You got to go, right?" he asked.

"'Here we go what? I'm working. What the fuck you want me to do?"

"I want you to call me. You know what? Fuck it, Kendra. Screw you," he said as the phone went silent. I took a breath and put my phone down. I tried calling him back when I got out of the shower but he didn't answer.

Corey was waiting in the studio when I arrived. He looked down at his watch and said, "You late." I playfully shrugged my shoulders as to say "so what?"

"Ms. Kendra Michelle, you better be honored. You know I get sixty thousand a track. I'm giving Thomas a heavy discount, but I know you are about to blow. So you better respect me," he joked.

I so didn't care. I just kept thinking about my cozy bed and how I should be asleep in it. I grabbed the headphones, placed them on my head and sang. The song was called "Amnesia." The beat was fast with heavy bass and drums. It was about a woman going back to her boyfriend, and forgetting about all the wrong he did to her. I liked the song.

"I must have forgot, how you did me wrong. I must have forgot how you didn't answer your phone. I must have forgot. I must have forgot."

Corey came across the speaker. "Give me some emotion. You love this dude and you want to go back to him but you can't. I want you to close your eyes. I want you to think about your man. Now sing."

He came into the booth with me and sang the song to show me how he wanted me to sing it. He was wearing Sean John cologne and it was smelling so good. I had just bought Marcus some and for some reason he hadn't put it on yet. I shook off the feeling. But damn, he was sexy and I felt a real connection. I guess he was like that with everybody. Our eyes kept locking, though. Was it me? It was very uncomfortable. If I didn't have a boyfriend I would talk to him. But I knew I shouldn't. I'd already heard that you can't mess with anybody in the industry without running the risk of getting a reputation.

"Come on, girl, sing. Don't scream," Corey said.

I was damn frustrated and tired.

"You want to take a break?" he asked.

"No."

He started the music over and I kept messing up. I was so tired and not feeling up to it. This shit was getting to me. This was like the sixtieth time.

"Take a break," he said. I took a sip of water and looked over the lyrics. I had to get myself together. I wanted to go home and it wasn't going to happen if I didn't get it right. I told him to start the music, and I sang it straight through without hesitation. I looked at him through the glass, and he gave me a thumbs-up.

"You got it!"

"That's it," I said.

"Yup. I knew you had it in you," he said over the speaker.

"Thanks, now I am going home and going to sleep," I said as I hung up my headphones and walked out of the booth.

The next day I had to meet up with another producer from the west coast named BayRon. He was from the San Francisco Bay area. Talk about gorgeous, all his features were. From his fawn-brown eyes to his golden-brown skin, to his six-three stature. He introduced himself by bending over and kissing my hand. He had a song for me called "The Side Chick." I liked him, but not the song. I studied the dumb lyrics. Then he played the track.

" 'The Side Chick' song—I'm not singing this. Who is happy about being the side chick?" I asked.

"Thomas wants you to sing this," BayRon said. Thomas

was fucking up. Who wants to sing about how they are happy about being the woman on the side? I looked over at BayRon, and he looked like he was getting frustrated. I didn't want to get a reputation for being hard to work with, so I said, "Okay, okay. I'll sing it." The music started and it was a sample of the beat from the D.O.C.'s "It's Funky Enough" but instead of saying, "It's Compton" somebody would be singing, "I'm the side chick, side chick. When you at work I'm gonna come and see your man, because I'm the side chick. I'm the side chick." I was singing it but the song was awful. You could tell a man wrote the song. But I was being a trouper and just hoped that song didn't make my album. The session went okay. I didn't know if BayRon thought I was a bitch or not, but I still thanked him and started getting ready to leave. Corey came into the studio, gave BayRon a pound and asked him if he wanted to go get a drink and something to eat. BayRon said he would go and then Corey asked me.

"No, that's okay. I don't drink, and I already ate," I said.

"Don't go in the house. Hang out with us," Corey said as he tried to stop me from leaving.

"No, I don't want to go out with a bunch of guys," I said as I grabbed my coat.

"I don't bite," BayRon said, eyeing me down with his focus being on my breasts.

"My artist, Bella, will be there, and she is supposed to perform," Corey said.

"I'm not even dressed," I said, looking down at my outfit.

"You should come out. You look good. This is not a really dressed-up place anyway," Corey said.

"No, I'm good. Plus, I don't even drink like that."

"Why not?" BayRon asked.

"Because I don't."

"There are only two reasons why a twenty-something doesn't drink: religion or recovering alcoholic," Corey said, laughing.

"I'm neither," I said, offended.

"Go home and get dressed. How long before you are ready?" Corey begged, saying since I had been out here I hadn't been anywhere. He was totally ignoring me saying no. I needed to go out and have some fun. It was true, I had been trapped in this studio the last few weeks. It was only twelve-thirty—I could hang out for a little.

"Give me an hour," I finally said.

"You going to meet us here or at the club?"

"I'll come back here."

I went home and threw on jeans and a coral-pink V-neck tank top, silver jewelry and matching sandals then hurried back to the studio.

I followed Corey, BayRon and their crew through the side door of the club. That was a first—no waiting in line. It was packed to capacity on a Wednesday.

"Damn! I never saw a club this good during the middle of the week."

"Only regular people party on the weekend. All industry events are during the week," Corey said.

Okay, I guess I've been a regular person my entire life, I thought as I took in the scene.

The music was loud, and people were dancing everywhere. There were two women standing on high columns on opposite ends of the club doing the same routine to the beat. The Ying Yang Twins' "Salt Shaker" was playing loudly. We walked up a few steps to the VIP section and the bouncer unhooked the red velvet rope. We had our own section right by the dance floor. We were able to look down at the rest of the club. The waitress was a tall girl with black fishnet stockings. She came over to our booth and asked us what we were having.

"Kendra, ladies first. What are you having?" BayRon said.

"Nothing. I'm cool."

"What? Man, you not sitting in this club all night with us and not drinking. Bring this lady a bottle of Moët," BayRon said jokingly.

"You never had a drink before?" Corey asked.

"Yeah, I've had a drink before. I just don't like the way they taste. I used to be a bartender."

"A bartender that don't drink?" They both took turns smiling, laughing and flirting with me. They kept insisting that they were going to make me have a drink. When the drinks arrived, Corey poured me a glass of champagne and put it in my hand.

"The virgin's having a drink tonight," Corey said.

They kept asking me, so I finally gave in. Corey and BayRon were both being very attentive to me. I guess they were looking at me as fresh meat. I had two glasses of champagne, and I was a little buzzed. So I just sat and sat on the sofa, not really saying anything. A lot of women were coming over near our section, just standing around trying to get noticed. They would walk past dancing provocatively or holding their friend's hands. One of them sat down next to me. She said, "How you doing?" She was dressed in a white dress with multicolor platform sandals. Her hair was brown and black with traces of blond. Her sides were curled down and the front was flicked up like a cute mohawk. She had light green eye shadow and clear peach lip gloss on. Corey gave the girl a hug.

"What's up, Core?"

"What's up with you, Shel?" he asked.

"I'm good," she said, looking over at me.

"Let me introduce you to Kendra. She just signed to Touchlight."

"Yeah?" I saw her eyes light up. "Really nice to meet

you, Kendra. Do you have a stylist?" the girl said, introducing herself as Shelly.

"No."

"I'm a stylist. I would love to style you. You can wear anything. You are built like a model."

"Thanks, but I heard stylists want all this money. I don't spend my money up like that," I told her.

"No, girl. Here you are. Take my card and give me a call. I have connects with so many boutiques. I know a lot of people." Then she said, "Let me get your number."

Every time I turned around she was smiling at me and asking was I okay. The rest of the evening she was trying really hard to hang on. The photographer came over to our booth and she said, "Get in the picture," like I was her new best friend. People act really funny if they think you can help them I thought.

BayRon was in the corner hugged up with these girls. Damn, he looked good. I was admiring him when Corey came over and said, "This is my artist Bella."

She shook my hand like a dude. She had on a rainbow bracelet, necklace and hoodie. She had a headband on her braids to the back. She was a cute girl but she was thugged out—Bella was straight-up a boy. How did she get the name Bella? That was such a soft, feminine name and she was the total opposite. She seemed like a man stuck in a short woman's body. All her mannerisms were so masculine.

"Bella, I'm going to put y'all on a song together. It is going to be crazy," he said excitedly.

"Sounds good Core, but I got to get ready to perform, I see you in a little. Nice meeting you," she said as she walked toward the back of the club.

"So she's a rapper?"

"Yeah, she is so sick. Wait until she gets onstage. She is going to turn into a whole other person. You know what would be so hot? If y'all did like a 'best of both worlds' type of thing. You singing and Bella rapping," Corey said.

"Yeah, that might be good."

"Only thing I want her to bring is the sexy girlie thing. Ain't no dudes checking for no hard-ass broad. She cute—I want her to show it. I don't care what she do off that stage but I want her to start looking like a girl. I want somebody to take her hard ass shopping. I would have my girl take her, but they're too opposite for me. My lady is a straight-up diva, and I can see them fighting now," Corey said.

"Whenever you ready," I said.

I was having a lot of fun. I was glad I'd come out. People kept coming up to our area. I hadn't realized how popular BayRon was. He was attracting all types of women. It was just something about his smile and his eyes. The black, Latin, white and Asian women were all on him. He was sexy as hell and flirting with me. The champagne was making me want to flirt back, but I didn't, because I thought about Marcus. BayRon was out on the dance floor with like six girls. All the women in the club must spot money, because they were flocking to him. I don't know how they knew who he was but they did. But he was on me hard. At first I didn't know if it was me or if I was just fantasizing. He confirmed my suspicions when he leaned over to me and whispered, "What's up?"

"You tell me," I said as I giggled and sipped some more of my champagne. Everything he said was funny. He whispered in my ear, "I'm two for two."

"Two for what? What are you talking about?" I asked flirtatiously.

"One, I persuaded you to come out, two, I persuaded you to have a drink. And now there is only one thing left to do, and that's to come home with me."

"I can't do that," I said, blushing.

"Why can't you?"

"I have someone."

"Who's going to tell?"

"Sorry, I can't. I'm a good girl."

"Yeah, sooner or later all good girls go bad. You going to breakfast with me?"

"I can't," I said.

"So when I going to see you again?"

"I can't." I explained to him that I didn't think my boyfriend would like that too much.

"I'll get with you next time," he said as he winked at me and said goodnight. Little did he know that next time wasn't ever going to happen. When he left I escaped. I was way too tipsy and the club was basically over. People were leaving; it was four in the morning. A bunch of other people were outside waiting for cabs, too. One girl took her shoes off, exposing her corn-filled toes. She was standing up against the wall. Her friend had too much to drink and was on the side of her trying to hold in all her liquor. I didn't want to be around if she failed, so I started walking toward the corner. I flagged a cab and went home.

I got home and fell back on the bed. My head was spinning a little. I was experiencing the start of my first hangover. My phone rang with a 410 area code. I answered.

"Hello?"

"Hey. You made it in, Miss?"

"Yeah, I did."

"You know who you talking to?" the voice asked.

"I think so. How did you get my number?" I asked. I knew it was BayRon.

"Um, I got my ways. I know people who know people. You left, and I just wanted to make sure you got home safely."

* * *

I went home to visit my family. I needed to be in my house and just take a few days off. I pulled onto my block and into my driveway. It was still hard to believe that I lived here and this was my house. I went in and surprised my mom in the kitchen.

"The superstar is home," my mom yelled as she hugged me. "I got the CD that you sent me. I played it for the ladies at work. Everybody was like, 'you sound good.'"

"Mom, I told you not to let anyone hear it."

"It's okay. They are not going to bootleg it. You are just in time for dinner," she said as I opened up the pots. My mom was making garlic noodles, grilled salmon and broccoli. She said it was almost done.

I went upstairs to take a quick nap. Everything was just like I had left it. I stretched out on the bed. It felt good to be home. I thought I was just going to close my eyes, but when I awoke it was dark outside and two hours later. I came downstairs and everybody was eating dinner—Nitra, John, Bubbles and Bilal. I pulled up a seat and my mom made me a plate. I caught up with everybody over our meal.

After dinner John said that he wanted to talk to me privately. Me, him and Nitra walked out to the driveway. I leaned on their truck and said, "What's up? What's going on?"

"Nothing. We just wanted to ask you something."

"What?"

"I don't know if I had mentioned it to you, but we are about to open a daycare. We wanted to see if you wanted to be a partner."

"A daycare?"

"Yeah, we did all the math. The startup is about fifteen thousand. We have to get equipment and find a building to lease. But we're going to make our money back in a matter of months. We are going to accept subsidies and get grants."

"That's nice. It seems like a good plan."

"We have five thousand and we need ten more."

"Ten thousand. That's how much y'all want me to invest?"

"Yeah. Your brother was talking about a detail shop, but I told him everybody don't care if they car clean. But people do need a clean, safe place to send their children. You know I just started early-childhood classes," Nitra said, smiling.

"No, I didn't know that," I said as she passed me the pamphlets they'd come up with. The daycare was going to be called Mind Garden. Nitra had the curriculum outline. It was very impressive, but I wasn't sure if I wanted to open a daycare. And ten thousand was a lot money. But I didn't know how to tell them no.

"So what do you think?" John asked.

"I think it is good," I lied. I mean, it was a good idea but I didn't want to be involved. They were investing five thousand of their savings. He had a five-year plan and even had a section about eventually allowing investors in and franchising.

"I guess I'm in. I'm going to give you the money, but you are going to have to tell Marcus you got it from somewhere else, because he keeps counting my money, telling me what I should do with it."

"What? Man! This is your money. You don't have to get his permission."

"I know. I just don't want to hear his mouth." I wasn't sure what I was getting myself into, but I did write them a check. I went to visit Marcus, who was happy to see me. He took me to TGI Friday's.

I went home and got ready for the next day. That girl Shelly I'd met at the club the other night was calling me. "Hello, Kendra? This is Shelly."

"Hi, Shelly."

"I just was calling to say I have already picked up some pieces for you. I hope you don't mind. I just need an address so I can send them to you."

"That is so nice of you. Thank you." I was impressed, but scared as well.

"Are you home? I can bring them to you."

"I live in the Yardley Court."

"I know where that is. I'll be right there."

When she arrived she had her hair pulled back into a long ponytail, and big sunglasses covered her eyes. She was wearing an aqua sweater tube top, with jean capri pants.

"Yes, girl, you are going to love this," she said as she walked into the living room. She placed her bag on the sofa and began to open up a big white box. She pulled the dress out of the box and said, "This is going to look so good on you." It was a pretty dress, pink with a high-waisted black belt.

"You should wear it to your next event. Try it on."

I went into the bathroom and changed. The dress wrapped my body so elegantly. Although it was nice, I didn't like Shelly's pushy manner. She was a name dropper and was looking around my place. I hate that shit. She seemed like the type to be all up in your business. I thanked her and told her that I just didn't need a stylist. She said she understood but that we still had to hang out.

Chapter 17

I had to get something to wear to Peter's party. That girl Shelly wanted to style me, but it was like, I'm not paying somebody hundreds of dollars to pick something out for me to wear. I knew what looked good on me and I could pick it out for myself.

I wore a purple dress, brown belt and brown high-platform sandals. I looked really nice without anyone's assistance. I'm not going to tell you I found the dress at Target. Yes, I was there buying some sheets and I saw it hanging on the rack. It was the last one. I'm not afraid to save money.

Peter's party was my first red-carpet event. It was being held on the roof of the Lexington Hotel in Manhattan. I went up to the twentieth floor. I walked in and realized I was at a major party. There was a pool and I could see the New York City skyline for miles away in every direction. I didn't see anyone I knew. A waiter came over and offered me a glass of champagne. At first I declined, until I realized I needed something to keep me company.

I saw Peter and wanted him to know that I had made it,

so I walked up to him. He had a black suit on with a white shirt.

"Hi, Peter."

"Oh, hello, Kendra. I'm glad you made it. I would like you to meet my wife, Molly." She looked me up and down and then gave me a firm handshake. She had translucent blue eyes with dark brown hair. She reminded me of Wonder Woman. "This is one our new artists," Peter told her. "She is about to perform."

"Nice to meet you. Enjoy yourself," his wife said. "I look forward to seeing your performance."

I saw Tashay and her manager Gil. I gave them a finger wave as I sat in the corner and sipped my drink.

She came over to me.

"Hi. Kendra, right?"

"Yes, how are you?"

"I'm good."

"You came alone?" she asked.

"Yes."

"I love your dress." I felt like, *who the hell needs a stylist? I can do this on my own.*

"Thanks. Did you see Beazie?" I asked.

"No, but he is here."

"Where?" I asked.

She pointed to the bar area. I thanked her, walked over to Beazie and gave him a tap on the arm. I was happy I'd found someone I knew.

"Hey, Kendra. What's good with you?"

"I just got here. How long have you been here?"

"A few minutes. I'm not staying at this stuffy party."

"Why not?"

"I have things to do."

"You can't leave me," I said as someone came and grabbed my waist. It was Thomas.

"Kendra, come with me," he said, holding my hand and leading me around the party. Everywhere I turned,

Thomas was pulling me around the party wanting me to meet different people at the label. He was introducing me to everyone we encountered in the party as the next Touchlight superstar. Then he didn't give me any warning—he just came out and said, "After I introduce you, I want you to just sing."

"Sing what?" I asked nervously.

"Good evening, everyone. I just wanted to thank everyone for coming out this evening. I have a musical treat for you. Touchlight's next superstar, Kendra Michelle, is going to sing for us," he said as he handed the microphone to me. I cleared my throat and then sang "Fallin' " by Alicia Keys. When I was done, everyone was clapping and commending me on my performance.

As I was leaving the party, Peter said, "You did great. Sorry I didn't get a chance to talk to you that much this evening. Make sure you come to see me on Monday." I thanked him for inviting me and said goodnight. It was raining and the security guard came up and let me stand under his umbrella.

"Thanks, Boo," I said.

"Anytime, anytime. When you come here ask for me—Marvin." He gave me his card. "I'll always make sure you get VIP service."

Chapter 18

Maya had set up an interview for me and Tashay with *Vibe* magazine. We were having lunch at Miramoso, an Italian restaurant on the West Side. The article was called "The Future of R&B." They were profiling five people for the article. Tashay was supposed to be with me, but she hadn't shown up yet. The journalist, Brenda, was a young, petite black woman with short dreads that were dyed brown at the tips. She had on a black suit jacket with a lacey white T-shirt underneath, and a short denim skirt and black knee boots. Her style was very different. We sat down and she turned on her tape recorder and started asking me basic questions like where I was from, who did I listen to growing up, and who did I think I was like who was already out. Tashay came up to the table and took a seat.

"How you doing? Sorry I'm late," she said, brushing her burgundy curly weave out of her face. She was wearing a short pantsuit with a red belt and red shoes. She looked like she was about to do a photo shoot—big hair and makeup done up.

"Let me see them shoes. They are so nice. Are they Christian Louboutins?" Brenda asked.

Tashay turned her foot out and showed off the red bottom of her shoe.

"Yes, aren't they cute? My boo bought them in L.A. off Rodeo Drive."

"They're nice, but now that is nicer," the reporter joked as she pointed to the big fake-looking diamond bracelet Tashay had on. After she complimented Tashay on the bracelet she went back to her shoes.

"What separates you from the rest, Tashay?" Brenda said, finally getting back to the interview.

"Well, I've been writing my own music since I was ten, and I took vocal classes and dance. My mother was a singer and her mother was singer. I also play the guitar and I read and write music. I also sang at church in the choir since I was seven."

Wow, that is so impressive, I thought. Brenda asked me the same question. All I could think to say was that I loved to sing. Brenda asked us a series of questions. Tashay answered effortlessly. I'd have to learn that skill. I felt like I was confusing my words and stumbling through answers. Tashay was what Tony was talking about—camera ready and poised, the kind of artist a man wants to bed and a woman wants to be like. I had to step up my game.

I got a call from Peter's secretary telling me to meet him at his office at six-thirty p.m. When I arrived, his secretary called Peter and he came to the door.

"Kendra, come in and have a seat. I'm finishing up some work." His office was big. There was a bookcase and a long mahogany table. Plants were near the window. I sat and looked at the stacks of reports on his desk. I smiled as he offered me something to drink.

"I just wanted to let you know that if you ever need

anything, I am available. You're going to do great. Thomas has told me about your amazing voice. Actually I was just listening to it," he said as he turned the volume up on the speaker and I heard myself singing "Amnesia."

"Thanks," I said.

Peter then came over to my chair and said, "Don't thank me, you are the talented one," and clasped my shoulder gently. "I just wanted to let you know if you needed anything don't be afraid to ask. Sometimes you need to have someone higher up looking out for you. But if that person looks out for you, you have to look out for him, too," he said. His hand brushed past my breast and then he let his finger circle my nipple. He was making me feel cheap and nasty. If he thought I was going to sleep with him for some extra favors, he was out of his damn mind.

"Mr. Sutton, if I need you I will ask. I'm going to leave. Okay?" I said as I walked out of his office. I couldn't believe that he had said that to me. Who did he think I was? I went home angry, shocked and in disbelief. I still felt his nasty hands on me. I felt like calling Marcus and John and having them come and kick his ass. But if they did that I would probably lose my deal. I wanted to tell someone, but who? He was the vice-president of the company. He probably did this all the time and I came to the conclusion that my best bet was to keep my mouth shut and act like nothing ever happened.

It was 11:00 a.m. the next morning and Bubbles sent me a text message asking me to call her immediately. Her butt should have been at school. I dialed her cell phone.

"What's up? Aren't you supposed to be in school?"

"There's no school today. I just wanted to tell you that this girl called Smilie on the radio was dissing you this afternoon."

"What are you talking about?"

"She has a picture of you off of this Web site, Wire Images, and she is laughing because she said her niece got the same outfit as you."

"Hold up! Slow down. Who said this?"

"This girl named Smilie said her niece wore a dress you had on at a party to church. Did you get it from Target?"

"What radio station?"

"It's the new hip-hop and R&B station. All my friends were calling me telling me she is talking about your sister. Right. She don't be talking about my sister. 'Cause I know you have money and don't have to buy a dress from Target. I should go up to that station and beat her up for lying."

"No, don't do that," I said. I didn't dare tell her that my dress was from Target.

"She don't want me to go up there and hurt her talking about my daughter. She don't know she won't have a job," my mom said as she jumped on the phone.

"Mom, it comes with the territory. Don't worry about it."

"I don't care about no damn territory. No, that ain't right. You trying to make something of your life and you got this chick talking about you on the radio. I'm going to beat her ass." I didn't let them know, but I was upset.

"Mom, did you check the account for the bill money?"

"Yes, I paid the bills yesterday."

"Okay. Mom please don't worry about it. I have to go, I'll talk to you later."

How was somebody going to be talking about me? *Fuck her,* I thought. *She don't even know me.* The good thing was that it was only a local radio station, so nobody out here would have heard of her. I got off the bed and I looked at my purple dress. To me it was still nice, but I guess I wasn't allowed to shop cheap anymore. I don't know why, since I wasn't rich. I had a few dollars in the bank, but was I supposed to spend all my money on clothes and stylists? I didn't have time for this mess. I got myself together, dressed and was on my way to meet Tony, Thomas and Beazie at the studio. I had fifteen songs recorded. All I needed was another five, Thomas would pick fourteen to go on my CD and I would be done.

Tashay was in the studio down the hall. Everybody was really jocking her hard. She had a nice shape and her face was just okay, but she must sing like heaven, 'cause they loved her. To be honest I was starting to get a little jealous. I hoped she didn't sing better than me. My fears were immediately put to rest. I walked into the studio, and Beazie and Davis were laughing.

"What's so funny?" I asked.

"All this hype around this nonsinging bitch," Beazie said, laughing.

"What are y'all talking about?" I said as I placed my bags down on the floor.

"Nothing. You ready?" he said, flagging the air.

"Beaz, tell me," I said, still trying to figure out what was going on.

"It's nothing. That chick can't sing and was trying to get smart with me."

"Who can't sing?"

"Tashay. She can't carry a note and she goes off on me. So I'm like, 'Calm down, Ma.' Then she was like she didn't have to and all this and that. Getting smart, right? So then I told her to her face that she can't sing and she started telling me what vocal training she had. So to make a long story short, she goes and calls Thomas. Then Thomas comes in and I told him I'm not working with that bitch no more. He put her in another studio and then goes off on me. So I'm off her project. Ain't nothing, though. It's not like she going to sell any units anyway," he said, throwing a piece of balled-up paper into the trash.

"Damn! For real?" I said.

"You should go listen to that nonsinging trick. Go to the end of the hall and just listen."

"She can't be that bad," I said. Then even Davis, who was her biggest hype man, gave me the craziest screw face.

"But y'all worked with her before."

"No, we didn't. They were playing stuff she already recorded. This is the first time I've heard her live, and she is bad. She is going to fall right on her face. People recognize real. She can't do no live shows singing like that. It don't matter how good you look," Beazie said.

I couldn't believe it—I had to hear it for myself. I had to see for myself. I walked to the end of the hall, and I heard it with my own ears.

Her voice was a combination of a duck whispering and a sheep straining loud. And it didn't help that she was flapping her arms around while she sang.

"Oh no," I said as I ran back down the hall, laughing my ass off. We were laughing hysterically. I had my hand in front of my mouth. I couldn't believe Tashay was sounding like that.

"That girl is tone-deaf. How did she get a deal? They are going to triple overdub that voice," Davis said.

We were all still laughing when Tashay came walking in with this big hair and super-tight jeans on. She found herself somewhat stepping to Beazie.

"Is there any reason why y'all keep coming into my studio? Did y'all want something?" she asked.

"Naw, you got it," Beazie said and started laughing again, right in front of her face.

"Is something funny?" she asked.

"Yeah, you bitch. You're funny 'cause you mad at me

because you can't sing," Beazie shouted as he started laughing again and playing my song "Amnesia" real loud.

"I thought you might want to hear what a real singer sound like." He laughed.

Why did he have to put me into it? Now, that was not funny.

She walked out of the studio switching hard, saying, "Whatever."

Chapter 19

Even though I didn't want to get with Peter, I still wanted to play nice with him. I told Tony what had happened, just to get a man's opinion. He said it was good that I'd resisted his advances, but I didn't want to totally turn him off either. So I went to his office just to let him know I appreciated the opportunity to sing at his party but was not interested in anything else. I got to his office as his secretary was coming down the hall.

"I'm here to see Mr. Sutton," I said.

"One minute," she said. She went to her desk, grabbed her keys and bag and said, "He's in there. You can go in." She raced out the door and said, "Sorry, I have to pick up my kid from daycare. My husband's stuck in traffic."

I shrugged and walked into Peter's office. He was sitting at his desk and a mop of black hair was bobbing up and down on Peter's lap. His eyes were closed and his pants were resting around his ankles. The person was on her knees and wasn't even coming up for air, she was going so hard. They were so into the act, neither of them heard me come in or leave. I tiptoed back out the door and shook my head as I replayed what I'd just seen. That's when it hit me—the woman on the floor in front of Peter had been wearing shoes with red soles. It was Tashay. Oh my God! Wow! Now I see how she got her deal. I wasn't with that shit. If that's how she got down, fine. I'm not her, and I'm not doing what she does. I didn't want any part of that. I walked out of the building like I didn't see anything.

The next day Corey called and asked if could I meet him and Bella at six at his place so we could discuss the songs he wanted me on. I was going to sing the hook for Bella's demo. She was not signed yet and Corey was trying to get her a big deal. He gave me his address and I took a taxi over. When I arrived his girlfriend, Aisha, answered the door. She had on jean shorts, a blue tank top and blue satin wedge sandals.

"Can I help you?"

"Yes, I'm here to see Corey," I said like, *Aren't you going to let me in?*

She looked me over and then said, "Oh, you're that singer. How you doing?"

"I'm okay."

"You can come in and have a seat."

I looked around his place. He lived in a bi-level condo. His kitchen was on my immediate right and the living room was straight in front of me. There were hardwood floors and a kitchen with an island. His microwave, dishwasher and refrigerator were all stainless steel. His sofa was white leather with red pillows. There were pictures all around.

"Baby, the singer girl is here," she said.

"My name is Kendra," I smiled, correcting her.

"Oh. Sorry," she said.

Corey told her to send me upstairs, and that's when I

found out he had a small studio set up in one of his bedrooms. I walked in said, "Hey," to him and Bella. She was there, once again looking like little Thug Misses. Corey was looking good as usual.

"Your place is nice," I told him.

"Thanks," he said, as he began to play the music for the song he wanted me and Bella on.

"So, what do you think about the track so far?"

"It's hot. I think the concept will work."

He started playing a few other beats when Aisha walked in the room and said, "Core, I'm leaving."

"Okay," he said.

"You not going to walk downstairs and say goodbye?" Aisha whined, standing in the doorway.

"Give me a moment," he said.

He started discussing the songs with us. When she came back in the room she said, "Core, you don't have to walk me because I'm leaving."

He finally got up and walked her downstairs.

"That chick is so needy," Bella said when Corey left the room. I didn't comment but I definitely agreed; her whiny voice was annoying. She seemed like she thrived off attention.

A few moments later he came back in the room and said, "Now that she is gone let's get down to business."

We went back and forth with ideas about the concept of my and Bella's song for over an hour. Corey wanted us to get everything ready before we booked studio time.

"So when are you trying to get in the studio to record this?" I asked.

"By next week, I hope."

Bella's phone started ringing. She answered it and then she said she had to go.

"Bella, we have to do this," Corey said as he tried to block her leaving.

"I got to meet my moms at the airport. Y'all finish

everything up, and then tell me what the songs are about. I'll spit my verses and that's it. Corey I've been here for two hours. I have to go."

Corey begged her not to leave but she left anyway. "I guess it's just me and you," he said finally. "So what do you think about the songs?"

"They're okay."

"You okay?"

"Yeah, I'm just a little tired," I said, yawning. "And a little stressed."

"You need to get a massage," he said as he attempted to rub me.

"I will when I get time," I said, removing his hand.

"I need one. I haven't slept in three days and I'm getting tired. Can you give me one?" Corey asked.

"I'm tired too. So I'm going to get out of here. When you have everything ready let me know," I said as I stood up to leave.

He stood and I followed him down the steps, and then he asked where my boyfriend was.

"He's home in Philadelphia."

"I guess he hasn't learned his lesson yet. He is still leaving you alone in the big city."

"I'm doing okay. He knows I know how to handle myself."

"You do?" he asked as he moved uncomfortably close to me. I could feel his body. Only six inches separated us. "Whew, if I didn't have a girl," he said.

"I'm taken," I said, reminding him that even if he didn't have a girl I wasn't an option. He made the six inches into three inches.

"Right now I'm not thinking about your man or my girl," he said as he began to move even closer to me. I tried stepping back, but he just kept stepping up. He finally backed me all the way against the wall. There was nowhere else to go.

"Don't your girlfriend have a key?" I asked, hoping that would make him scared.

"She is gone for a couple of days."

"Please get away from me," I said as I felt my heart beat rapidly. I was trying to flee. I turned my back to him but that made him push his body up to mine. I asked him to back up off me and stop touching me.

"I'm not touching you. Do you want me to touch you?" he asked.

I wanted him not only to touch me but to take every part of me, to sensually devour me. I could feel his wet tongue going up and down my neck.

"Stop. Please, stop. Please," I said.

I was right by the front door, but I didn't want to leave. He was who and what I wanted at that point. But then the next thing I knew he began swabbing his round dick on my ass. I knew my pants were coming down. I tried to pull them back up.

"Get out of them," he demanded. He was rough and I was loving it. He wasn't even inside me yet and I was feeling him.

I was trying my best not to give in to temptation. I was wrestling away and telling him to get off me. "Corey, I don't move this fast. Plus I have a boyfriend."

He wasn't listening to me. His focus was getting me out of my clothes and onto the floor. And I wanted to be on the floor. Just the thought of him prying my legs apart and tearing my insides up made me want to stop fighting. He wrapped his arms around me and squeezed so tightly I thought I was going to pop.

"What's wrong? You're not feeling me?" he asked as he kissed my neck. For some reason I felt like I couldn't lie to him.

"Yes, I'm feeling you. But I have a boyfriend, and this just can't happen."

"We want each other. I see the way you been looking at

me in the studio. We are grown and can do whatever we like."

"No, no. I have to go."

"You don't really want to go, do you?"

"Yes, I do."

"Okay, I'll stop," he said as he pulled away from me.

Damn! The moment he stopped I wanted him closer to me. I thought about him pushing me against the wall and sticking his thickness in me, and I wanted to let him do whatever with me. I wanted to suck on him and just put every inch of him in my mouth and swallow him whole. As I attempted to leave he walked up on me and blew on my neck. I almost lost it. It was really time for me to go. Then he wrapped his warm arms around me. I turned around and his lips were right in front of mine and he took a kiss.

My thoughts kept going from yes, to no, to maybe so, to take me now. But I put my hand on the knob, opened the door and walked into the hallway. As I adjusted my clothes, he came out and accompanied me to the elevator. The elevator opened and he pushed up against the elevator wall and passionately sucked on my lips and tongue until we reached the ground floor. I was so into it I wanted to get back on the elevator and let him do whatever he wanted with me.

"You really leaving?" he asked as he kissed my forehead.

"I have to," I said.

"In a perfect world I would take you back upstairs and make love to you. You just like I like 'em—brown, thin and gorgeous."

"Thanks for the compliment, but I have to go."

Lucky me, as soon as I waved for a cab, one stopped. Corey kissed me again on the cheek and closed the door. I felt instant relief. I slouched down in the cab and thought about what just happened. I could taste his cologne on my lips. I felt so proud of myself for not giving in to temptation.

"Hey, baby, you called me?" I asked Marcus after I got in my apartment. I was still shaking off the tingling of Corey.

"Yeah, I did. Where were you?" he asked.

"In the studio."

"Damn. They always got you in the studio. They better give my baby a break. Well, I be there on Friday. You know I love you."

"I love you too, baby," I said as my other line started ringing. It was Corey.

"Babe, it's Tony on the other line. I have to take his call." That was wrong, but now that me and Corey were apart I wanted to hear what he had to say to me.

"Why you leave?" Corey said when I switched to the other line.

"I had to go."

"No, you didn't. We were just getting started. I think I'm about to come over there and get you and bring you back here. Or I'll just stay there with you."

"No, I'm good. I'll talk to you later," I said.

Knowing that my man would be here soon made me that much stronger. I couldn't be getting caught up with Corey. He had a situation, and I had one too. Plus we worked together and I had to stay focused. And I'd never cheated on Marcus, so why would I start now?

Shelly called to invite me to the *Fusion* magazine party on Friday and said I needed something to wear. I told her I would only go if she could help me get my look together. I couldn't afford another fashion mishap.

"This is why you need a stylist. You can't show up at these big events with nondescript clothes on. I'll have someone send you some things over. How are you going to take care of the charges?" she asked.

"I'll pay with a credit card," I said as I gave her my credit card information.

Shelly picked out the perfect outfit for me, a black dress with a plunging neckline that showed off my ample cleavage. I wore a gold charm necklace, a gold clutch bag and black pumps.

"I wish we could stay in and relax. I haven't seen you in almost a month," Marcus said, watching me get dressed.

"We can stay in tomorrow. We have to go to this party," I said as I looked in the mirror and put my earrings in.

"Kendra, this is killing me. I miss you. I need you back home," he said as he came behind me, tugged on my waist and attempted to nibble on my ear. "I don't want to share you tonight. I miss my baby. You know we never been apart this much."

"Okay, baby. I miss you too! But we have to leave," I said as I was sliding on my shoes.

The party was at 40/40 Club. There was a wait and a long line outside, but I gave them my name and they let me right in. People were everywhere. Flat screen televisions were playing music videos. Initially, I didn't see anyone I knew, so I decided until I ran into someone I would spend the time catering to Marcus. He seemed uncomfortable and needed my attention.

We sat down at the bar and I got the bartender's attention.

"What can I get you?" he asked.

"A bottle of Moët," I said as I handed him my credit card. "You okay, Marcus?"

"Yes, baby," he said, kissing my cheek. He smiled. He was getting a little more comfortable with the environment.

"I wanted to tell you, you look real sexy in that black dress," he said, bending over and kissing my neck.

"Thanks. The girl Shelly picked it out for me. She is now my unofficial stylist-slash-PR person." I laughed.

"You got a stylist? You're going Hollywood," he joked. The bartender brought the bottle uncorked. I poured our glasses, then I gave one to Marcus and sipped on the other.

"What's this?" he asked.

"Champagne."

"When you start drinking?"

"Um, I don't know. I just did. It is not so bad," I said, sipping from my glass. He looked at me, shook his head a little and then took his back. I noticed Shelly was walking past me. I got up. I tapped her on the shoulder.

"Hey, girl, I was looking for you," she said, flashing me a smile.

"We just got here not too long ago," I said as I introduced her to Marcus.

"Come to the room where I'm at," she said as she took my hand and led us through the crowded club. We followed her upstairs to the VIP room. Marcus was in front of me and I was holding onto his hand as we went up the steps. Then I felt someone squeeze my ass. I jumped a little, and Marcus turned around to see what was going on. I looked around and saw Corey wink at me.

"You okay, babe?" Marcus asked.

"Yes, the champagne must be getting to me. I felt a little chill." I couldn't believe Corey would do that all while he was holding Aisha's hand and I was walking with Marcus. I was glad we were walking in opposite directions. I wouldn't know how to react if he came over and tried to talk to me in front of my boyfriend.

Shelly brought us to the table she was sitting at and said, "I'm glad y'all could make it. I'll be back." Me and Marcus was just sitting back catching up. When I saw people I knew, I said, "What's up?" and made sure I introduced Marcus as *my man* to everyone I spoke to. I sat extra close to him, and I was leaning into him. I wanted him to know that I appreciated him and nothing would come between us. I laughed at all of his jokes and was showing him extra attention. Even when I saw Beazie and he said hello, I practically ignored him. I felt bad throwing him shade, but protecting my man's feelings was more important. Then Shelly came over with a guy named Ashton Phillips, who worked for Nike. I said hello and got his card.

Shelly then came back to the table and said, "Make sure you call him. He'll send you all the Nikes you want." Then she told me, "Kendra, I have some other people I want you to meet."

"Babe, I be right back," I said as I took one more sip of my drink. We walked out of the VIP room into the main floor and she introduced me to the editor of *Fusion* and a few of the writers, and we started chatting about a whole lot of nothing. Then I walked Shelly to the bathroom, and on the way out we posed for pictures with a party Web site and made some more contacts. I looked down at my watch and realized thirty minutes had passed since we'd left the table. I had left Marcus alone for all that time. I knew he was probably steaming. I had to get back to him. Shelly kept talking and meeting and hugging people, so I finally left her. I went back to the table and apologized to Marcus, but he was just sitting there looking like he was enjoying the atmosphere.

"I want you to meet this photographer Johnny Nunez; he takes everybody's picture." Shelly flagged down the photographer and said, "Johnny—hey I wanted you to meet my friend Kendra Michelle, she is a singer on Touchlight." He said hello and put his camera up and told us to smile. By now I had perfected my face-to-the-side, lips-pouted-out smile. He gave me his card and said, "Nice meeting you." I said likewise and put his card in my pocket.

As soon as I sat down Shelly walked back to me.

"Kendra, come here. Sorry, I have to steal her again," Shelly said as she pulled me away from Marcus for the second time. I returned to the table but Marcus was gone. I called his cell phone, hoping he'd gone to the bathroom, but he didn't answer. I waited around for a few moments and he still didn't come back. I walked to the men's bathroom and stood outside the door for a few minutes. Then a drunk guy walked out and I asked him if there was anyone else in there and he said no. Just to be sure, when he left I peeked in and didn't see Marcus.

I searched all over the club. I ran into Corey again. He was leaning on the wall and Aisha was dancing all over him like a stripper. He was looking side to side at all the women passing by, like she wasn't even there. He was so not into her—but that was their thing. I had to find my man.

He wouldn't leave me, I thought. He wouldn't not support his woman when she was trying to make moves; he wouldn't do that. At least I thought that way. But I finally gave up looking for Marcus after I passed the same crowd of people three times. I tried to dial him one more time.

"Baby, where are you?" I asked.

"I left," Marcus said.

"You did what? Why you leave?"

"You left me sitting by myself for an hour Kendra."

"Where are you at now?"

"I'm on my way back to your place."

"I'll be right there." I left the party. I didn't even tell Shelly I was leaving. I was so fucking pissed off. Yeah, I left Marcus for a few minutes, but he should have been like, *Look at my lady. She's trying to make connects. Let me sip this champagne and relax until she get back.* He couldn't do any of that; he just left me.

I met up with him at the apartment. I walked in,

slammed my bag down, looked him directly in the face and said, "Baby, what's wrong with you?"

"Nothing."

"So why did you leave the party? You are acting weird, Marcus. You're changing."

"I'm not changing, you are. When did you start drinking?" he said as he tapped the side of his head and then pointed to me as if to say, *think about it.*

"Okay. So what? I drink now. And what?"

"I'm just saying, Kendra, that's your shit. I didn't feel comfortable. All that fake shit. That's not me. So I left." He played with his water with his index finger. I swear sometimes I felt like I was sleeping with the damn enemy. I mean, he was supposed to be there supporting me, pumping his fist for me, telling me I'm doing good. But I didn't feel like he was supporting my dream at all.

"Kendra, you know I love you, but I don't know about all this. I need you home with me. This shit ain't working out."

"Well, I can't stop working. I need you to be a little more supportive."

"I'm not asking you to choose me or choose the music, but I don't know how much more I can handle," he said, sighing, and palmed his face down taking a long pause.

"Let's not talk about this right now." I was still so mad. We lay in the bed.

"Baby, okay, when your album comes out, do you get downtime?"

"Probably not. Why?"

"Okay, can you take nine months to have a baby? Then I can have the baby with me." He was still talking this baby mess. I couldn't believe it.

"Marcus are you serious, look at me. Don't you see what's going on? I'm not having a baby next week or next year, so stop asking me."

"All my friends have family, Kendra. I need that. I

want that in my life. I want kids and a wife home when I get there. I don't want to stop your dreams, but I have to live my life too!"

"So what are you saying?" I asked.

"Now that you are doing what you want to do with your life I am trying to figure out what I need to do in my life. I wrote a list of all the things I want to do. First, I know I have to get my home together and I can't do that with my dad there, so I'm going to send him to Fayetteville with his sister. Then I'm going to try to get in the sheet metal union. And I want a family. It is only me. I'm the only child—no sisters, no brothers. My dad was the baby, and all his peoples are almost gone. My mom's family—I don't fuck with them like that. So when my dad go I'm going to be all alone."

"You won't be alone. You have me."

"It's not the same Kendra."

"Baby, let's talk about this later." I was not thinking about having a baby no time soon. I was trying to get my career together. I was trying to enjoy us. Then maybe have a baby. I got back in the bed and he came and held me and said that he loved me.

My phone began to ring at 3:30 in the morning. I scrambled to look down at the screen and saw that damn 410 area code. I knew it was nobody but Corey, so I didn't answer it. Then he called back twice. He was definitely tripping. Luckily Marcus was not a light sleeper. I walked into the kitchen and answered the phone.

"Hello?" I said with an attitude.

"What's up?"

"Nothing. I'm sleeping and you are tripping. Please don't call me this late again," I whispered.

"Oh, your man must still be in town. All right, holla at me when he leaves."

"Okay."

"Yo, you know I'm really feeling you, right? I don't

know what it is, but there's something about you," he said. I looked down at the phone, closed it and went back in the bedroom.

"Who was that on the phone?" Marcus asked.

"That girl Shelly from the party."

"What she want? Why she callin' three in the morning?"

"She was making sure we got in all right." He didn't ask any more questions. I was happy, because I just wanted to go to sleep and forget about the entire night.

The next morning I was awakened by Marcus telling me that he was leaving.

"Where are you going?" I asked.

"I'm going home. I think we need time off," he said. I sat up and said, "What are you talking about? I thought you were going to stay until Monday."

"I was, but I think you need time alone. Kendra, if you want this life you going to have to live it without me. I want to settle down and have a family, and you're chasing this music. I can't have my woman all over the place."

"What? What are you trying to say?"

"Nothing. Basically, I am here for you if you are home. I can't deal with you being away, and until things calm down for you we should be apart."

"Don't do this, Marcus. I need you, Marcus. Baby, don't do this," I said as I leapt out of the bed and asked him to sit down.

"Stop acting like you care. Now you don't have to call me back. You can party with all your new friends," he said, trying to be smart.

"Marcus, why can't you just understand?"

"I do understand. This is your new life and I'm not a part of it. Your life is to go to parties, take pictures and drink champagne," he said sarcastically.

I started laughing at Marcus; that was the furthest thing from the truth. I walked up on him and he pushed me away.

"So you think this shit is funny?" Marcus asked.

"No, but you think that's all I do is party. You don't see when I be having twelve-hour studio sessions. This shit isn't fun all the time. All I do is work. Marcus, stop this. Let's talk about this."

"I got to go to work. Some people have real jobs. I'm not no leech-ass nigga, Kendra. Here you go. Take this," he said as he threw the watch I'd bought him at me. "I don't need your watch, your clothes or this life."

He was acting like a baby and I couldn't stop what I was doing. I tried lying down and taking a nap. But I wound up just thinking more about my relationship with Marcus. I was aggravated. Why couldn't he just understand? The phone rang. I was hoping it was Marcus.

"Hello. Can I speak to Kendra Michelle, the next R&B diva?"

I laughed and asked, "Who is this?"

"Your soul mate."

"My soul mate?" I asked.

"Yeah, your soul mate. What's up, Boo?" I realized it was Corey.

"Why did you grab me? That was so not cool."

"So, I felt like grabbing you. You didn't have a problem with me grabbing you the other night."

"That was a mistake."

"I don't think so. You really wanted me. You need me in your life. You're the type of woman who should have your man at her feet doing whatever she needs. If you were my woman, I'd give you whatever you wanted—foot massages, warm milk bubble baths and back rubs," he said. Then he began to laugh and said, "No. When I'm going to see you again?"

"I don't know why you're saying all this and you have a woman."

"Not anymore."

"What happened?"

"I got rid of my dead weight. She is gone. You need to drop Mr. UPS and get somebody that knows how to take care of their woman."

"He does know how to take care of me."

"Dude looks like a clown. He's insecure, too. He was looking all around, making sure nobody wasn't looking at you the whole night."

"You can't keep talking about my man like that," I said.

"Why you getting mad? It's the truth. He's a boy. I'm a man and you have outgrown that nine-to-five loser. When you're ready for someone like me, get at me."

"I'm going to talk to you later," I said. He was making me mad—mostly because everything he was saying was true.

Marcus hadn't called me in two weeks. I'd been too busy to pay attention because I was working with this other producer, Agent. He was a perfectionist asshole. He wanted every note completely on point. So between him and photo shoots I didn't even know what day it was.

I had to go make sure Marcus was okay. I gave him two weeks to calm down. Eventually I knew we were going to try to work it out with him. He was my man and I needed to make him feel more comfortable. I just had to do whatever it took to do that. One way was to start going home more and to persuade him to come up here more.

* * *

I arrived at Philadelphia's Thirtieth Street train station and took a cab to Marcus's house. As I drove down his block I noticed two little kids with yellow ShopRite bags getting out of my car and a short heavy woman unloading with them. I know Marcus wasn't driving anyone around in my car because that would be straight-up disrespectful shit. She was closing my door and hit the alarm on my car. *Oh, really?* I paid the cab driver and got out. Marcus was coming to assist her. He still hadn't seen me yet.

The second he grabbed the bag I yelled, "Marcus, who is this girl?"

Marcus started walking toward me dumbfounded. He was stuttering. "Kendra, this is Tamika. Tamika, this is Kendra," he said.

"Why was she taking groceries out of my car?" I said very loud. He tried to pull me to the side.

"No! Get off me." I yanked my arm away and turned to the girl. "Who are you?"

"Ask Marcus," she said.

"I don't got to ask Marcus shit. I asked you." She looked at me and her kids were looking like, *what is going on?* She walked them up the steps into the house.

I turned my attention back to Marcus.

"What's going on, Marcus? Who the fuck is this girl? Who are those kids? And why is she taking groceries up out of my car?"

"Baby, listen. Tamika is my friend from work. She got kicked out of her place and I'm letting her and her boys stay here until she gets another place. Ain't nothing going on between us."

"So you were driving her around in my car?" I asked.

"Not like that. I just let her pick some things up from the market."

"You let her drive my car? I gave you a few weeks to get yourself together and you already moved somebody in and you're letting them drive my car. Are you kidding me?"

"It's not like that. Listen, Kendra . . ." he said, trying to calm me down.

"It's like something. I don't believe this shit. You got some homeless bitch all up in your house."

"Let's talk," he said as he followed me, trying to get me to listen to him.

"Talk about what? I don't want to hear nothing you got to say. Give me my keys." I stood tapping my foot with my arms crossed. I looked at him. Tears were forming. I wanted to punch him directly in his head, but he wasn't worth it.

"Marcus, this how you do me, huh? All these years, Marcus. We been together since I was seventeen." I went to smack the shit out of him but he grabbed my open hand right before it landed on his cheek.

"What kind of woman are you dating? You got a woman out here making money trying to do right for you and you want to fuck with a broke-ass bitch with two kids. You are so damn sorry," I yelled at him.

The girl gave me a look like, *hold up, I'm not no broke-ass bitch.* Then she had the nerve to say something.

"I'm not going to be listening to too many 'broke-ass bitches'."

"Fuck you. You're a nothing-ass bitch. Please," I said, looking down at her like she was a piece of trash.

"Marcus, you better get your girl," she said while standing in the door.

"He ain't got to get me, bitch," I said as I lunged for her. Marcus grabbed the girl and asked her to go in the house. He told me to take the car keys and go home.

"Go home Marcus. You telling me to go home for this bitch! You going to protect her instead of me? Tell her to go in the house?" I said as he let me go. I walked to my car and began pointing and yelling and screaming. "Fuck you, Marcus. I did everything I could do for you. Keep on slumming, you fucking nothing-ass bitch. Look how you living. Look at this dump. Look at where you live at. Fuck you and fuck that dirty bitch. I'm above both of y'all lowlifes."

"Kendra, come here," he said as he ran up to my car.

I pulled off. There wasn't anything he could say to me to justify—one, having someone driving my car, and two, letting them live in the house with him. Ooh, I was steaming mad. Somebody was going to get hurt.

As I pulled off I wanted to back my car up and run Marcus over. I wanted to go beat that girl's brains out of her for trying to get smart. I stopped at a light and calmed myself down. *Kendra, you have too much at stake. If you beat his ass, you're going to jail and you won't be able to finish your album.* And I knew Marcus wasn't worth it. *Look at him. Let him stay right there where he at. He don't want anything with his life.*

Instead of turning around I drove straight to the New Jersey Turnpike, but I still felt the need to cuss Marcus out. He didn't pick up his phone, so I left him a message.

"Fuck you, Marcus. I don't want to talk to you ever again in life. You hear me? I have nothing to say to you. Nothing."

After I left that message I called back and left ten more messages. I was so mad. I know I was a little guilty by flirting with Corey, but that's all I did—flirt. Yeah, I kissed him, but he didn't live with me and he wasn't driving Marcus's car. I'd wanted to get with Corey, but I hadn't because I was loyal, and Marcus didn't know anything about loyalty.

Marcus must have gotten all my messages and began

ringing my phone. Each time he called I would send him to voice mail. I finally picked up the phone.

"Hello?" I shouted angrily.

"Kendra, just listen. I know you are mad, but let me explain myself."

"Do you mess with her?" I asked.

"No."

"You never slept with her?" I asked.

There was a long pause and then he said, "No."

"You're lying, I can tell. Don't lie to me. I'm not a stupid bitch," I said as I hung up the phone.

He called back and said, "Please listen. I did sleep with her, but I just was so upset you weren't here with me."

"You are a nasty dirty dick dog. I don't want to talk to you ever again in life. You are a broke-ass loser. You hear me. You are dead to me. I hate you. I hate the bitch that birthed you. I got too much to lose to fuck with a nothing-ass nigga like you. I tried to bring you up to my level, but that's impossible. I'm too good for you, Marcus, you know that. You ain't shit. I can get much better but you are going to live in that dump with your dad the rest of your life. You tried to play me? Sit back and watch me come up on your ass. Watch while shit continues to crumble around you and you go nowhere. I'm going to come up."

"Kendra, you don't mean any of this. Stop talking to me like this."

"I do mean it. Don't call my phone ever again," I screamed as I turned my phone off. I had had enough of Marcus.

My ride home I felt so alone. I didn't even turn the radio on. I mean, I thought we were going to be together for the rest of our lives. I thought he was going to be my husband. But it was not my fault that he couldn't handle my success. I tried to patch things up with him. I gave him a few weeks to get himself together. But he's with somebody else already? That means he was cheating all along. It was not my fault that he left me. I'd come to try to work it out with him and he had next girl in my car. I did everything right by him. He messed up, not me. He should know better. I didn't want to talk to anyone. I felt so foolish.

When I got back in the city I called Shelly. I wanted to go shopping and hang out. At first I thought of Shelly as a hanger, but she wasn't—she called me so much, she became my friend. She was in her second year of law school and wanted to be an entertainment lawyer. She had taken a few semesters off and was a genuinely nice person trying to break into the business.

"I thought you went to Philly," she said as I invited her out.

"I did, but I decided to come back." I was so messed up about what went down with me and Marcus. I needed an ear and hers was there. I told her everything that had just happened and she told me she would meet me at my place and we would go shopping. She was sitting in the lobby when I arrived. Although I had called her I was a little embarrassed that I had been crying.

"So what happened?"

"He broke up with me a few weeks ago. I thought I was doing the right thing and letting him have some time to hisself. I went home to make everything right and he had a bitch in my car."

"That's messed up. A man needs to feel needed. If you are doing too much he feels alone and he has to have someone who is less than him and makes him feel like a man. You too much woman for him."

"You're probably right." We got something to eat and it made me feel better. After that we went boutique shopping in the Village. I didn't really need anything, but I didn't have my man and I needed something to make up for it.

Chapter 20

I had to head back to the studio. One of the last songs I was recording was called "Don't Wait," an uptempo song about a girl telling a guy not to wait to ask her for her phone number because she was about to leave. Beazie kept making me sing over and over again. He asked me what was wrong with me but I just told him nothing. I couldn't tell him I was still upset from breaking up with my boyfriend. My voice was straining and I was tired.

"I don't feel good. I'm going home," I said.

"If you go home you still have to pay for this session."

"I know. Whatever. I'm tired," I said as I left.

I went home and began to cry. I was just breaking down. It was so hard on me, not having Marcus in my life. But I couldn't take him back, because he had done me wrong. I needed someone to comfort me, so I called Corey.

"This is Core," he answered.

"Where your girlfriend at?" I asked, somewhat disguising my voice.

"Who is this?" he asked.

"I'll tell you who it is, after you tell me where your girlfriend is."

"I don't have a girlfriend."

"Since when? What happened to Aisha?" I said, laughing revealing my natural voice.

"What's up, Kendra? I broke up with her. I'm tired of her mess. She was stressing me. Her job was to be a professional shopper and it was killing my accounts."

I didn't tell him that Marcus had broken up with me. He was probably lying about Aisha; that gold digger wasn't letting him go anywhere. I just wanted to talk to him. I actually wanted to finish what we had begun the other night.

"What's up with you? This is the first time you called me. Something is up. What you need?" he asked.

"Nothing."

"When I'm going to see you?"

"Whenever you want," I said seductively.

"Really? You mean that? The last time you were near me you ran away."

"I promise I won't run this time."

"All right. Meet me at Charlie's in an hour."

"Okay," I said. I didn't know what I was going to wear, but I was just happy that I was meeting up with Corey.

I met up with Corey at Charlie's, a sports bar. There were big flat-screen televisions playing. I wore a denim miniskirt, red stiletto sandals and a red blouse. I had done my makeup and curled my hair a little.

"Mr. Washington," I said as soon as I saw him.

He gave me a hug and we sat down. He was smelling so good. His hair was lying down perfectly, and his beard was trimmed just right. We were in a booth in the back of the restaurant. We ordered a few drinks and nibbled on hot wings and quesadillas.

"So you don't have a girl anymore. Why not?" I asked.

"Because she just doesn't understand me or this industry. I have to make money and be on my grind while I can. So that means I can't be available all the time. I give her everything she asks for and she wants to complain. So I just finally said fuck it. I'm not going to ever be able to give her all the attention she requires."

"That must be going around, because I broke up with my boyfriend too!"

"You broke up with ol' UPS boy? Stop," he said as I laughed.

"What for?" he asked.

"Basically the same reason. He just wanted me to be home and I couldn't be right now."

"So now we are free to date each other," he said.

"Maybe."

We had about three drinks each. The liquor made it okay to be all flirty. We were all cozy up in the booth when Corey turned to me and said, "You going home with me, right?"

"Maybe," I said, knowing I was.

"What's up with all these maybes? Say yes or no," he said playfully. He wrapped his arm around me and brought me to him and said you are coming home with me.

After our meal and drinks we hailed a cab. He began sloppily kissing me in the cab. It was unexpected, but I was with it. Then I felt his hands slide my panties over and I tried not to make any noise as he let his fingers roughly glide in and out of me. I was feeling so good, so into it.

Out of nowhere I felt like something wasn't right. I tried to get my thoughts together. My supersexiness was being ruined by a lightheaded feeling. I made eye contact with the cab driver through the rearview mirror, to make sure he didn't know what was going on. And he didn't—he was talking on his cell phone.

"Hold up, Corey," I said as I nudged him off of my body. I was trying to sit up. He didn't get the hint. So I pushed him off of me and said, "Yo tell him to pull over."

"What's wrong?"

"Just tell him to pull over."

The minute the car stopped I opened the door and threw up everything in my stomach plus some. I was so embarrassed, and even the cab driver was disgusted. Corey was looking like, *yuck*, and my head was still spinning. He patted me on my back. I thought I was okay, but two lights later we had to stop again.

"Are you mad at me?" I asked, drunk.

"No. No I'm not. You're fine."

"You sure?"

"Yes, it's cool. Don't worry about it."

"I am so sorry," I said, embarrassed.

"Stop tripping, Kendra."

By the time we arrived to his place I was feeling really sick. He gave me a glass of cold water and two slices of wheat bread to soak up the liquor in my stomach.

I awoke with a *crick* in my neck and a stiff back. I looked over and there was Corey across from me, asleep on the other sofa. We had gone to his place. I did remember that, and all I did was run back and forth to the bathroom all night. Our first night together was spent with him patting my back and telling me I was going to be okay.

"Good morning," I said as I saw him open his eyes.

"You feeling better?" he asked.

"Yes."

"You want some breakfast?" he asked.

"Are you going to make it?"

"No, I'm going to have some delivered." He dialed the restaurant while I sat on the sofa. He came over to me and asked again if I was feeling better. He pushed my hair out of my face and gave me a kiss on my cheek. He handed me a wash cloth, towel and tooth brush. While we waited for the food I showered. Once I came out he said, "You are so gorgeous," as he let his tongue massage my arms, my legs, and down to my fingertips. I was ready for him. I wanted him and I wasn't drunk anymore.

"Baby, your body looks amazing. You don't have any tattoos. I love your breasts. They are perfect," he said as he took one in his mouth and feverishly nibbled on it while looking up at me. Every slight twirl of his tongue on the tip of my ripe nipple stirred my internal juices. If he continued I would have easily reached my satisfaction point. His size was stout and solid. My walls had to expand to make room for all of him.

"Girl you got some claws in your pussy, out of sight," he said whispering, as I clasped on to him. He was tossing my body all around.

"Uhm baby, I want you girl," he moaned as he traveled up and down my inner walls.

"You can have me," I moaned back.

"No, I want you I want you to be mine. I want you to be around, Kendra."

"I am going to be around," I yelled.

"You not going back to ole boy?" he asked.

"No, not at all."

"You sure?"

"I promise you," I said as I had reached every climactic stage that I could. I was out of breath and my legs were exhausted. Corey kept going on like he was having a competition with himself. The only thing that stopped him was the arrival of our food.

My phone rang and it was Tony. I let him go to voice mail. When I finally checked my messages Tony was all on my phone cussing me out because I'd left the studio session. And I couldn't say, "Sorry, Tony. Yes, I know. I didn't make it because I was in the bed snuggled up all cozy relaxing with Corey."

"You just ate that," he yelled.

Oh well. I really had forgot. And getting with Corey was well worth it.

I had only been dating Corey for two weeks and I liked him. There was nothing about him I didn't like. Corey just made everybody feel special. I thought that was one of his good qualities. Because he was so sweet and nice it seemed like he was flirting all the time, but he wasn't.

Every day since we got together he has called and told me I was special and that he thought he was falling in love with me. Right now he was over in London working on this new girl rapper signed to a J Records project, and I was missing him already. I called him on the number he'd given me—I had to dial like ten extra numbers to get him in London. He answered, sounding like I'd awakened him.

"Hey, you asleep?" I asked Corey.

"Yeah."

"I'm sorry for waking you. What time is it there?"

"It is three in the morning. It's five hours ahead."

"You okay?"

"Yes."

"I can't believe you are all the way over there," I said.

"London is not that far."

"It's far to me. I've never been out of the country."

"You will go one day. You have to see the world. I've been everywhere—Germany, Denmark and even Japan."

"I want to go on vacation somewhere far like that."

"We'll do that real soon. I can't wait to see you when I get back."

"I can't wait to see you either," I sighed.

"Why don't you go apply for a passport today so the next time I go I can bring you with me?"

"Okay."

I went and applied for my passport. I did want to be worldly. I was twenty-five and had never been anywhere. That was insane.

I missed Corey so much. When he arrived in baggage claim I was there waiting for him. As soon as he saw me he gave me a hug.

"I'm glad you came. You can drop me off over at Quad," he said.

"Why? What you got to do?" I asked, disappointed.

"I have to meet a group there."

"Oh. I thought you didn't have anything scheduled."

"No?" He looked at me and I knew he could tell I was upset. "Listen, if you want you can go with me."

"No, just call me when you finish working." I was not about to be the next Aisha, waiting around for him in the studio. I dropped him off, went home and checked my mail.

Nitra had sent me a package with brochures for the daycare. There was a little note attached that read:

> *Dear Kendra, Thank you so much for going into business with us. Everything is coming along great. I just wanted to get your opinion on some of the furniture.*

I called Nitra. I wanted to let her know she didn't need my approval on everything. She had children and she was a better judge of furniture and toys.

"Hey, Kendra."

"Hey. I was just calling to tell you that whatever you decide on at the daycare is fine. I'm just an investor."

"You sure?"

"Yeah, just keep me in the loop, but I trust your judgment. Okay?"

"Okay, thank you so much, Kendra. I can't wait until we open and I can quit my job. Thanks for helping us out. You don't know how much this means to me."

"You're welcome."

"Oh, I've been meaning to call you to tell you that Marcus has been asking for you."

"I'm not talking to him. We're over, girl. I got somebody new."

"I know that's right," she laughed.

Chapter 21

Corey took taking me somewhere to heart. He called me and asked if I had anything to do tomorrow. I told him no and he instructed me to pack.

"Where are we going?"

"Somewhere hot and beautiful, like you," he said as we arrived at the airport. He wanted it to be a surprise. But I looked at the plane ticket as soon as he handed it to me. I was on my way to Hawaii. It was my first time on a plane. I tried to remain calm, but I was terrified. I had a window seat, and after the plane took off I looked out and saw I was flying over clouds. The sight scared me so much I closed my eyes. Corey was trying to make me open them but I wouldn't. All I could feel was the plane shaking and my body leaning back.

"Open your eyes."

"No."

"Why not?" he said as he held my hand, but I just shook my head. I kept them closed until we switched to our second plane. By then I was a little more relaxed and able to watch a movie.

We arrived in Hawaii and I was silly to think that women in hula skirts were going to be waiting for us to put leis around our necks. We went to baggage claim and there was an older Hawaiian man waiting with a white sign that read."Corey Washington."

"Hello, Mister Washington, welcome to Honolulu. Let me get your bags." He grabbed our luggage and walked us out to a black Lincoln Town Car. The driver drove us to our hotel. Our hotel was not far from the main street. It was a beachfront property. I couldn't wait to go and change my clothes and see everything. I felt so special that Corey had brought me here. We went upstairs, put our luggage down and took a walk around the hotel. Everything was open and breezy.

Hawaii was the most beautiful place. The sky was blue with traces of white, thin clouds. The water was a clear baby-boy blue, and the sun was beating down on me, nice and hot. Palm trees were all around, swaying. There were white sailboats in the distance. It was the most serene thing I'd ever seen. I really wished my mom and family could see this. *I have to bring them here so they can experience this,* I thought. *This is living.*

Dinner was cooked by our own personal chef, who was wearing a big white hat. He served us a four-course meal. After dinner the island band played music. Corey took me on a romantic walk on the beach. He reached out for my hand and kissed it. I smiled and couldn't believe how lucky I had become.

"Thanks for this trip," I said as we walked in the sand.

"No thank you," he said as he raised my chin up to kiss him. He then brought me in closer as he gently raised my dress, placed me on the sand and began kissing me all over my body. I heard the waves coming in crashing and I had my legs wide open not caring if someone was looking out their hotel room. He kissed on my lower half so succulently that I felt like my clitoris was going to burst. The sand was in my hair and the water was crashing in the distance. I looked up in the dark sky and saw the moon and my only thought was that I was literally in paradise.

The next day I was pampered all day. Corey arranged for us to have side-by-side massages. He reached out and kissed my hand. I felt so good, so loved, so relaxed. I wished it would never end.

The next morning I awoke to light, gentle kisses all over my neck. Corey did not stop with his affection and attention. Aisha was a damn fool. He had been saying the same thing about Marcus. Like, why wouldn't they appreciate good people like us?

"I'm hungry. I'm about to order room service," he said. I grabbed a white robe out of the closet and looked over the menu. He ordered a frittata—mushrooms, spinach, diced tomatoes and onion.

"Order me Belgian waffles and fruit," I said.

After we ordered breakfast I lay back in the bed in Corey's arms. He kissed me one more time and said, "I think I might love you."

"How can you love me already?" I asked, lifting my head and turning to him.

"You don't believe in love at first sight?"

"No. I think it can be lust at first sight, but not love." I laughed.

"Well, how about, I adore you. And I knew from the moment I saw you that I wanted to be with you. Yes, I did. I even remember what you had on that day in the studio."

"What?" I asked.

"I forgot, but I still adore you, Boo. And I think I want to marry you."

"Yeah, right," I laughed.

"You wouldn't marry me?"

"No, not yet."

"So you wouldn't marry me if I asked you?"

"No, because you wouldn't be serious."

"Yes, I would. If I asked you would you say yes?"

"No."

"Why not? We're soul mates. You know that, don't you? I never felt like this about anyone so soon. So will you marry me?" he said as he got on bended knee and placed an imaginary ring on my finger.

"No. Ask me again in six months when you are serious," I said as I threw a pillow at his head.

We spent the weekend swimming, snorkeling, riding and lying around by the pool and beach. I felt so inspired and refreshed. Being there made me want to tackle the world.

On the last day an island woman asked to read our fortune. She grabbed Corey's hand and traced his palm. Then she said, "Your love is standing right in front of you."

"What about my career?"

"In your career you will need hard work and dedication to make your dreams come true."

Then it was my turn, but I was reluctant.

"I don't believe in that stuff," I told Corey. "My mom said when you let someone read your future you are inviting evil into your life."

"Girl, be quiet and let her read your palm." Corey laughed as he forced me to hold my hand out.

The woman traced my hand and said, "Fire surrounds you, and you can't always put out the flames, although you will try."

"Fire?"

"Yes, fire in your heart and something from your past,"

she said as she traced the lines in my hand. They usually gave vague answers that would fit any situation, but her talking about fire hit close to home. So I asked her about my career. She said I was going to make it and that Corey was my true love. I somewhat believed her.

I was so excited that I was in love with Corey. It was the first time I'd ever loved anyone besides Marcus. He called me regularly just to say, "I adore you." Me and Corey were all over the place—at every party and event. We were the official new couple. I knew Aisha was probably somewhere sick, taking a razor to her wrist. I told Corey everything about growing up: my mom, my dad, the fire. He even told me I should probably talk to my dad. With him life was fun. Everything was obtainable and he never said "no." We haven't argued yet. Me and Marcus was arguing over why didn't you pay a bill and whose turn it is to treat. I never looked at a phone bill. He didn't come home complaining to me about how hard life was because he made it easy. He went out every day and made opportunities happen for himself. He was good with the music, but he still had other business. He even had a rim shop in Maryland with one of his frat brothers, Aaron. And Marcus was sending messages through John, but I wasn't thinking about him. Why would I go back to him? I had a man who looked good, had money and treated me like royalty.

Chapter 22

I had finished my project. I was so excited. The album was called *The Songstress.* It was going to be released in May. So from now until then I was going to be doing a lot of promo stuff and putting in time with Corey. I thought our relationship worked because we both were in the business and knew what we were going through.

I loved everything about Corey. He wasn't jealous, and I knew he wanted me to succeed. He had even been talking to me about us doing the marketing for my project in addition to what the label was going to do. His only flaw was he was too materialistic. I wasn't complaining, though. He always says, "My girl got to be seen in the best." He likes to buy me things only people that know would know what it is.

He bought me a red and black Marc Jacobs bag and Bulgari sunglasses with crystal rhinestone flowers on the side. Then today he sent me for a surprise spa service at the Claudia La'Betue Alexander Salon. He bought me the

Ultimate Relaxation package—three people working on me at once. It was heavenly. One man was giving me a pedicure and foot massage. Another one was giving me a manicure and hand massage. The last person was doing a treatment to my scalp. It was so relaxing.

I had to get ready to go on a twelve-city tour with Tashay to promote our albums. Shelly was going with me as my unofficial stylist/personal assistant and friend. We had to be at Newark International by ten in the morning, and it was eight, but I hadn't showered or packed yet. Shelly was knocking on my door.

"You ready?" she asked once I let her in.

"No."

"You have ten minutes."

"I didn't even pack yet." My stuff was all over the place. I was so embarrassed that I was running late and that my place looked a mess.

"Listen, just get in the shower and tell me what you want to bring and I'll pack it. I am your personal assistant." She laughed.

"You right. All my clothes were cleaned. I just tried to pull out the right shoes to go with the outfits." When I came out of the bathroom, everything was neatly packed and at the door. She had my plane ticket and driver's license in her hand. I thanked her and we were on our way to the airport.

Tashay was building a reputation as a bitch. Everyone was talking about her—they said she had no talent and thought the world revolved around her. I just hoped she didn't try that shit with me. She might still be mad at me about what Beazie had said about her that day in the studio. That was him talking, not me. But if she didn't understand, oh well. I don't need to be friends with her—she didn't pay my bills. Our tour consisted of doing shows at a bunch of historically black colleges. The first school we did was Prairie View A&M University in Texas.

Tashay was my opening act but she was getting treated like the superstar and I wasn't feeling that. She had a whole production team with her. She had a stylist, hairdresser, publicist, manager, dancers and a whole choreographed routine. Meanwhile, I was in the bathroom trying to put on my own makeup and curl my own hair.

"Hey, girl. You need my people to get you ready?" she asked.

"No, I'm okay." I didn't know if she was for real or being smart. Not only did this bitch have a makeup team, she had a camera crew following her around. She said she was getting footage for a possible reality show called "Tashay: The Making of a Star."

She went on first. And I was happy—at least that let her know my rank. I was Touchlight's hottest up-and-coming artist, not her. And no matter how much fluff she had around her, she wasn't better than me. Shelly and me watched from backstage. I was curious to see her perform. The music started loudly. When Tashay got onstage she turned into a baby Shakira. She had on a pair of jeans with a split going straight down the crack, and both of her butt cheeks were exposed. She wasn't even a little sexy—she was so disgustingly slutty. The white light was following her. She started singing. There was silence—the audience was not enthused. The crowd was just sitting there unmoved. Then she began clapping her hands, shaking her hips from side to side, and said, "I want y'all to sing along with me and do what I do."

People were looking around like, *who is this girl?*

Then she got desperate, put the mic back in its hook and said, "Listen, I want y'all to sing along with me. *What's up? Okay. All right. And then you clap clap. Okay. All right. And then you clap clap.*" She began shaking her ass one butt cheek at a time. I thought surely the women would say, *Who is this trick?*, but everybody started cheering her on. The crowd began participating, "Okay. All right. And then you clap clap," singing the song with her. She was walking back and forth on the stage with her dancers. She made these ugly faces like something was hurting on her as she tried to sing again. Then she pulled a guy from the audience up onstage with her and grinded on him like he was a pole. She wasn't singing at all. She was shouting into the microphone sounding a mess. But her crew said, "You did great, baby," as she exited the stage. It was hard for me to go on after that. Unbelievable I thought.

The crowd was so hyped from Tashay shaking her ass when I came onstage and I didn't have my ass out, I almost got booed, until I began to sing "Don't Wait" and hit some high notes. I did good, but not as good as Tashay.

The next night we were performing at Texas Southern University in Houston. Right before the show, I called home to check on my family. It was so hard being away from them. I really missed everybody and wasn't keeping in touch the way that I should have.

"How is Texas?" my mother asked.

"Mom, I get off the plane, do the show, go to a hotel, and get back on the plane. I never really get to see any of the city but the airport."

"Well, other than that, how is it going?" my mother asked.

"Good. I'm getting tired. We have six more stops and then I'll be back in New York. Maybe y'all can come and meet me and we can have dinner."

"We can do that and oh I forgot to tell you something."

"What, Mom?"

"You know Marcus has a baby on the way?"

"With who?" I said in shock.

"Some girl from his job with two kids already."

"Why would you tell her that?" I heard John say in the background.

My mom responded, "She doesn't care."

John grabbed the phone.

"I don't know why Mommy told you that mess. You don't need that while you are on the road."

"Is she serious? How? When? How he feel about it?" I asked.

"I don't really know. I guess he's happy. He sent Mr. Skip down south with his sister, so he got his dream. Don't worry about him. Do what you got to do okay? I'm going to put Mommy back on the phone."

Wow, is all I could say repeatedly to myself. I couldn't be mad at Marcus. If I wasn't willing to have a baby, he was going to have one—one way or another. It's just messed up; he started a family without me. He moved on and I had moved on too. I was just mad he went and had his first child with somebody who had two kids already. I wasn't upset. I didn't care. I really didn't—at least that's what I told myself. I had to get myself together, get onstage and still give a good performance.

"Kendra are you okay? Are you upset?" my mom asked, breaking the silence.

"No, not at all. Good for him. I'm not worried about Marcus."

"That's what I was trying to tell your brother, that you didn't care. We need to go and thank that woman for having that sorry-ass man's sorry-ass baby. I'm glad you left him." I agreed with my mom but I was still a little hurt.

"Mom, I've got to go," I said, rushing her off the phone and standing momentarily shaking my head. Shelly ran over and asked what's going on. I told her nothing.

I was glad she was on the road with me. I had someone to talk to. She was helping me with everything. She was my entire posse all rolled into one. She was my eyes and ears as to what was going on. Tony really should have been here on the road with me, I thought.

"Look at Tashay. She's in *Vibe* magazine in the 'Next' section," Shelly said. I looked at the magazine and there she was with a big picture, talking about her album.

"And she has a sampler CD hosted by DJ Mines."

"Really? Let me see," I said as she showed me her CD. "I wonder how she got in there," I said aloud.

"You should be in here. You need to get in your manager's ear. He's running around with his other group when he needs to be trying to get your situation right."

Shelly was thinking exactly what I was thinking. I had to call Tony. He had signed this teenage boy group called Handsome. He said he wanted them to be the next big boy group, but ever since then I hadn't been a priority. I dialed him up. His answering machine came on and I demanded for him to call me back.

The next night we were in Georgia doing a show at Clark Atlanta. I looked outside my window and saw a truck that said TASHAY WORLD on a wrapped, big pink Hummer truck. Her name was in diamond sparkling letters and there was a picture of her wearing bright pink jeans with COMING SOON! written on her ass. She was leaning over, holding a globe and winking. I couldn't hate. That truck was so major.

Once we drove up to the Clark Atlanta campus a crowd was already waiting for us. Tashay's people were handing out T-shirts and her sampler CDs from the side of her Hummer. She got out of the van and her stylist screamed, "Tashay is in the building." The students looked at her, then at the truck and rushed her to get her autograph.

Meanwhile, me and Shelly got out of the van and nobody even looked my way except for this one guy who asked us if we were part of Tashay's camp.

"No!" I snapped. Shelly turned to the guy and said, "She is a singer too! She is Kendra Michelle."

His demeanor changed and then he gave me his card and told me he could help get me signed.

"I already have a deal. I'm signed to Touchlight."

"Yeah? I never heard of you before. Well, now that I met you, I will definitely show you love," he said, rubbing his ear. "You coming out next year?"

"No, this May."

"What? And I didn't hear of you yet? I get everything that's hot," he said.

"Thanks," I said as I walked into the building, passing Tashay and all her fans. I didn't appreciate getting treated like a stepchild.

As soon as I got back in New York the first person I called was Tony again. He really needed to step up his game. Why was Tashay getting all this attention? She ain't hot. She can't sing and right now she was looking like a star and I was looking like, *Who are you?* She is even in this month's Sophisticated Black Hair magazine. This is too much. Tony better get on his job.

The moment he answered the phone I yelled, "Why is it I can't get in touch with you, Tony? Why is it that Tashay got all this promotion and I don't have any? I'm tired of hearing about this bitch and how hot she is. She is not better than me and I want you to make sure people know that. On tour she had her stylist, her publicist and her maaaannnnnagggger. Meanwhile, I was there all alone. I was doing my own damn makeup and shit." I screamed, "She can't sing and she is blowing up because she has good management. She even has a blog."

"I can get you a blog. I'm going to make some things happen."

I called Beazie to tell him about everything that happened on tour. I knew he hated her and I could confide in him.

"She is whack; don't sweat that chick. She is not going to sell like you. She doesn't have any talent. I wouldn't even worry about her. All that hype is nothing, ya mean? We know the real. Everybody else will find out. And when they do, she won't be able to give away a CD."

"You right. I got to go. That's Tony on the other line," I said as I clicked over to speak with him. "Tony, what's up?"

"I called Maya and spoke to a bunch of people in PR. And they said they don't know anything about the promotional CDs and truck. They said she must be doing all of that on her own. She has a sponsor."

"Who is her sponsor?"

"She is the new face of Alisanye Jeans."

"Well, get on your job and find someone to sponsor me," I said as I hung up on him.

Chapter 23

When I told Corey about everything he told me not to worry and he would try to get me some help, giving my project more buzz. He even said that I should fire Tony.

"Why?"

"Because he eatin' off you. What has he done for you since he got you signed?" He was right but I wasn't ready to fire Tony just yet.

"Look, I'm going to hire you a PR team. Don't worry about nobody else. Just do you, and you are going to do great. You are very talented and you will get your turn, Boo," he said.

"I know. I just feel like I should have more going on. Like people still don't even know who I am and my album is going to be out in a few months."

"Don't worry. When we get back we'll sit down and make everything happen. Right now let's just take this ride to Maryland. My brother has some tickets to the Wizards game."

"I don't feel like going anywhere. I want to stay here

and make sure Tony's doing what he supposed to do. I have so much at stake. Corey I have to make it."

"And you will. One day ain't going to hurt you. You need to go, and it will take your mind off of everything. When we get home we are going to get on it. I have too many connects in this city for my baby not to blow."

We drove to Maryland in his black Range Rover. "I need you to drive. I have to make some calls and I need to concentrate," he said as I got in the driver's seat. My boo was about his business all the time even when he was supposed to be relaxing. I listened in on his conversation; he was negotiating with an artist to pay him more money for his track. I listened quietly and let him handle his business.

I met Corey's brother, Walter. They didn't favor at all. Walter was tall and brown, and worked as an engineer for the government. His wife, Tianna, was a teacher and was also tall and brown and very simple. They were dressed in sneakers, jeans and sweatshirts, while me and Corey looked like we were going to the club. I had on an army fatigue-colored hat. My curls were cascaded down the sides of my face. My short black jacket had a few rhinestones on it. My Frankie B. jeans were hugging my waist. I felt silly for having on heels and being all dolled up at a basketball game. As we walked to our seats I kept feeling like I was about to fall. Corey held my hand so I wouldn't. We walked down to our seats by the floor right behind the court. I knew a little about basketball from John but didn't know any of the players. I was texting back and forth with Shelly the entire game. I wanted her honest opinion about my situation.

After the game Walter and his wife went home. Corey wanted us to go past this club called Love. We rode up and it was real crowded. It was huge, like a big warehouse. We checked the car into valet and walked right in the front door past the people waiting in line. Corey was a local celebrity. People were saying "What's up?" and shaking his hand. It was so crowded—people were pushing and shoving because some guy decided he was going to throw money in the air and make it rain. We walked upstairs to the second level and straight to the back of the club. It was just me and him, but then his frat brother Aaron walked up, said hello, and took a seat. He was five-eleven, an Indian-red shade of brown, and had dark, wavy close-cut hair on his head and face. Corey kissed my hand and then said he would be right back.

"Where you going, Corey?" I asked.

"I'll be right back," he said as he winked at me and blew me a kiss.

I didn't like being alone in this club with all these people I didn't know.

I heard the deejay announcing all the celebs in the building. Then I heard him say, "We have Corey Washington aka Core, super producer, and his lady Kendra Michelle in the house. Here's her new song, "Don't Wait." Corey came back to the table and made me stand up, and then everyone started dancing.

"You didn't have to do that."

"Yes, I did, babe. I told you I got you. We going to make this thing right for you. We are going to be an industry power couple." I smiled.

Then out of the corner of my eye I saw Aisha. She had on a navy blue and gold suit jacket that she was wearing as a dress. Her arm was all wrapped on this big light-skinned guy. Corey saw her but didn't acknowledge her. He looked up at her once and then at me to see if I had seen her. I acted like I didn't.

Then Aaron asked, "You see Aisha?"

"Yeah, I saw her," he said.

"That dude she with play with the Redskins. She's a straight-up gold digger," Aaron said, shaking his head.

"I know. That's why I left her," he said as he swallowed the remainder of his drink.

The rest of the evening we partied hard. People kept coming over to our table. We danced and I met a few more of Corey's friends. On the way out we walked past Aisha, who had this smirk on her face. I just turned my head the other way. The valet pulled up with the car. Her and her dude was waiting for their car to pull up.

Her dude was hugging her waist from behind. She was all over the place looking a mess. Then Aisha broke away from her date and said, "Corey, I need to talk to you. We need to talk right now."

"Man, get out of here. I don't have time for this," he said as he opened my door and I got in. She was tripping big time. Then the stupid girl actually jumped in the backseat of the car.

"Aisha, get out the car now!" Corey yelled.

I'm looking like, *what the fuck?* I got out of the car and just watched. She wouldn't budge. She wrapped her arms around the head rest like it was a teddy bear and was crying, "Corey, please talk to me."

"Aisha, I'm not playing. Get out this car." She was making a scene and people were looking at us trying to figure out what was going on. I wanted to pull the bitch out of the car myself but I was trying to stay out of it. Corey looked over at me and said, "I'm sorry babe." I turned my head. I couldn't believe he had me outside the club with people looking at us. A few minutes later, tired of asking her to leave, Corey said, "I'm going to call the cops. Move!" as he tried to pull her out.

"No, I'm not moving until you talk to me. Talk to me, Corey. I love you. I love you. Please, Corey. I'm sorry I left you. I'm sorry I was wrong. I was wrong for cheating on you. Don't you still love me? Don't you?" she said, crying. I was getting more than an earful. So she left him.

He said that he'd left her. I didn't say anything—I just listened.

"Aisha, get out. I mean it, I'm going to call the cops on you. You're causing a scene."

"Call them, I don't care. I love you, Corey," she screamed. She then got out of the car and onto her knees and started pleading for him to take her back. She said, "Sorry, I was wrong. Please forgive me."

"Yo, don't do this here. Stop, Aisha. I can't deal with this right now," Corey said, madly walking away.

She got off her knees and Corey got in the car. I got back in and we pulled off. Instantly, his phone started ringing nonstop. He turned it off and there was silence. I wanted to say something, but there was nothing to be said, really. He tried to turn the radio on. I turned it off.

"What was that all about? Corey, why is she saying she is sorry for breaking up with you? You said you broke up with her," I questioned him.

"I did break up with her. She is crazy. She doesn't know what she is talking about. What does it matter who broke up with who? We're not together and I'm with you, right?"

"Yeah, but why you have to lie about everything? She said you still calling her."

"I didn't lie to you. I don't call her. I'm with who I want to be with." We rode all the way home without talking.

Bubbles and my mom called with an earsplitting yell in my ear. "Kendra, why didn't you tell me your song got released?"

"What are y'all talking about?"

"The one you gave me. 'Cause they playing it on the radio," Bubbles said.

"You sure?" I asked.

"Yeah. Me and Mommy just heard it. Didn't we hear it, Mommy? It came on at five o'clock, then I heard it right before the countdown came on. I've been trying to call you since yesterday to tell you."

"My bad. I've been busy. I don't know what's going on. Let me call you back." I hadn't talked to Tony in a couple of days, since I'd cussed him out.

"Tony, do you know anything about my song being played on the radio?"

"Who heard it?"

"My mom and sister. They playing it at home, on the radio. Who you think leaked my song? Is this good?"

"I leaked it, Kendra. You wanted them to pay attention—right now they are. And I got you more interviews lined up too. One is on Sirius Radio. I put in a call into *Hype Hair* magazine; and Academiks is sending you a bunch of clothes over and they might sign you for an endorsement deal. I'm going to take care of you."

"Thanks Tony."

"No problem." I felt a little relieved. It was about to happen for me.

My song "Don't Wait" was getting played all over the country. And it was doing so good, getting almost three thousand spins a week. I was so happy Tony made that executive decision to get me out there and let the world know my name and it was working. I was about to get the respect that I deserved. I called Corey to tell him the good news. I got his voicemail. So I just left a message.

Chapter 24

It was March and Shelly told me Tashay was shooting her video and having a listening party the next week. Shelly saw the invite list and all these high-powered names who were supposed to make cameos, everyone from Kelly Rowland to Young Jeezy. That would mean they would be cosigning for her. I called Corey and told him all about it. His answer to me was, "Stop being obsessed with what Tashay is doing. You are looking a little jealous."

"I'm not jealous. Far from it. It's just that I know I'm ten times hotter than her. It's just like, when is it going to be my turn? This shit ain't fair. They have her plastered everywhere."

"Kendra, I'm telling you. You need to spend more time worrying about your career than worrying about Tashay. Tashay is getting hers."

"And what is that supposed to mean?"

"I'm just saying she is making it. Be happy for her and you will get your turn. Jealousy is like a cancer."

"So you saying I'm jealous of her?"

"No, but your focus should be on you, not her. Call Tony and tell him to set up a meeting at Touchlight. We need to see what they are doing for you."

Corey was not understanding what I was going through. He of all people should have known where I was coming from.

"I'll call you back. I have to pack," he said.

"Where are you going?" I asked.

"To L.A."

"You didn't even tell me."

"I did tell you. You would have been going with me if you weren't acting childish."

"Whatever," I said.

"Well, I'm going to L.A. and I'll be back in a few days. I'll holla at you then."

"So what's up with us? Are we together or what? 'Cause you acting funny."

"I don't know. You tell me."

"You don't know? Really," I repeated.

"Nope. I don't know. All right, I got to go."

"Corey, how about you use that time in L.A. to decide if we are together or not?"

"I'll do that," he said.

Chapter 25

Thomas called me and said, "Kendra, we like your style, and we think you are going to do big things. However, we want to rework your project a little bit, so we're moving you back three months." Although "Don't Wait" was getting spins, my project was getting pushed back from May 2005 to August 2005. It didn't seem like a big deal but it was. In August people were thinking that the summer was just about over and it was time to go back to school. They were buying school clothes, not albums. They should have kept my project where it was. I was steaming mad—the summer was the time when everyone rides around with windows down listening to their favorite songs.

I hung up with him and felt so lonely, the loneliest I'd ever felt in my life. When I finished speaking with Thomas, Tony called.

"Tony, why are they doing this to me?" I asked.

"They want you to change your album around a little," Tony told me.

"Kendra, having your album pushed back is a good

thing. It gives us more time to promote and get everybody to know your name. It's only March. By the time August comes you are going to be on fire."

I knew what would get my situation right. I had to take things into my own hands—literally. Tony suggested for me to go pay Peter Sutton a visit. Fuck Thomas. He didn't have any real weight. I had to go and see the big man.

I went to see Peter in his office. It was five-thirty. I hoped he was still there. His receptionist was typing and told me I could have a seat. I didn't know if I would come right out and tell him I would fuck him and say something seductive like you can have me daddy if you help me. I decided I would play it by ear.

I knocked on the door.

"Who is it?" Peter asked.

I opened the door without answering and walked up to his dark brown wood desk.

"Peter, I'm having some problems with my album. I need the label to get behind me. My project is getting pushed all around."

"Well, I tried to help you," he said as he brought his fingers together and folded them into a clasp.

"I know you tried, but back then I had a boyfriend and I was faithful to him. And now I don't have a man and I'm ready to do whatever it takes to get where I need to be."

"You sure about that?" he said, smiling.

"Yes. I'm certain."

"Have a seat," he said as he pulled out the chair for me. "You need my help?" he said as stepped in front of me.

"Yes, I do," I said as he unzipped his pants and put his dick in my hand. At this point I could do what he said and be a signed artist or have pride and not have anything. He was trimmed and shaven. I began stroking him up and down trying to get him aroused. His peach flesh was smooth and firm. After ten minutes of heavy stroking, he closed his eyes and he came. He was making these crazy faces. I thought that would be enough, but then he said, "Kiss it." Jerking him off was not enough. His fluids were still all over him; I was disgusted but I had to do it. He began smiling as I got on my knees. He placed his dick in my mouth, and I closed my eyes and did what I had to do to stay in this game. I sucked so hard my jaws hurt and his veins were popping up. I let globs of spit come out of my mouth on to him. He was moving his hips real quick, huffing and puffing. I felt nothing. It was like an out-of-body experience. He came all over my lips, chin and neck. He then handed me a napkin and I wiped myself off.

"Peter, when is my album going to come out?" I asked him.

"I will let you know next week when you come to see me."

I didn't like my life being in limbo. I didn't know what was going on with my album. I still didn't have an actual date in August just a month and I didn't know what was up with me and Corey. He had not called me one time since he had been in Los Angeles. So I called him.

"Corey, this is Kendra. Give me a call when you get back home." I knew he was returning Friday. I felt like he was avoiding me. He finally answered his damn phone.

"I've been calling you," I said.

"I know. Well, I was mad busy."

"Okay, so what's up with us?" I asked.

"Kendra, I don't think I want to jump back in a relationship so soon. We had fun, but I think we were rushing. I realized that when we were in D.C. and you was giving me attitude."

"What?"

"Yeah, I did some soul searching and I think I want to be by myself."

"You want to be by yourself, huh? So, what you back with Aisha?"

"No, I'm not with her."

"Well, why are you breaking up with me?"

"I don't want to be with anybody. I want to be by myself."

"So that's it."

"Yeah, basically. I'll holla at you some time. We'll still keep in touch."

And just like that me and Corey were over.

Chapter 26

I still had to wait and see what was going to happen. Tony called me and said that they were going to give me another release date because August might not work. They were just getting everything in order. I was making some progress though. I wasn't dealing with Peter's ass for nothing. I had been to his office twice. Both times, I'd come in, and got onto my knees and left. I tried to give him the best head possible. He'd never asked me to do anything else until today. Today when I walked into his office he was watching television. I looked over and on the screen were two naked men; one was penetrating the other roughly. I couldn't believe he was watching gay male porn. I wasn't sure if he was into it—until he placed K-Y Jelly on two of my fingers and asked me to ram them in his ass. I was shocked. "Kendra just do it," he said as he got on all fours and took off his pants and pushed his booty towards me. I closed my eyes, and he squirmed and moaned. His hole felt squishy and wide. It felt like my fingers weren't the first to be inside as I poked his inner hole. He jerked his own dick back and forth towards the television screen. After he was done my finger was filled with moisture. I couldn't look down. I ran out of his office to wash my hands. All the other times I was with him I never felt sick, but today I felt like I couldn't move. As I walked out the door Peter asked me to come to his house for the weekend.

"You think you can make it?"

"Where will your wife be?" I asked.

"She is out of town. Come around nine tonight. Here's my address," he said while writing the information down. "And I'll make sure it's worth your while. We will discuss a little business and a little pleasure."

I drove to his house in Long Island. The house was amazing. It looked like too much space for one couple.

"I'm glad you came," he said, rubbing both my arms simultaneously. "Now relax. Have some wine," he said as I entered and had a seat.

"I'll take a glass," I said.

I didn't know what to expect with Peter. I wanted to be so drunk that I didn't remember anything the next day. He might want to do something even nastier. I figured I only had to do this a little while longer, until my project was set to be released. In all I had about eight glasses of wine to relax my nerves to allow me to be able to tolerate him.

Peter took my hand and walked me into the bedroom he shared with his wife. It was a big room, with two walk-in closets, a flat-screen television in the wall and a fireplace. The bedroom set was black lacquer. He didn't waste any time in attacking me. Peter pushed me on the bed and began licking all my fingers one by one. I went right along with it. I started kissing him like I liked him. I made my hands scratch his back roughly through his shirt. He bent me over, pulling my dress up far enough that he could see my ass. Then he slapped it, giving it a slight sting. He pulled my nipples, stretching them apart, and inserted two of his fingers inside my body.

All of a sudden, out of nowhere I saw someone in the doorway. His wife, Molly, walked in the room and began to watch us. I jumped up, but he didn't. Her eyes were piercing and her dark hair was pulled into a ponytail, and she wore a see-through dress. She sat on the bed and stroked his back and kissed his neck. I sat back on the bed and he re-entered his finger deep inside of me. That's when it clicked that this was all a setup. I didn't know what to do. I just closed my eyes and acted like I didn't know what was going on. I opened my eyes to see what she was about to do. Then she pulled out a double-headed dildo and put lubricant on both ends. Then Molly stuck the dildo in herself and me, and we both began moving back and forth on it. I moved my hips on it. It felt just as good as the real thing. Peter was fondling both of our breasts. I opened my eyes and saw her jerking at the other end of the dildo. It was like we were in each other because every move she made, I could feel. I wanted to get up and leave, but I knew that I couldn't. No matter how unwilling I was to participate, I had to. The sad thing was I felt myself enjoying it.

Peter then put his dick in my face. I sucked on him until I almost choked. She licked the right side, and I took care of the left. Our tongues met at the tip of his dick. He watched in enjoyment. Now that he was aroused, he thrust himself in me. My breasts were bouncing back and forth, and my mind was racing. He kept going and going between the both of us. I felt like their personal sex slave. They didn't want to stop. They never were satisfied. They were sexual beasts with animalistic appetites. I cried during every position they put my body in.

When I awoke I was at the end of the bed. Molly was on the floor and I heard the shower running. Peter must have been in there. I grabbed my dress and left out the door. I went home and soaked. I felt so dirty and disgusting. The vision of last night kept appearing in my head. I got back in the tub thirty minutes later because I still didn't feel clean. I couldn't stop crying.

Chapter 27

My album had a new release date—Tuesday, August 16, 2005. They had set me up with more interviews and I had to go on another promotional tour. Tony thought he was responsible for the change but actually I could thank myself, because in the last three months I'd had to sleep with Peter and Molly so many times I lost track. They were swingers all around the board. I didn't like being intimate with Molly, though. I felt so nasty every time she looked at me. I had actually convinced Peter that I was really into him. So now me and him would meet up for cocktails, and he even gave me his American Express card. I had been on three shopping sprees courtesy of him. He really had been fighting for me, so much that I was about to shoot my video next month.

Even though they had leaked "Don't Wait," it was too late for a video. The label decided that "What's It Going to Be" was going to be the first official single.

Shit was finally coming together and I was so grateful.

I was working with this choreographer, Mina. My career was about to take off, and fuck anybody who wasn't down with me. I heard Corey got back with Aisha. That's cool. He was a distraction anyway.

Chapter 28

I was scheduled to film my video at this warehouse in Brooklyn on Thursday. I was so excited. Me and Shelly went out shopping for some different looks for me when I got a call from Maya saying that it was canceled with no explanation. I was about to get gangsta on somebody if they didn't call me and tell me what the hell was going on. Something had better give. I called Tony but he wasn't calling me back. I went off on him on his answering machine. I dialed him four times in a row. Then he finally picked up.

"Hello?" I said angrily.

"What's wrong?"

"Did you know my video shoot is canceled?"

"No, I didn't. I'll call you right back. I'll make some calls today. Calm down. Something probably came up."

"No, you calm the fuck down. Somebody needs to be hype. That's the problem—you been too busy running behind those fake-ass singing boys that you haven't been paying attention to me. You call them and call me back," I said as I hung up on him in disgust. I thought about going up to the office myself and going off on them. I heard that had worked for this rapper back in the day. I needed to show them I wasn't playing. My phone rang again.

"Hello?"

"What's wrong with you?" my mom asked.

"Nothing. Mom, I can't talk to you right now."

"I'm about to take Bubbles to school. You know she has to start her summer program at college so if you need me just call my cell phone. I didn't want you to come home and I wasn't there."

"I'm not coming home. I have to go. I'm busy," I said as I cut her off.

I saw Tony's number come across the screen of my phone. I clicked back over and Tony asked, "Kendra, where are you?"

"I'm at the apartment. Why?"

"Well, you know, some changes been going on at Touchlight. They are merging with Millennium/Aprise Records, and I'm going to make some calls tomorrow. And don't worry. I got everything in control because you're going to do all right."

"Stop rambling, Tony. What are you saying? Don't beat around the damn bush. What's going on?"

"Kendra, they are not putting your CD out. Your project was shelved indefinitely."

"Huh. You're joking, right? What do you mean?" I knew that it was a possibility that it could happen, but not like this. Damn it.

"I talked to Thomas this morning. It wasn't his decision. He tried to fight for you but he couldn't. They wanted to take the project that was already up and running. They heard the album and they just aren't feeling it. Plus they feel like they already have another artist like you."

"Who is the other artist close to me?" I asked.

"I think they talking about Tashay."

"That bitch ain't nowhere next to me as an artist," I screamed.

"Tashay has a name. They just really like her. Don't worry. We can find you a new home."

"What about everything I already recorded. All my hard work."

"It belongs to them."

"And I can't get none of my songs back?" I asked.

"No, they own them. The good thing is you don't have to pay back your living allowance."

"The good thing? There ain't no good thing. I don't have a deal. You know what? You are a fucked-up-ass manager."

"Yo, I know you are upset, but come on now. Don't talk to me like that. I'm here for you."

"No, I mean it. You let this go down. You suppose to have my back. Whoever is at Millennium they're sitting behind the desks. They don't know what's hot, they don't know what it takes to make a good artist. They get a paycheck every two weeks while I'm out here trying to survive."

"Kendra, you have till the end of the week to move out of the apartment."

I didn't even know what to say. I didn't even get till the end of the month?

"Ain't that something," I said aloud to myself. I hung up on him again and called Peter—Mr. Vice President—Sutton.

"So, I guess all that sucking dick went to waste," I screamed at the top of my lungs as soon as he picked up.

"Who is this?" he asked nervously.

"It's me Peter, Kendra. I fucked your ass for nothing."

"Calm down. What are you talking about?"

"You knew I was getting dropped."

"Kendra, I had no idea. When did this happen?"

"What-the-fuck-ever," I said as I madly kicked a hole in the wall.

"Fuck you and your fucked-up-ass wife. Peter you are going to pay."

I started packing my things. I didn't need this apartment. I didn't need them. How could they do this to me? The only thing I could think of was that I had a good album that nobody would ever get to hear. I was so mad. All those hours, all that fucking work. I was so damn frustrated. I knew I had done everything in my power to make shit happen.

Tony called me back and told me that he knew another manager who had a girl group that needed a lead singer. I was so not interested in being in a group, I screamed.

"Hell no. I am a solo artist. Why would I get in a group?"

He pleaded with me to give him a few days to make some calls to see what he can do. Sometimes, he said, a hungry A&R will pick an artist up and sign them when he knows they were dropped just because of the label politics.

"That's all fine but what am I going to do for now?"

"I can get you some dates overseas."

"I'm not going overseas to perform," I told him. "Fuck it. I give up—it ain't meant to be. It ain't meant to be. I'm going to move out of their stupid ass apartment. I have my own house."

Actually I didn't know what I was going to do. I couldn't go home. I couldn't believe this bullshit. I went to the label's official website to see if I was on there but my name was already deleted. So it wasn't a mistake—I was officially off the roster.

Chapter 29

I drove down the Atlantic City Expressway. I had all the windows down and the wind was blowing all over me. I had the radio blasting, but I didn't even know what song was playing—everything was a blur. I was so miserable I couldn't think. I didn't even know where I was going. I was still trying to come to terms with the fact that I had been dropped. That my album was not coming out. How could have this happened? Why didn't Tony fight for me? Who made the decision to ruin my life and say I'm not good enough? I can sing and I looked good. Why me? Why not somebody else who didn't deserve it—like Tashay? She can't sing. But she still got a record deal. How? Why? This shit ain't fair. All those thoughts flooded my mind at once.

I was too frustrated to even think right now. I punched the steering wheel. I didn't expect this to happen to me. To me, Kendra Michelle. I was supposed to be coming up. Everybody said that I was the next big thing. I was about to be rich. Thomas told me that, Beazie told me that, and now look at me. I was tired of trying, God, I was so tired. I tried and I tried and nothing seemed to pan out for me. Why did they let me go? I'm a good person. I couldn't understand why I wasn't blessed, if I was doing right. I didn't deserve this. I was a real good person. I did right. I took care of my family. And look what I got. Look at what I got. Fucking nothing. Not a thing. I shouldn't have felt this way but I did. I felt so drained, so powerless and frustrated. My hard work for nothing. I felt like I was by myself. I didn't know what to do. I felt like I was so behind in life. I needed to give up on the dream. I wasn't going to be famous, I wasn't going to be rich, I was going to be who I was—just another person with a dream unfulfilled. I needed to go to work like everybody else, get paid every two weeks, take a vacation once a year, and have the weekends off to yell at my kids and argue with my husband. I didn't know how I was going to pay my bills. I didn't know nobody who had my back. I wanted to take a bus somewhere and go off far away from everybody and disappear.

I got to get money some other way. This was not going to happen. I was chasing a fucking dream. This shit was for the damn birds. I wish I hadn't tried at fame. Marcus was right. I must have been a fool to think I really was going to be somebody.

I couldn't go home, so I found myself parking in valet at the Bally's Hotel and Casino and getting a room using the American Express credit card Peter gave me, so all charges would go to him. I was going to stay there for a few days because I didn't want to talk to anyone—I just wanted to get my thoughts together. I went upstairs to the room and closed the drapes. I didn't even want the sun in there with me. I wanted everything to be dark and quiet. No noise, just me with my thoughts. Maybe I would wake up and this would all be a bad dream.

Tony, Beazie and other people who had heard what had happened kept calling. Fuck them all. I was so tired and not in the mood. Nothing anyone said could change the way I felt. I was going to stay right there in that room until I got kicked out.

I spread my body across the bed and began to think about where I went wrong and what I was going to do for money. I had thirty-five hundred a month in mortgage and a nine-hundred–dollar car note and other bills. My money wouldn't last any time. I used the hotel stationery and tried to add up what I'd spent my money on. What did I do with eighty thousand dollars? How did I spend all that money? I kept thinking about how I could have bought a car and house and still had money in the bank. All these fucking boots and shoes. I bought my car and house, and loaned my brother ten thousand, and now I had exactly twenty thousand dollars left. If I had a gun right now I'd kill myself. I mean, I really wanted to die. I'm sorry—that's how I felt. My phone kept ringing and I shut it off. I felt like throwing it out the window. Everybody was thinking I was about to be this big star, and now I wasn't going to be nothing. I was so embarrassed. I felt like the biggest failure. I didn't know what to do. I gave this business my life. All that freaky shit with Peter and Molly—I sold my soul. Before I started in this business I never smoked or drank. It was not only the in thing, it was the only thing to do. I got these stupid breast implants in my body for fucking the rest of my life. I screamed loudly and fell into the bed.

I had been asleep for four hours and awoke to find it wasn't a bad dream. It was true life. It was real life. My album was not coming out. I kept having the same thoughts.

Can't I call somebody? Can't I do something to make this work? I will do whatever they want me to do. I can make more changes. I can wear whatever they want me to wear. I could do whatever they want me to do. What am I going to tell my family? How am I going to make it through this?

I squeezed my forehead to halt the pressure that was building inside of it. I couldn't take it. I needed a Tylenol and a drink. I looked in the mini bar and opened the green bottle of Tanqueray and drank it straight. It burned my throat a little. I ran in the bathroom and got some water to chase the Tanqueray down. I sat on my bed. *What do I do now?* I couldn't think of anything, so I took another sip of what was left of my drink and went back to sleep.

I heard "Housekeeping," then a knock.

I didn't get up fast enough to tell her no thanks, so the woman entered the dark room said, "Sorry," and then left. I looked at the time. It was ten in the morning on Sunday and I was still in my same clothes from Friday. I had another headache and I wanted to take a shower. My shower turned into a bath as I sat down in the shower and let the hot water run over my hair, head and neck. I closed my eyes, balled myself up, and cried and cried.

I called for room service and ordered potatoes au gratin, shrimp, lobster and a steak. I hadn't eaten in two days and I was in the mood for everything.

When room service came I sat on the bed, pulled the food cart over to me, turned on the television and flipped the channels. *My Super Sweet Sixteen* was on MTV. I couldn't stomach it. It was about a rich girl thinking that the world revolved around her. She was spoiled, mean and rude. I wanted to go in the television and smack her. The girl was arguing with her parents because they didn't buy her a Benz that she wanted. I didn't get a lot of shit when I was sixteen. I didn't get what I wanted when I was twenty-six, I thought as I changed the channel.

* * *

Monday I went to my car and got some of my things, then walked from my hotel down to the Taj Mahal at the other end of the boardwalk. I thought about Marcus and wondered what was he doing and if he was thinking about me. He'd wanted his baby and he'd gotten it. Everybody got what they wanted out of life except for me. I walked on the beach and just thought about my purpose. I kicked at the sand a little. The waves were going out and then coming back in. The water was more peaceful and serene. Seagulls flew over my head. I sat in the sand and just looked out into the ocean. I felt a little better after reflecting on the beach. So I walked back to the boardwalk and noticed this lady in a wheelchair all smiling and happy to just be alive. She looked up at me and said, "God bless you, honey." I almost didn't say it back but then I thought about it and said, "God bless you too, miss."

Chapter 30

I couldn't go home and tell my family I was dropped. I didn't want to see the looks on their faces. I felt like I let them down. I knew they were going to be so upset, especially my little sister and brother. They had been telling everyone their sister was about to come out—"She's a singer, we're going to be rich, she bought us a house, she lives in New York City, she drives a Benz."

But staying here at this hotel was not an option anymore. The front desk had left me several messages telling me to come down. I don't think so. I know what time it is. Peter must have just caught on and canceled that card. I began packing my things and headed for the lobby. I went to the valet and got my car and sat in it for another thirty minutes contemplating what I was going to do. I guess there was only one thing to do—go home.

I went home and the first things I saw were my mother's three brown paper bags from Macy's. Joanne had been shopping again. She looked at me and said, "You're not getting enough rest. You look stressed. You drinking your water and taking your vitamins?"

"Yeah, Mom."

"You don't look so good. You better get some rest."

"I get rest."

"I bought some pots and things from Macy's," she said as she showed all of the things she had bought. "That was a great sale," she said like she was proud.

"Where you been at?" she asked. "I have been calling you the last three days."

"I have been busy." I went and sat on the sofa. I didn't know how I was going to tell my mom I wasn't signed anymore. She had really gotten accustomed to going in the store and buying whatever the hell she wanted. But I had to say something to her before she went shopping again. She followed me in the living room and said, "You're probably coming down with something. You don't look like yourself. Why don't you go lay down."

"I'm not sick. I have to tell you something," I said as I directed her to sit. She saw how serious I was and sat next to me, her legs twisted toward me, and said, "Whatever it is, it is going to be okay."

"Mom, my label was taken over by another label and they dropped me."

"What does that mean?"

"They let me go."

"What? Why?" she said, standing up.

"They said they had another artist similar to me and a bunch of other things. So we going to have cut back on the spending."

She pulled me in to her chest and hugged me. "Can't you get another record deal?"

"Maybe, maybe not. Tony making some calls for me," I said as I began to cry again.

"This ain't right. Oh, hell, no. How they going to do this to my baby? Can't you sue?"

"No, Mom. Listen, something will happen. But for right now, I just want you to keep this to yourself. Don't tell anyone," I said as I rubbed my eyebrows and took a deep breath. I got up from the table.

"I won't." She grabbed my shoulder and assured me again that it was going to be okay.

Bubbles came in and sat at the table, and I saw she had dyed her hair blond. She was becoming a grown woman.

"Why are you home? When are you going back to school?" I asked.

"I'm not," she said.

"What do you mean you're not?"

"School isn't for me," she said as she slumped in the kitchen chair.

"What is wrong with this girl? Why is she home?" I asked my mother like Bubbles wasn't sitting in front of me.

"Her playing around, not handling her financial aid. I asked her did she need help filling out her forms. She told me she had everything straightened out and it wasn't. So she has to sit out until the spring."

"Mom, you are all wrong. That's not what happened. I filled out my paperwork but they made a mistake. I didn't get my financial aid. They called me down to student finances and told me I had forty-eight hours to pay my tuition or I had to leave," Bubbles said.

"What? They can't do that," I said.

"Yes, they can and they did."

"Why didn't y'all call me? How much is your tuition?"

"Mommy said not to bother you. It is four thousand for my tuition, and my room and board is another two thousand for the semester."

"Six thousand dollars."

"Yes."

"Did you at least try to call and talk to somebody?

They probably could put you on some type of payment arrangement."

"Already asked them, and they said no."

I opened my cell phone. "What's the number? I'll call. They can't do that to you."

She gave me the number and sat and looked at me like I was wasting my time.

"I already talked to them. They are going to tell you the same thing," she yelled.

I ignored her and I asked for the financial aid office. They put me on hold for ten minutes, then I got a financial aid representative. She asked me for Bubbles's social security number. I gave it to her and nicely explained the situation. The woman placed me on hold and came back on the line and said that her aid hadn't come in from the state and that she needed $7,806 to return.

"They told her six thousand."

"Whoever told her that didn't include the late fee and the student activity fees," the woman said.

"Okay. Thank you, ma'am," I said as I hung up.

"I told you," Bubbles said as I stood up from the table.

"Bubbles, be quiet," my mother said. "Somebody's trying to help you."

"But I knew what I was talking about. It's cool. I'll just get a job and then go back next year."

She went upstairs. Damn. I felt bad I couldn't even help her. If I paid for her to go back to school it would be almost every dollar I had. Knowing that still didn't stop me from saying, "Bubbles, get your things."

"Where I'm going?"

"To school."

"I'm not sure if they still have housing for me," she said.

My mother came up the steps and asked me, "Kendra? Are you sure you can afford this?"

"The girl got to go school. Now pack, Bubbles."

Bubbles had never really unpacked. Even though she was acting like she didn't care, she was happy to be going back to school. We took the two-hour ride to Penn State Berks campus. It was a little campus with all-new buildings and green grass everywhere. Kids were walking, books in hand, and talking on cell phones. We went to the bursar's office. They still hadn't canceled her classes, but they had given away her housing. She had to stay in an older building, but at least she was there. Her dorm room was small—there were two beds, two closets, and she had to share a bathroom with four other girls. We brought all of her stuff from the car.

"Thank you so much, Kendra."

"You're welcome," I said. I felt good that she was going to be able to stay in school.

"Amira, you have to take school serious, because if you don't finish college you won't be anything. You can't get a job. I wish I wouldn't have never left school and I had a college degree."

"But you took care of us, and look, you're still rich. You have a record deal without school."

"I'm not rich. Listen, do not play. I just wrote a check for almost eight thousand. You have to get all A's."

"I will. Thank you."

Tony called me but I still didn't want to talk to him, so I told him I would call him back. Beazie had been calling me like crazy too. I finally had the heart to speak to him.

"What's up Kendra?"

"Nothing much."

"So when you coming back to the city?" he asked.

"I'm not."

"Why not?"

"I give up. Ain't no sense. You know what I'm saying. I just feel like maybe it ain't for me."

"That's not true. But I understand—keep in touch."

"I will."

After I got home I went straight to the daycare I had with John and Nitra. The door was open and there was sawdust everywhere, and a man hammering another one was drilling. Nitra was standing behind the contractor making sure he wasn't making the holes too big in the wall. Nitra was shocked to see me. She immediately gave me a hug and said, "Hey what are you doing here?"

"Just stopping by. This is a real daycare," I said as I looked around. "It is really coming together."

"Yeah. They're almost finished wiring, but we still need to paint and lay the carpet down."

"How long before we be open?"

"It's July—I'd say about the end of August, right before school starts."

"Well, I'm home, so I can help." Looking around I thought that I was glad I invested in the day care. At least I would have some money coming in.

Chapter 31

It was only me and my mother in our house, and she kept checking on me. I was okay. I was over the whole dropped thing. It was what it was. I was trying to refocus and plan the rest of my life. I was dodging calls from Beazie—he was the only one who still called constantly even though I didn't answer my phone. When I got a chance I was going to call him back. I hadn't heard from Shelly one time yet, though. I knew she knows about everything. I think that is kind of fucked up, that she hasn't checked on me. Fuck them all.

I was looking through all my bills trying to do a budget. I wanted to see how much money we needed to survive each month. I used to give my mom money to pay the bills, so why weren't they paid? I had a bunch of cut off notices. I ran downstairs and turned off the television.

"Mom, why are all these bills behind?" My car note was three months behind and the house was two months late and in pre-foreclosure.

"No, I didn't know that. Let me see."

"I've been sending you money. Why wouldn't you pay the bills?"

"Oh, a lot of these bills are from May. That's the month I tried to flip the bill money."

"How did you try to flip the bill money?"

"I took some of it down to Atlantic City with me."

I was livid. I couldn't even speak. I know my mother didn't say she'd spent my bill money in the casino. I went off on her.

"Do you know they can come and take this house and my car? What is wrong with you?" I asked her. I was so upset. If she wasn't my mom, I would go off on her. Instead I started crying uncontrollably and walked into the kitchen. My mother followed me and said, "You right, Kendra, I was wrong. I can take that stuff back I just bought at Macy's," she said.

I couldn't listen to her explanation. I walked away from her.

"Mom, leave me alone. You couldn't even pay the bills. I can't trust you. Don't you know if you don't pay bills, things get taken and turned off? When will you learn? First the drinking, and now you have to keep gambling. You don't gamble with other people's money, Mom."

I tried to get the mortgage company on the phone. They said I had to make three mortgage payments. After catching up with all the other bills I was almost broke.

I guess I really was going to have to get a job. I was so sick of being generous and people taking advantage of me. Nobody ever appreciated what I was doing for them. I wished I could go back to a year ago. I would do things so differently with that money.

I got the newspaper and began looking for a damn job. There was nothing in the paper for bartenders. At this point I would do anything. I can't go back to the bar; everybody thinks I'm supposed to be a star. Everybody was rooting for me. I know my boss would give me my job back, but I just couldn't go back. I'd be too embarrassed.

John called me and said that he needed to talk to me urgently about the daycare and to come down immediately. I drove down and saw our new Mind Garden daycare sign hanging up.

"What's going on?"

"We got shut down by L&I."

"Who is L&I?"

"It's license and inspection. Kendra, I'm sorry," he said as he handed me a piece of paper. I reviewed the yellow and pink slips of paper. I looked them over and read that there were code violations and fines in the thousands of dollars.

"How did this happen?"

"The contractor said that he would take care of everything and he knew someone at City Hall who could get everything approved."

"So I guess he didn't come through."

I didn't know what to say. I was upset that John had neglected to tell me and Nitra that he'd cut a few corners with the building. One, the building that we were leasing was not in a commercial zoning area. Second, we didn't have any permits for all the work we were doing. And lastly, the contractor we were using was not returning John's calls and he was already paid. And we couldn't get anybody else to finish the job because we were out of money. So basically it was a wrap.

Chapter 32

Nitra and John had been calling me apologizing. I actually wasn't that mad. They thought I was upset with them, but I wasn't—we all tried and it didn't work out. That's the way it happens sometimes. I went to see them. I hadn't been doing anything but staying in the house. I hadn't wanted to go anywhere. I decided to go over in person and talk to Nitra.

Nitra was in the kitchen making dinner. She took the pot of noodles off the stove and dumped them in the strainer. "You're staying for dinner, aren't you? I'm making spaghetti."

"No," I said.

"Please don't be down, 'cause we feel like we are responsible. Like if you wouldn't have invested with us at least you would still have ten thousand dollars."

"I'm not mad at y'all. Shit happens," I said, taking a seat.

"I know it may not be something that you want to do, but my job is hiring."

"Really, I'll take anything right now. What do I have to do?"

"It's a customer service rep job. You only get paid like fourteen an hour, but all you have to do is answer the phone. You know how to use Word?"

"Yeah."

"Come up to my job and fill out an application. My supervisor loves me. I can definitely get you in," she said as the doorbell rang.

"Are you expecting someone?" I said as I went and answered the door.

"No."

I opened to the door and saw Marcus. The moment I saw him I knew I wasn't over what we went through. I wasn't mad at Nitra and John for messing up the daycare, but I was mad at them for remaining friends with Marcus after all we'd been through.

"Hey," I said as I opened the door. He walked in behind me, and I grabbed my coat and told Nitra I would see her later.

"You don't have to leave," Marcus said.

"I know I don't, but I was leaving anyway." Nitra stood still; she didn't know what to say.

He followed me out the door and said, "Look, Kendra, I still want to be your friend. We're still cool. I want you to meet my daughter." He handed me a picture of her.

"She's adorable. What's her name?"

"Taylor."

"That's cute. How things working out with her mother?" I asked.

"We was never together. That was a mistake. She's still trying to get herself together. She let me have custody of her."

"How is Mr. Skip?"

"He is doing good."

"Yeah, well, it was nice seeing you," I said, handing the photo back to him.

"Yeah, you too."

I went down the steps toward my car.

"Kendra?"

"Yes?"' I said, turning around.

"Do you think we can talk sometime, go out or do something?"

"No, I don't really think we have anything to talk about."

"We can still be friends. I want you in my life."

My mother had made dinner. It was just me and her. Bilal was out playing basketball with his friends.

"Marcus was over at John's house," I said.

"How's he doing?"

"Okay. His baby is cute. He has a daughter named Taylor."

"And you don't have a problem with that?"

"No, I didn't want to have his baby," I said, shrugging my shoulders. I think I had time to get over it. Worse shit had happened to me since Marcus. My mom cleared the table and I pondered over my thoughts. The cordless phone rang. I knew it wasn't for me, but my mom was doing dishes, so I stood up and grabbed the receiver.

"Hello, Kendra? Put Mommy on the phone. I want to come home," Bubbles said.

"What's wrong?" I asked.

"I hate it here," Bubbles said.

"Why?"

"Because I feel so poor. I don't have a job. And if I work on campus I'm not going to make any money. I want to come home."

"And do what? No, you are not coming home." I took a

deep breath and said, "I just paid all this money for you to go to school and you think you're going to come home?"

"I'll get a job and pay you back. I just want to come home. I hate college."

I couldn't get my words together quick enough.

"You know what, you little dumb bitch? If you want to be a fucking loser like your sister, like me, like your mother, like your father, then come the fuck home. You are the first one in the family to go to college and you want to come home? Go right ahead. Come home and do nothing with your life."

"Man, you not up here. It is so hard, and I don't have a computer," Bubbles yelled in my ear.

"I don't care. I didn't have a lot of shit, but I did what the fuck I had to do."

"These white kids have rich parents that send them food and money. They have computers and Ipods in their room. I have to walk all the way across campus to use the stupid computer."

"Well, you know what? Just thank God that you can walk. I don't care what you do. Come home and be a failure, Amira Thomas. Come on home, be a bum, get pregnant, have six baby daddies and get a welfare check. Or come home and do some crack. Fuck you. I'm tired of you, Amira," I screamed as I slammed down the phone.

I went to Nitra's job and filled out an application. She told me what to write and introduced me to her supervisor and she said he would call me. I went home and started cleaning.

"Bilal, come and put this trash out," I yelled, purposely trying to embarrass him in front of all his friends. Everyone in this family made me sick. The house was a damn mess. I walked in the garage and there he was playing the drums like he was in the movie *Drumline*. The other two boys were playing the guitar and keyboard.

"Didn't I tell you to take the trash out?"

"Yeah. I'm going to. I'm practicing. This is my band."

"Is that your sister that sing?" one of the boys asked.

"Yeah, that's her."

"Can you sing for us?"

"She doesn't sing anymore," Bilal whispered and answered for me to his friend. He didn't think I'd heard him, but I did. He was right—I didn't sing anymore. I didn't do a lot of things anymore. I was tired of everyone, and I wished I had somewhere to go instead of this house. Everyone was driving me crazy as I walked up the steps to my room. I heard my mom yell, "Damn it. I missed the lottery by one number. It came two, three, six. I played two, four, six." She was sickening because she didn't get it. She wasn't ever going to win. I was still mad at her from not paying bills. I couldn't have another conversation with her on why she shouldn't gamble. How we were behind on our bills. How I was fed up with her and this house. I had to get out of this damn house and right now.

Chapter 33

Nitra's supervisor at Medical Alliance called to let me know I got the job. I was so happy I was going to have some stable income. I really needed it. I was going to be in training for thirty days learning the computer system. Then all I had to do was answer patients' questions about their primary doctors. That seemed pretty easy, but it wasn't. There were all these systems to learn, HIPAA, code of ethics, patient responsibility—stuff that made no sense but that I had to follow.

I finished training and was on the floor as they called it. It just meant I was ready to take calls.

My desk was in a small cubicle. There were no windows and very bland tan and off-white walls and carpet. I had a computer and a bunch of files on my desk. It was very dull and boring, but they paid for you to go back to school, and I had full benefits. And I'm going back to school for something. But first I have to get my GED. My days went by slow but at least it would help pay the bills. One evening I came home from work tired as hell. I opened the door and saw flowers on the table.

"Mom, who sent you flowers?" I asked her as she watched the evening news.

"They are for you," she said, not bothering to look away from the television.

"Really?" I said, smiling. I took the card and read it.

Thinking of you. I miss you being in my life. Love, Marcus.

I was touched. I called Marcus and said thank you. I heard a baby crying in the background.

"You're welcome. Won't you come see me?"

"No, I was just thanking you for the flowers."

"I really miss you, Kendra."

I thought about it briefly and then said, "All right. I'll be over."

Before I got out of the car Marcus was at the door waiting for me. He had a shirt, slippers, and basketball shorts on.

"You look good. Can I get a hug?" he said, reaching out to me. I gave him one and sat down.

His daughter was asleep on the sofa. The first thing I noticed was everything in the house was remodeled. The living room had a brown and gold sectional and the carpet was a dark shade of brown. "You want to take a look around?" he asked proudly.

I told him no and remained seated.

"Go ahead, look around. I want you to see what I did around here."

I hesitantly got up and walked into the kitchen. It was very nice, like a kitchen out of a home magazine. There were plants and a new big window that used to be two separate windows, brown granite countertop, brown and white flooring and new pine cabinets. Marcus had fixed up the house like he had promised. He really did everything. I walked upstairs. The bathroom had shiny new tile, and his bedroom had a new bedroom set and wallpaper. The other two rooms were closed. Marcus was definitely piecing his life together. I felt happy for him but deep down I was a little jealous. I had talked about him so bad but he got his self together.

I came back downstairs to find Marcus on the phone. He had the baby in one hand and the cordless phone in another. "Man, I can't call it," he said as he spoke to someone on the phone and motioned for me to sit. He told the person he would call them back.

"Hold her. She just woke up," he said as he handed me the baby.

"No I don't want to hold her," I said as I gazed at her. She had on a blue sleeper and she was yawning. Her hair was full of tight curls, and she was chubby and a cinnamon color.

"So what's going on with you? When does your record come out?" he asked.

"It's not coming out," I said. I waited for his response. Telling Marcus I got dropped wasn't easy at all.

"Damn, what happened? What are you going to do?" he asked while putting Taylor into her swing.

"I'm working at Nitra's job now."

"Well, you tried. They don't know what they are missing. I'm sorry to hear that." Everything he said seemed so bogus to me. He had a tiny smirk on his face. It wasn't an "I'm so happy" smirk, it was more like an "I told you so" grin.

"You'll be all right."

"I know I will."

"You sure?"

"Yeah, I'm sure. It's just messed up," I said as I broke down in tears in his arms and started feeling sorry for myself.

"It's going to be okay," he said as he held me. His body was filled with warmth and comfort. I felt like not letting him go. "I love you Kendra. I never stopped caring about you."

"I love you too, Marcus."

"Why you leave me?" he said almost tearfully.

"It don't even matter just I'm glad you're here with me now. Don't you ever leave me again. I wasn't trying to kill your dream. I just didn't want them to hurt you like this. I'm still here for you. I don't mess with that girl, she just had a baby for me. I wanted you to be the mother of my children. I want us to be together. Please forgive me." I didn't say anything. We both just cried together.

Chapter 34

I'd never fallen out of love with Marcus. I know me and him had been through a lot, but being with him now was like I never left. When we were apart it must have been a reality check for him because he really has changed. He makes me and the baby dinner and runs my bathwater after work. I feel like a surrogate had my baby, Taylor, for me because some days I think Taylor is mine. She favors Marcus a little but she really got her own look. She is the most precious, sweet, cute baby. She was always smiling up at me.

Nobody in my family understands why I went back to Marcus and why I've been playing mommy to his daughter, but I told them it is not for them to understand. I'm happy. This is where I belong—with my family. No, it's not the ideal family. But it is working for me.

My job is another story. Already I hated it. I was sick of this loud and stupid clique of women who sat in my cubicle area. There was Sharon, Melody and Felicia. Felicia was the gossip—searching the Internet, reading blogs, talking about people, forwarding "God loves you" e-mails. Melody was just fat and always asking if you wanted to order food with her. And there was Sharon, my supervisor. She was just about thirty, and mean for no reason. She walked past my desk to see what I was doing all the time. I didn't like that shit. I wasn't a kid and I didn't need to be monitored.

Chapter 35

I've been at my job for four weeks and I have hated every moment of it. My desk is still empty. I don't have any pictures, plants, radios, or magnets. Because I don't plan on staying. Today I am ready to quit. This is a good job for a regular person. I'm not saying I'm not regular. It's just not for me. I don't belong here. The only thing making me not quit was I knew I didn't have any money. I kept telling myself to turn everybody off in the office and just get paid, but I can't just sit somewhere for eight hours. I never had this type of job in my life. I hated answering the phone a hundred times a day. It was so boring. I walked to Nitra's desk to tell her I was about to quit, but she wasn't there. The woman who sat behind her said, "I think Nitra went to lunch."

I thanked her, went back to my desk and I logged on to my computer. "Thank you for calling Medical Alliance. How may I help you?"

"I want to change my doctor."

I placed that lady on hold and changed her doctor, then

told her, "Thank you. Have a nice day." My next call was not as easy.

"Hello, is my daughter eligible for bracelets?"

"What type of bracelets?" I asked.

"You know, the ones for your teeth."

"You mean braces." I pushed my phone on mute and took a deep breath. I didn't need this right now. This is why I wanted to quit, because of stupid people like her.

"Yeah, braces. You know what the hell I mean. Can my daughter get something to fix her teeth?"

I told her she would have to make an appointment with her dental provider and they would schedule her appointment with an orthodontist. She didn't like my answer so she said just do your job you stupid bitch. I looked around to see who was looking and disconnected the call. I took my headset off. I didn't want to talk to another person. I just wanted to leave.

That was the last call. I couldn't imagine getting more calls like that each day.

A few more minutes went past and I was still thinking about my next move. I kept rubbing Bath & Body Works vanilla body lotion on my hands. I want to leave. I want to quit. I hate this job. It is stupid, I thought.

Instead of leaving I went to the vending machine and I got some Famous Amos oatmeal cookies, then sat and ate the bag in the breakroom. I went to the bathroom and then I went back to the desk. I was trying not to quit. I was trying not to give up. If I quit what would I do? I have to take care of the bills. I didn't know how I was going to do it. So I sat back down. But then I looked around and said this is not for me. I have to get out of here. I have to quit.

I walked away from my desk to the fire escape. I didn't want to run into Sharon or Nitra, but it was time for me to break free, time for me to get away. Step by step my heart pumped faster and faster and faster. Then I ran down the steps and out of that job. I opened the large door that said

EMERGENCY EXIT ONLY and saw the beaming bright sunlight and clear blue sky. I inhaled the fresh, cold air. It felt so good. I got in my car and I was officially free.

I am going to have to call Nitra to tell her what happened; I didn't want her to find out I quit from anybody but me. I dialed her extension an hour later. As soon as she heard my voice she whispered, "Why did you quit?"

"I couldn't take it."

"Now what are you going to do?" she asked.

"I don't know. I will have to do something."

"You should have just stayed until you found something else."

"I'm sorry I just couldn't take it. I'll talk to you later, okay."

"All right."

I felt bad. Nitra had got me the job but the nine-to-five thing wasn't for me. I felt trapped at that job. I have to do what I love even if it means being broke while I'm doing it. Another year was approaching, I was getting older and I had to do something with my life. I was about to be twenty-seven years old. That's three years away from thirty and I still didn't know what I was supposed to be doing with my life. I went home and went to sleep. When I awake I'll have the answer. Until then I buried myself in my pillows.

Chapter 36

John was at my house when I awoke; he had been going through it since the daycare had closed. Nitra has been chewing him out daily. She probably sent him over to check on me after I quit.

"I heard what happened at the job. So what are you going to do now?" he asked, sitting on the edge of my bed.

"I don't know," I said as I sat up.

"I think you're not going to be happy until you are doing what you love."

"No, that's not true. I did what I loved and I got played. Now I'm stuck. I'll figure it out."

"You're not stuck."

"Yes, I am. I don't know what I'm going to do with my life John."

"I think you need to just go back to New York and make it happen for yourself. Since you been back you have not been happy."

"I've been happy. I just know I can't work a nine-to-five. I have to find the right kind of job for me. Plus, it's too late for me. I had my chance. I'm not dreaming no more, I'm going to live my life."

"Stop saying that. There is no expiration on dreams. Forget everything that happened the last time."

"No, I can't do it."

"Yes you can. Why can't you? This time around it would be different."

"I don't want to go and I have nothing to go back to."

"Don't that guy Beazie call you all the time still?"

"Yeah, he probably could you help you find a place."

"I don't have any money."

"I'll give you money. I owe you ten thousand dollars."

I smiled then thought of another reason why I couldn't leave.

"All right, I hear you. But if I did go back to New York I don't have anywhere to go. Plus, I just started back with Marcus. I can't leave him again."

"If he wants you he will support you. But I don't see it happening, though. To tell the truth he doesn't want you to succeed. Everything Nitra tries to do, I support her. Even with that daycare, that was her thing, not mine. And he don't feel the same way about your dreams."

"Yes, he does."

"No, he doesn't."

"Marcus has changed a lot. He told me he supports me."

"I was talking to him and, fuck it, let me just tell you. Kendra, I knew that nigga for ten years. I know that man. He ain't for you, sister. I love you. He and I were talking and I'm listening and this dude was saying like he knew it wasn't going to work out for you. He's just stunting your growth. Y'all shouldn't even be back together. He can't handle you trying to live your dreams."

"That's not true, John."

"Yes, it is. You just need to get yourself together and go

back to New York. You need to go and live your life and realize your dreams."

"Marcus loves me and I'm getting too old to be chasing some dream. This is my reality. Plus, I don't have a manager or a place to stay."

"Man, forget what Marcus says. He don't want to see you grow. I can be your manager. I can read some books. I know how to read a contract. You got to go live your life and not sit back and live it for anyone else. Especially not for Marcus. He ain't right."

"What are you talking about, John?"

"I'm talking about Marcus, man. You fire, he is water. Water puts fire out. He just wants to sit back and be in charge. He's used to you needing him. And when you don't need him he be hurting because he don't know how it is for you not to need him. He used to y'all being fucked up. And when you wasn't he didn't know how to act. And it's not your fault, 'cause you tried to stick it out with him. You need to leave him in that house. I mean, soon as you stop messing with him what's he go do? Get a dirty chick with nowhere to live pregnant. I'm not going to watch you forget about your dreams to make him happy."

Everything John was saying made sense. But why was he telling me all this now?

"Stop. You're about to make me cry," I said.

"Kendra, I want you to start packing and leave him."

"Who is going to pay the bills?"

"The bills are going to get paid. Forget about them for once in your life. Think about you."

"I am thinking about me."

"No, you are not. You really need to think about what I'm saying. I will quit my job to help you succeed if I have to. Life is not a joke. When you're trying to get to the next level, everybody can't go with you. Sometimes you got to leave somebody behind. There is no such thing as luck, only preparation and opportunity meeting at the same time. It's not over, it's not too late. It's not over until you're dead and in your coffin," John said as he rambled off every inspirational cliché he ever heard.

"Shut up," I said as I laughed and wiped my eyes. He was starting to sound like a bootleg inspirational speaker. What John was saying made sense, but when do you give up on your dream and say, "Fuck it, let me get a real job"?

"Think about what I'm saying."

I thought about it a little then. I went to Marcus's house to tell him about me quitting. I had to see if what John was telling me was true. I did want to go back to New York and try singing again, but I didn't want to lose Marcus again. I knew he would support me this time. I went in his house and told him to sit.

"What's going on, Kendra? I have to go and pick Taylor up from daycare."

"I'm going to make it, Marcus," I said as I paced back and forth in the living room. "I quit my job today."

"You did what? How are you going to pay your bills?" he asked.

"I don't know." I paused. "And I think I'm going to sing again."

"You tried that before. It didn't work out."

"Well, I'm going to try it again."

"For what? You getting too old to be trying to hold on to a dream. We already talked about that."

"Who says so? If I start back singing, will you support me? I need to know, Marcus," I said, waiting for his reaction.

"No, I won't support you. You just need to stop dreaming. You better call and see if you can get your job back. That was a good job. You complain that you don't have any money? Now you really not going to have any money. Why would you quit?"

"I'm not sitting in the office. I want to sing. Marcus, I

was talking to John and since I have been home I have been miserable."

"You need to stop tripping. I don't know what's wrong with you. You can have a good regular life, but you want to be Miss Famous and it's not going to happen for you."

Marcus's words enraged me. How could he say I wasn't going to make it? I was his woman. John was right, he was supposed to be supporting my dreams, not tearing them down.

"Marcus, how could you say that?"

"Because it's true. You not going to make it, so you need to stop even trying. That's your problem—dreaming. Reality check—it ain't going to happen," he shouted.

I couldn't believe what he was saying. I got up and walked toward the door, tears flowing down my cheeks.

He tried to hold me back, but I pushed him away from me and said, "No, Marcus. The problem isn't me having dreams. The problem is I need to stop dealing with your dream-killing hating ass. I must be crazy trying to make it work with you. I can't take you anymore."

"If you leave me again I'm not going to be here when you get back," he said as I turned the knob to walk out the door. "Go ahead and get hurt and get played again."

"Fuck you, and I mean it. I'm never coming back to you," I yelled back at him. I left Marcus for good.

Yeah, I took a chance and messed up before. I made some mistakes, but no one has ever come up by sitting still. You got to go out there and make something happen. This can't be it for me. I am going to be great. It is going to happen for me. Marcus was trying to discourage me but all he did was pump me up even more.

"Hey, Beazie. This Kendra."

"What up, baby? I miss you. You straight?"

"Yeah. Listen, I wanted to thank you for calling me."

"So you did get all one hundred of my messages?"

"Yeah, I did. I appreciate you calling. Matter of fact,

you was the only dude that called me. You know, I haven't even heard from Corey or Shelly."

"Yeah, I be seeing Dude. Forget him, he ain't about nothing. So what's up, Ma?"

"Well, I had a couple of months off and I was thinking about trying to get on again."

"I think you should. A lot has changed. I'm not even doing any recording with Touchlight. And I moved to another studio. And I got an artist I'm producing. I'm trying to get him a deal now. So when a label come to me they going to come to me correct. Come to the city and let's talk."

"I just got to find a place and I don't really have any money."

"Kendra, don't waste your talent. You had your vacation, now come back and grind it out. Come and get yours."

John was right. Beazie was right. It was now or never. I went home and started packing. I sat my mom and Bilal down and told them I was leaving. It was all about me, Kendra Michelle Thomas. My dreams, my goals, my life. I was really out and I meant it. There was nothing here for me.

Chapter 37

"Go hard or go home" was my new motto. I was back in New York and I wasn't going home. It was freezing cold outside but I was warmed by the city's promise and opportunity. This time I had to take advantage of it. But first I had to find a place to live. All I needed was a room with a bathroom.

I went and met Beazie at Premier Recording Studio. He looked a little different. He had cut his dreds.

"When did you do that?"

"You didn't know I cut my hair," he said as he reached out and gave me a hug. "This is my artist, Authentic." I said hello.

He was a short, dark brown–skinned guy with all these muscles. He was wearing a sweatshirt, leather jacket and jeans. He had a tattooed teardrop under his eye. Underneath the tattoo he had in scripted letters FATHER FORGIVE ME. He looked intimidating, but when he spoke he was very nice. I took a seat and asked what was going on with him.

"Basically, I'm hating this game right now. I'm anti-industry. People like me and you going to come up. We are going to get ours. We going to do this from the bottom up. I promise you," Beazie said.

"So where is Davis?"

"He is gone. He is doing him. Did you find a place to stay?"

"No, not yet."

"You can just stay with me, until you find a place."

After our session was over we got in his black Denali truck and drove over to his apartment in New Jersey. You could see the entire apartment from the front door—the small kitchen was to the left; the living room, bedroom and bathroom were on your right. He had a black cotton low-to-the-ground IKEA sofa. The place was small but welcoming. I put my bag down on the floor.

"You can take my room and I'll sleep on the sofa," he said.

"No, I can't do that. I'll sleep on the sofa."

He didn't argue with me. He threw me a tan pillow and a blanket. He went in his room and shut the door. Even though I was on his sofa I was happy I was back.

I was spending eighteen hours of twenty-four-hour days in the studio. I was writing my ass off. I had no choice actually because Beazie was my ride in and out the city. But I didn't mind because it was my passion. "I want you to write," he told me. "Write about how you feel. About everybody not believing in you. Write about how you going to tell these motherfuckers to kiss your ass when you make it. Write about your life."

I wrote about how everybody else was coming up around me and I still was in the same place. I wrote a song for Marcus called "Didn't I Tell You?" I just started writing songs and more songs. Every emotion I had trapped inside of me, I let it out. I was writing a freestyle about my life called "All I Want." It was the story of my life.

Being in the studio with Beazie was all good, but I still needed money. He was feeding me and providing my transportation. I tried paying him back by singing the hooks on Authentic's songs for free and he was selling them all over the country. Me and Beazie have been working on a bunch of songs for me too!

Chapter 38

I was making food runs, cleaning Beazie's house. I just wanted to earn my keep. He couldn't even bring his dates home 'cause I had my butt on his sofa. No one was believing that I was his little sister and he was just helping me out.

I had just left the studio. I was making a food run to go get pizza for all of us when Beazie called me on my cell.

"What's up? You forgot to order your cheese fries?"

"Miss Kendra Michelle I need a big favor from you. Go to Tashay's party with me," Beazie said.

"Hell no, why would I go?"

"Because there is going to be some influential people there. I need you to do this for me. I need to put Authentic's demo in somebody's hands."

"I don't have anything to wear."

"Yes, you do. I'll meet you there."

"I can't go."

"You have to. There's going to be so many people there you need to meet."

"So what about the food?"

"Forget it. Yeah. Go find something to wear, get nice and meet me at Marquee."

I had sixty-two dollars on me, and what could I find to wear for that little bit of money? I went to H&M and found a black dress on the clearance rack marked down to twenty-four dollars. I tried it on. It wasn't a perfect fit, but it would do. I had a dress, and now I needed shoes. I bought black Payless pumps for twenty-three dollars. I had enough money left over to buy a slice of pizza and a soda, and a tube of lipstick that doubled as eye shadow.

I pushed my hair up in the front and pinned it up and wore it long in the back. You never knew who would be at the party.

I walked in and instantly I felt like I was back on the scene. People were finger waving me like I'd never left. There was a lot of "hey how yo doin'," "where yo been hiding," a lot of fakery but I smiled and accepted business cards. I met Ryan Marcell, an A&R at Def Jam. That was so major. He told me to call him. Then I was speaking to this girl from Koch, an independent distributor. I made a lot of good connects.

I was trying to avoid Tashay. I didn't want to see her. Right now she was everything that I was supposed to be but wasn't a big star.

I was heading for the bathroom when I bumped into Miss Princess Tashay. She acted like we were girls.

"Hey, girl," she said, giving me a fake industry hug. "How you doing? How's it going?"

"Good," I said.

"And you know I'm doing good. I'm kind of like a big deal," she bragged as she pointed to herself and winked at me.

"What have you been doing with yourself?"

"I just got back in town, actually."

"Oh, okay. Working on anything new?"

"Not yet."

"Well, do you have another deal?"

"No, not yet."

"Well I need a backup singer for my tour. Are you available?"

"A backup singer," I said, as I almost choked on my own saliva.

"Yeah, I think you would sound great behind me. Think about it and give me a call." *Yeah, okay,* I thought as she proceeded to give me her cell phone number.

"K.I.T.," she said as she floated around the party meeting and greeting. She looked even more polished than when I'd first met her, and just like she belonged. She really was a star and I still wasn't. I went to the restroom and checked my make-up. I put all the business cards I collected in my wallet. I took a deep breath and walked back in the party. Exiting the restroom, Beazie grabbed my arm and said, "I made some connects. How about you?"

"Yeah? Me too!" We walked to his truck and I said, "You want to hear something funny? Tashay asked me to be her backup singer."

"So what did you tell her?" he asked.

"I didn't tell her anything. How I look like being her backup singer when I can sing rings around her? I almost laughed in her face."

"That's true, but Tashay is the hottest thing out now."

"Yeah, I know."

"I'm not trying to tell you what to do, but why don't you at least try it out and see what happens? Sometimes you have to let go of your ego and fund the dream or continue to be a starving artist. I think you should do it. It's exposure. We are going to make it work."

"How could singing backup for Tashay help me?"

"I think you going on tour with Tashay is going to open so many doors for you."

Beazie was right. The more I thought about it the more

I had to think of reasons why I wouldn't. I didn't have any money coming in, and I could make money and meet people working with her. It definitely couldn't hurt.

I reluctantly called Tashay.

"Hey, girl," I said. I hated being fake, but it was necessary.

"Who is this?" she asked.

"It's Kendra."

"Oh, hey, Kendra. What's up?" she asked like how did I get her number and what did I want.

I told her I was calling about her backup singing position. She told me she was busy but to call her manager and that he would give me the details. She said it all in a rush like she was important. *What-the-fuck-ever,* I thought. I called her manager Gil's number.

"Who gave you this number?" he questioned.

"Tashay."

"I told her to stop giving people this number. Yeah, just meet us on Saturday."

"When does the tour begin?"

"In a month, but we are recording some remixes and have to practice the choreography. See you there."

Chapter 39

When I met up with Tashay at Demand Practice Studio she was still looking red-carpet pretty. She was pushing her Louis Vuitton doggie stroller. It looked just like a baby stroller but smaller, and she had her little doggy dressed up with shoes on and pink sweats. She started rehearsal and singing. She was steadily flapping her arms again. This time I didn't laugh. I just went along with the charade. Whatever pays the bills. She was untalented, I knew that, but she did something in her past life, because God was looking out for her. Some people just get all the luck.

She was in the front of the studio trying to get me and the other two background singers to follow her directions.

"Okay, I'm going to sing *You want me. But you can't have me. I'm taken. My man is home waiting. So stop asking me for my number.* Then I want you to come behind me and sing *Yeah yeah yeah stop asking my girl for her number.*"

* * *

Tashay had sold almost seven hundred thousand copies of her album, but her people said she was platinum, building the hype. We were doing spot dates all across the country. We went to Hartford, Columbia, South Carolina, Orlando and a bunch of other places. Promoters were bringing her in at thirty thousand a show. However, Tashay's star was somewhat dimming. There were petitions all over the Internet saying they wished she'd shut the fuck up and stop trying to sing and go back to being a video girl. She didn't care—she was selling albums. She wasn't even nice to the people who bought her records.

We were backstage when a guy approached and said, "Could you please sign this? I'm a really big fan." He was a tall, skinny young guy with bad acne, around seventeen.

Tashay looked at him and said, "No, not right now."

The guy said, "Please? I'm your biggest fan, Tashay. Come on, I took off of work to come and see you. Can I get a picture?"

"Huh," she said as she got in the picture with her fan. Even though she was dissing him right in his face, he was still so happy to have her attention.

"You are the best," he said as he scurried away in awe.

The only way I was able to put up with her is because as soon as we were done with each show I left. I knew there was a bigger picture. I didn't hang out, I just went back to my room and wrote songs and tried to remain focused.

Chapter 40

Beazie had just gotten Authentic a mid–six-figure-deal with Universal Records. He said I was up next and just to hang in there, but first he had to get my name to ring. Buzz is what got Authentic signed. We put ten songs on a CD. I was going to sell it on the streets, and I had a five-song snippet CD I was giving out for free.

"Kendra, first we're going to get our street team to give out your posters and CDs everywhere in NYC. We are going to run this like a campaign like you're running for president," Beazie said.

Tashay was paying for me to go from city to city, and Beazie told me to take full advantage of it. Every night after the show I went and found the afterparty and gave the deejays my CD. Bubbles became my online PR machine, hyping me up all over the Internet. She got a guy at school who liked her to set up a Web site and a MySpace page. I had twenty thousand friends in a matter of weeks.

John and Beazie were working together as a team. They were going to co-manage me and split the 20 percent commission. Authentic had just moved ten thousand copies of his CDs in a matter of months, just in the five boroughs. That helped a lot in getting him signed. So Beazie wanted me to do the same thing. He told me I had to get out there and get my grind on. I had no idea how to do that. I just wanted to be a star. Authentic was a rap dude. People expect the hustle from a man, but what I look like selling R&B CDs? But I trusted Beazie, and he knew what he was talking about. If he said it was going to work, then it is. I'm going to do whatever it takes. What I got to lose?

John believes in me so much. He really quit his job. We had to win. He drove up from Philadelphia to help me sell the CDs, and I really needed the help. I was at Beazie's apartment with about twenty cases of CDs in my car. Beazie was all hyped on selling CDs, but I felt so stupid going from being "about to be the next big thing" to selling my own CD out of my trunk. The more I thought about it the angrier I got. "Why do I have to do this? I mean, can't we just go to the record label?"

"No, you know why you are doing this? Because you want them to come to you. You want them to be like, 'Where is Kendra Michelle? Who is this girl? I have to sign her.'"

Beazie sent us to 125th Street in Harlem to sell CDs. We had a portable CD player in case anyone wanted to listen to my music. I was trying to be hype, but I didn't know about this. My fears were confirmed when the first couple of people I approached just ignored me like I was crazy. Then I got enough courage to approach this woman. She was walking with her toddler grandson. I went up to her somewhat stuttering and said, "How you doing, Miss? I'm a singer and I'm selling my CD." I handed her one because she looked interested and then she said, "Is it in stores yet?"

"No, not yet."

"Well, I'll get it when it is in stores," she said. I wanted to smack her. What was the difference? People thought we were trying to scam them for some reason so no one would stop. New York was a hard city to conquer. John stopped this older man, but he said if it wasn't gospel he couldn't buy it.

Finally we had our first sale. This woman stopped and said, "I'm going to support you because you're trying. I don't listen to that kind of music, but here is twenty dollars for you." She took the twenty and placed it in my hand. I thanked her and began to believe that it was doable.

"Thanks," I said. She made me feel real insignificant, though she thought she was helping the cause.

The next day we went to Brooklyn and went into a nail and hair salon. People were looking at me like, *what the hell is she selling?* John cleared his throat and said, "Ladies, this is my sister Kendra Michelle, and she is a great singer. We are selling her CD today for ten dollars." The whole nail salon looked at us like we were crazy. Nobody bought a CD, and I began to get discouraged. We had been out two days and only sold nine CDs. This was too hard. How was I ever going to get to the tens of thousands sold? We walked back to the car and I put my face in my hands. John got in the car and gave me another lecture about staying positive and not giving up.

"I don't want to do this. This is too hard," I said.

"Kendra you have to become immune to people. Fuck whoever diss you. It's not about them. It is about us getting your name out there." Then he began blasting Rick Ross's "Everyday I'm Hustling" CD to get me hyped. The hustling anthem lifted my spirits a little. I had to sell CDs. I had to move units. After we left the nail salon on Fulton

Avenue, we went to the parking lot of the King's Plaza Mall. We parked the car and John started playing my CD. He opened the trunk and we began to wait for people to walk by. As people passed into the mall we gave them a postcard with all my info on it.

This old man stopped, looked down at the card and said, "You her? Let me hear you sing. If this is you I'm going to buy ten CDs."

I looked over at John. I wanted to sell ten CDs but I wasn't about to sing in a mall parking lot. But John gave me a look like I didn't have any other choice. This was awful. All I needed was a cup. I started singing along to the song. The man said I sounded good and really did buy ten CDs, and then he encouraged other people to come over to me. The next thing I knew there was a crowd and we had sold fifty-nine CDs in an hour.

I went back on tour with Tashay and it wasn't so bad. I had John and Bubbles with me. They began following the tour from city to city. We all stayed in the room together, me and Bubbles sharing the bed and John on the floor. I went to every radio deejay in each city from San Francisco to Miami. All I had to say was I was down with Tashay. They would say, "Tashay? Really? Okay, I'll spin it." Everyone was helping to sell my CD. My mom and Bilal was even selling CDs on the street for me back home.

Instantly the buzz started. A&Rs started showing up backstage at Tashay shows looking for me. Then I started getting calls on my cell phone. Tony even called Beazie to find out who was my new manager. I was trying to just stay focused, so I let John and Beazie handle everything. I was too scared of getting caught up in the hype again. I told them when they had a real offer on the table to let me know about it. I didn't want to be all pumped up and get knocked down all over again.

But John told me it was going to be different this time. He said I had bargaining power and had proven myself. He was back and forth with Beazie all day on the phone.

"You are getting really into this managing thing. John, I don't think I can do all of that again. I just went through too much. Plus I'm about to go overseas with Tashay, my bills are getting paid, and I want to play it safe. Maybe I'll start trying to figure all this out when I come back," I said. I didn't know what to think. I couldn't believe that labels were interested in me again, but it also scared me and I didn't want to deal with it. Beazie called and John passed me his cell phone.

"Kendra you are quitting the tour."

"Why?"

"Why—because we have some major labels interested in you. You will never be singing back up for anyone ever again."

I stayed silent. I didn't know what to think.

"Say something Kendra."

"I don't know what to say."

"Well, come on home. I already bought your ticket."

"Are you sure I should leave the tour Beaz?"

"Yes, Kendra it is for real this time. There's about to be a bidding war for your album."

"What does that mean?"

"We are going to have like an auction and the highest bidder with the best deal wins." I was happy but I couldn't get excited. I couldn't get caught up in the hype again.

"I'm leaving everything up to you and John. Work it out for me."

"You know I will. I see you when you get here. I think you should think this through. These offers more than likely are not going to be lightweight. Go on tour, think it over and I'll call you to let you know what's going on."

Chapter 41

Today was the day I had been waiting for all my life. It had been three years in the making. It was Tuesday, June 12, 2007, the release date of my new CD, *All I Want.* I had signed in February with Interscope to a three-album deal. This time I was in control. I didn't go all out of control—I paid some bills and went back to the studio. I wasn't about to make the same mistake twice. I knew I wanted to get property and live comfortably and not blow one dollar of my money. I had an album ready when I signed, so all I had to do was go in the studio and re-record the tracks. That only took a few weeks. Beazie and me were the executive producers.

I was so nervous. I barely slept and I would need extra makeup to hide the bags underneath my eyes. The video had been getting good play on 106 & Park and *TRL*. My Website and my MySpace page were getting hit up for the last two months. My first single "All I Want" was released six weeks ago and the album was coming out right on time.

* * *

In fact, everything was moving the way it was supposed to be. I was in *Vibe Vixen,* the *Source* and *Essence*. *Sister 2 Sister* did a nice article on me, too. They gave me a publicist. Her name was Shannon. She went over what I was supposed to say on interviews. She told me to talk about my experience over the last ten years. She said it was my testimony, that I persevered through things. She told me people needed to know who I was. They know you want them to know you're not a regular chick trying to sing. That this was my dream and how much I gave up for it. My new label was putting so much effort and money behind me to the point that it was scary. I knew I was talented, but I just hoped I lived up to everyone else's expectations.

I was under the covers. I got a knock on the door. I looked over, and it was four a.m.

"You have to get up and get ready," Shannon said. Already she had a phone glued to her head.

It was time for me to get my hair and makeup done. My heart was beating so fast—I didn't know why. I guess all this was still so unreal to me, being here in this beautiful suite and having people make a fuss about me. I was so used to not being a diva. In fact, I made a bad diva. I was carrying my own bags and parking my own car. My family had come up to support me. John and my mom were staying next door and Bubbles was in my room with me. John came in and sat next to me as I got my hair curled.

"You look worried."

"I've just been thinking."

"About what?"

"How about now that I got all these people behind me and I fought so hard, how about if I don't make it?"

"Girl, you're going to make it. You deserve this. Look at everything you been through to get to this point." He gave me a kiss on my cheek. Then Shannon came in, reading my itinerary for the day.

"You have a local NYC morning show. I want you to talk about your album and your appearance today in Times Square Virgin record store. Remember also to be very diplomatic in all your answers. Don't let her pull you into commenting on anything you don't want to." I okayed everything.

By seven a.m. I walked into the studio of the radio station for the Missy Brown wakeup show on 102.7.

"Good morning, Kendra Michelle," Missy said as she looked down into her notes and spoke into the microphone.

"Good morning, Tri-State."

"So your first single, 'All I Want,' is blazing."

"Thank you."

I was still nervous. I was looking at her and waiting for her to ask the next question. She was known for getting smart, asking questions you weren't prepared for or bringing up your back-in-the-day business. I was good so far. She didn't ask anything out of the ordinary. Then she asked about the producers on my project. "I have a lot of hot producers and I think I bring something different to the table. I sing and I write my own songs."

"So you not one of these manufactured artists like Tashay? I hate her. I think she is untalented."

"Tashay is a great artist. Shout out to her. She is doing her thing," I said diplomatically.

"So who are you feeling right now?"

"Um, I don't really listen—to the radio."

Before I could get my response she poked me in the breast and asked, "Are those things real?" I was so embarrassed.

"No, they real," I said as I looked down at my shirt and

her finger was still poking me. I was too shocked to react. She asked me to tell her about my experiences. I told her as briefly as possible about my life and all that I had overcome. She kept the questions coming.

"So you never gave up even after you was broke and down and out?"

"No, I stayed focused and here I am."

"Well, that's nice. I mean that. You are really talented and that is uncommon these days. Well we have to go to commercial, Tri-State. So let's play some cuts off your new album, *All I Want*. Dial us up to talk to Kendra Michelle. It's the Missy Brown Show—we will be right back."

When we went to a commercial break, she took a sip of water and went to the bathroom. While she was gone, Shannon my publicist came up to me and said, "Don't forget to tell them where you are going to be signing and your Web site when she come back from commercial break."

When we got back on the air I said, "My Web site is Kendra Michelle dot com and I want everybody to come out today at 5 p.m. to the Virgin Megastore to meet me and get an autograph."

After my interview was over, Missy Brown said, "Good luck, much success," and that she would be pushing the CD for me. I was relieved she didn't come for me.

"That went well," John said as he pushed the button to the elevator.

"I didn't want to have to give it to her, because she be all in people's business." We left the radio station and turned on the car radio. She was still talking about me.

"John, turn it up. I want to see if she is going to diss me." We all listened as she said, "Yeah, I like her. I think she is hot. She is really nice. Her boobs aren't real, but whatever, go support the album. It's called *All I Want.*" I laughed.

"You lucky she didn't badmouth you."

"No, she's lucky. I would have met her in the lobby," I joked.

After that we went to a meet and greet private luncheon with another radio station. Everyone was all excited and wanted to take pictures with me. There were people there of all ages who were asking me questions about my life and music. After the luncheon I had an hour, which I used to sit back and relax. They refreshed my makeup and hair. Back at the hotel, I had something light to eat and got ready for my instore.

"It's time," Beazie said as he opened the door on the truck.

I entered the black SUV. Beazie was with me, along with my assistant, Shannon, John and my mom.

"Look at this traffic," I said as I looked around, trying to see if we could go another way. I didn't want to be late for my first autographing session.

"The street is blocked off," Bubbles said.

I looked around and saw there were people holding my posters. There was a big crowd with posters and magazine covers.

"Is this for me?" I asked.

"Yes, we wanted to surprise you and tell you that your album shipped gold. The single is number five in the country and number two on the R&B charts."

"You doing it, girl," Bubbles yelled as she hugged me sideways.

"Don't make me cry, y'all. Are you serious?" I looked at the crowd. There were fans with T-shirts, people holding signs and screaming, "Kendra Michelle."

I got out of the SUV and people were shouting my name.

"I love you, Kendra!" this guy shouted from the side of the barrier.

"I love you, too," I shouted back.

"Can I get a picture?"

I turned around and smiled. I signed autographs going in and posed for a few pictures. There were rows and rows of photographers. The lights were blinding me—*click click click.* The gleam of the light was so bright. I just stood in one place and smiled. Shannon told them that was enough.

"Can I get a hug?" this boy said. He had a hand-painted picture of my album cover on his shirt.

The line was out the door with people waiting to meet me and to get their CDs signed. I was so shocked, but I had to act like *Yeah, I know this is me. This is how I do and I'm used to it.*

"Do you see this?" John asked.

"Yes, can you believe it?" I yelled.

"Yes, I can. You deserve it," Beezie said.

They gave me a black Sharpie marker and I got ready to start signing.

The first girl in line said, "I was in line since this afternoon. I love your voice and you are so beautiful."

"Thank you," I said, smiling. "How you spell your name?"

"Kamaya. K-A-M-A-Y-A."

I signed her autograph and took a picture with her. The line was still growing. I was still taking it all in. This young lady with a baby asked me if I could take a picture with her son.

"Sure," I said as I stood up and smiled.

"I read your story and heard you on the radio. You really inspired me to come down and meet you."

"Thank you so much." I gave her a hug. I don't know how many records I signed, but my arm was sore.

"You don't have to sign all those albums," said Chrissy from the label as she coached me to stop.

"Yes, I do." I took a short break and kept signing until the store closed.

Epilogue

October 2007

They say nothing comes easy or without a price. Attitude determines your altitude. And I believe it all. I'm so blessed to be at a place where I am right now. I am the headliner at the Power House at the Wachovia Center. It is the biggest yearly concert in Philly. I can remember seeing shows here back in the day. I used to watch people onstage, wishing it was me. Now I am here about to perform in front of my hometown. I was backstage trying to digest it all. There were people everywhere—reporters, photographers and local celebrities. I saw groupies trying to get pictures, athletes and everyone in between. Everyone was coming up to me wanting to take a picture and meet me. I still felt like I was dreaming. I'd been doing shows since the album came out last year. I'm at double platinum and counting. I had three hit singles and they are thinking about releasing one more. The funniest thing about all of this, people recognize me everywhere I go now. I can't go in the market anymore without someone saying, "Hey, aren't you the girl from the video?" And people have been sending me movie scripts, and I never thought about acting. All these other artists want me on their projects. It is all so overwhelming. It feels like last week, I just wanted someone to listen to me sing. Now everyone wants a piece of me. My mother and John and Bubbles being around me all the time is helping me adjust to the fame. My brother and Beazie are still my managers. Bubbles is my assistant. She has two years left of school. She is getting her degree in finance with a minor in accounting. She wants to be able to handle my money for me. My mom is with me almost all the time for support. My makeup artist was applying the finishing touches onto my face. I was trying not to ruin my painted lips. I sat in my dressing room sipping on honey and lemon when my mom walked in with her Kendra Michelle T-shirt on. She was always representing.

"I have a surprise for you. Guess who is out here," she said. "Who?" I asked as I stepped out of my dressing room and saw Marcus standing with a huge arrangement of roses. I hadn't talked to him since I left home.

"Hey, lady," he said as he gave me a kiss on the cheek. He was holding Taylor's hand. She had gotten so big. She had on a pink corduroy dress with pink ballies and barrettes in her hair. I bent down and spoke to her. "How are you?" I said. She pulled away from me and held on tightly to Marcus's leg.

"Say hi, mom mom. Stop acting shy, Taylor," Marcus said.

"She probably forgot me," I said, smiling.

"So how you been?" Marcus asked.

"Good," I said, standing up.

"I see. I am so proud of you. You really did it. Look around, Kendra. You did it. We used to talk about this."

"Yeah, I know. Isn't life crazy?" I paused for a moment and walked back to the mirror and looked at myself and him through the mirror. He walked closer to me. I turned around as he said, "I've missed you." I didn't respond. It was an uncomfortable silence. Then Marcus said, "I'm so damn proud of you. I be telling everybody at my job, my baby said she was going to do it. And look at you. Then I'm riding down the street and I saw you on the side of the bus. That big picture on your album cover. I was so proud. You know I always believed in you. I just didn't want you to get hurt. I didn't think it was possible," he said as he looked me directly in the eyes. He pulled me into his chest and gave me a hug. It was a long, silent hug. I knew he was sorry. I knew he didn't mean it. I pulled away from him. His presence alone was bringing back memories. Then him apologizing made it hard for me to keep my composure. I felt the tears about to come, so I started fanning my face. I began holding my head back, trying not to mess up my makeup.

"I am so sorry. Look, Kendra, I'm not trying to make you cry. Let's talk about something else. It is so nice to see your mom and Bubbles. I can't believe how she is grown now."

"Yup, she is entering in her third year of college," I said, relieved that I was able to keep the tears back.

"Wow!"

"How is your dad?"

"He is doing good. I'm still trying to get him to stop smoking."

"Mr. Skip ain't letting go of his cigarettes."

"So where are you going next?"

"To Los Angeles. I'm reading for this movie."

"Wow, a movie. You are really doing it."

"I'm trying," I said.

"Maybe we can have dinner when you come back?" Marcus said.

"Okay, I'll see."

John came in the room and said, "Hey, man, what's

up?" and shook Marcus's hand. Then he said, "Kendra, come on." I said goodbye to Taylor and Marcus. He gave me another kiss on the cheek.

"I hope you enjoy the show," John said to Marcus as he pulled me away. Marcus picked up Taylor and had her wave bye to me. Marcus looked so sad; he knew he had messed up with me. I wanted to forgive him and be with him, but I couldn't. His outlook on life was too small. And I wasn't seventeen anymore. I couldn't be with him. He was right there, a part of the dream since the beginning, but he wasn't man enough to stick around to see it manifest. It was too little too late. John was right—he needed a lesser woman to feel like he was in control, and I wasn't the one.

It was time for me to go on. The host introduced me and the crowd applauded loudly. He said, "Philly, welcome home your very own Kendra Michelle." I heard the crowd go crazy. They played the introduction of my song "All I Want" and people started screaming louder. I stood under the stage. They lifted me up to the stage on this crane. My ten dancers ran out on the stage with me. I walked out and stood and put my head down and began to sing. The music was so loud. I could hear the screams through my earplugs. I was in the middle of the stage and yelled into the mic, "It is good to be home. It's good to be here. I have been all around the country, but nothing feels like this." People in the front row were trying to get my attention. I smiled and waved to everybody in the audience. "I see you in the balcony," I said. The yellow, red and purple lights were flashing in my face. I closed my eyes and sang, *"All I want is everything and everything is all I want. Been on this grind since ninety-nine, it's time for me to get mine. I paid my dues. Let me tell you what I've been through. Sometimes life ain't fair. Almost lost my brother in a fire. A long time ago should have retired. But I didn't give up. Dad pulled out, left mom alone. She didn't have nobody else to lean on. She started drinking. Didn't know what she was thinking. I basically raised myself. Going to work and giving her help. Doin' hair and checking homework. People was telling me that it won't work. I didn't listen and now I'm here because all I want is everything. And everything is all I want."* When I opened my eyes I looked out into the crowd of twenty thousand plus. They were yelling my name and singing along with me. I almost forgot my lyrics because I was so excited. I took the mic away from my mouth, and the crowd of thousands completed my next verse. It was an indescribable feeling. I didn't want it to end.

Everything I have been through has kept me grounded, although in my mind I felt like I should have been here years ago. I am happy everything happened the way it did. Sometimes when you are too big too fast, it doesn't last. I am in is for the long haul. I have so much to be grateful for. I'm happy that I have seen the other side of the business. I'm smarter because of it. I value all my hardships, because I know at any time it can all be taken away. But I'm never going back. This feels too good. I want to be a timeless singer. I'm here to stay, like Aretha Franklin, Diana Ross and Patti LaBelle. All I ever wanted is everything, and I'm on my way to getting it.

If you enjoyed ALL I WANT IS EVERYTHING,
read on for a special preview of
Daaimah S. Poole's hot new novel,

SOMEBODY ELSE'S MAN

A Dafina trade paperback, on sale in October 2009!

Prologue

"Your father is dead," my mother's voice said dryly over the phone.

"Huh? What father?" I sat up straight, my heart picking up speed.

"Your biological. He passed away a few days ago." Her tone was calm and casual. I didn't say anything. I think I was in shock.

"Nicole, you there?" she asked.

"Yeah, I'm here," I said as I clutched the phone tight and processed that the man I never got to call father was no longer walking this earth. "How do you know?"

"I read it today in the obituary section of the paper. His funeral is Saturday."

"Really?" I asked, knowing it was true, because after retiring from the post office my mother read the column every day, right after checking her horoscope. Every once in a while she ran across a death notice for someone she knew.

"Well, I have to go. I just thought you should know. I'm going out and Ernest got overtime."

"Okay, I'll call you when I'm on my way home from work," I said as I slumped in my chair, dazed. I loved my mother to death, but why would she think it was a good idea to call me in the middle of my workday and give me that kind of news? She was acting like it was no big deal to tell me that my father is dead. Especially under the circumstances. The circumstance being, I had only seen my father once in my life, back when I was thirteen, and that was fifteen years ago.

I never missed having a father until I was in second grade. I remember my best friend Tia's father coming up to our school and bringing cake, ice cream, and balloons to our classroom for his only daughter's birthday. Tia came back to school on Monday bragging about how she had the best dad in the world. Then this other girl named Felicia joined in and started talking about her father and all the fun they had together. That's when it clicked. Where was *my* dad? But worse than that—who was my dad? I didn't even know his name. I suddenly realized I had never heard his name and didn't have a clue what he looked like. He was completely absent from my life. I had no pictures, and no memories. I couldn't even recognize him if he walked past me on the street. For years I asked my mom who was my dad, and why wasn't he a part of my life, and she would never answer me. One time she told me he was in the army and the next time in the navy. Then she told me he got killed in Vietnam. I believed her until I found out that the war ended before I was born.

When I was thirteen, I begged her to tell me who my father was, like so many time before. She usually would tell me to leave her alone and get the fuck out her face. But this time I didn't leave her alone, because I had to get an answer. I was working her nerves. And just so I would get out her face she finally told me his name. The words came out of her mouth real slow . . . "Ray-mond Haw-k." She would have been better off not telling me his name because once she did, I had more questions. "Where is he? Where does he live? Why doesn't he come around?" I asked breathlessly.

She explained to me that she met him through a friend when she used to hang in south Philly. She told me that he really was in the army and that she had gotten pregnant with me right before he went to basic training. She said by the time he got back from training, she tried to tell him she was pregnant, but she found out he was already married to a woman he met near his base. She said she confided in his cousin and told his cousin to tell him she was pregnant, but she never heard anything from my father, so she left it alone.

I still wasn't satisfied and wanted more information. So, the next day she went to work and I searched through her dresser drawers for my birth certificate. I found it and his name was on it. I went to the white pages and called a few Raymond Hawks. By the time I got to the sixth name I was tired and hoped I didn't get another answering machine. The sixth name on the list was the only address in south Philly. He lived on Wharton Street in a neighborhood where my mom used to hang out. I figured he had to be the right Raymond Hawk.

I rode the number seven bus to south Philly. I felt nervous and excited at the same time. Throughout the bus ride, I couldn't stop thinking about what was going to happen next. I didn't know how my father was going to react to meeting me. I wondered if he would reject me, or would he love me like a father should?

I got off the bus, one block away from his house. I walked up to Twenty-fourth Street and made a left. I saw a store on the corner with a big sign that read Delicatessen, and brick row houses in every direction. I looked at the address and went straight to 2416. Taking a deep breath, I walked up to the top step and knocked on the door. As I waited for someone to answer I became a little nauseous and my palms were dripping sweat. A woman with brown kinky-curled hair answered. Her skin was light brown with specks of freckles scattered on her nose and her cheeks. A pair of black, round glasses sat on the tip of her freckled nose. She was wearing a pink terry cloth robe and blue-and-white flowered nightgown.

"Can I help you?" she asked.

"Uhm, is Raymond Hawk here?"

"What's this about?" Her eyes narrowed suspiciously as they began to rove up and down, peering at me through her black glasses.

"I'm his daughter, Nicole," I said.

"Daughter? Raymond only got one daughter and she's in this house playing with her toys."

"My mother said he is my father." I unfolded the birth certificate that was clutched in my hand.

She bent down and examined my birth certificate. "How old are you?" she asked, breathing hard, her eyes narrowed at me.

"Thirteen," I said, straightening my shoulders.

She flung the birth certificate at me. "That's impossible!" Then she screamed at the top of her lungs, "Raymond, get out here . . . now!"

I got the first glimpse of my father as he came to the door, out of breath. He was a tall, beautiful man with smooth, Indian, deep red-brown skin, like mine.

"Yeah, baby," he said, looking out the white screen door to see why she was yelling.

They both stared down at me and she said, "This young lady says she's your daughter. Is that true?"

He looked at me, startled, and then he started backing up a little as he shook his head, saying, "No. No. I don't know her. She's not my child."

"You sure there's not something you forgot to tell me?" she yelled as she swung out and punched him in his side. He bowed over and she walked away from the door. As he was bent over I recognized even more features that looked just like mine. We had the same straight, black hair, mink eyebrows and long eyelashes.

"Who told you I was your father?" he asked, frowning.

"You dated my mom, Lois Edwards—they call her Lolo. She was friends with one of your cousins." I let out a breath as I waited for his face to change.

"Lois?" He wrinkled his brow and scratched his head. "I don't know anybody named Lois. Look, I'm sorry, I never met your mother in my life. I'm not your father, but I hope you find him." And then he closed the door in my face. I could hear the woman cussing him about me.

Hurt and confused, I stood there for a moment. I thought about knocking on the door again and demanding that he admit that he was my father. But all the lies my mother had told me over the years started swirling around in my head and I decided to just leave.

As I walked back to the bus stop my sadness and disappointment turned to anger. I was in tears for the entire hour-long ride home. I wanted to kill my mother. Why did she insist on lying to me? In my mind my mother was a stupid lying whore. How could she not know who my father was? How could she keep this information from me in the first place? I asked myself those questions until I got off the bus and ran home.

I usually tried to stay out of my mother's way because she was just so evil. But being scared of her didn't stop me from barging into her room and disturbing her nap.

"Mom, how could you? I went to that man's house in south Philly and he said he wasn't my father," I screamed.

"What man!" she said as she jolted upright.

I explained the entire story to her in detail, even throwing in how embarrassing it was to be told he wasn't my father. She didn't even respond to me as I cried and kept asking over and over, "How could you?" When she didn't respond, I ran out of her room in tears.

Ten minutes later, she came out of her bedroom with a baseball bat in her hand and ordered me to get in the car with her. I wasn't sure if I liked the way she planned on handling the situation, but I got in the car and put my seat belt on. What else could I do? We were at Raymond Hawk's door in less than fifteen minutes. I was surprised that my mom knew exactly where he lived. She blew her horn repeatedly in loud, drawn-out stretches. Then she got out of the car, stomped up the steps to his house, and hit the door several times with her balled-up fist. Two children, a girl and a boy, who looked to be about seven or eight years old, peeked out the window.

"Raymond, open this door," my mom yelled. He came to the door with his eyes bugged out, gawking at my mom like he was seeing a ghost.

"Raymond, why did you lie to this child?" my mother demanded.

Instead of answering the question, he walked away and the freckled-faced woman took his place in the doorway.

"He ain't lie to her, he ain't her daddy. He told her the truth," she yelled, with her hand planted on her small hip.

With her nose turned up, my mom looked her up and down and said, "Listen, you need to mind your fucking business. This ain't got shit to do with you."

"It's got a lot to do with me because it is my husband you are talking about," the lady yelled back.

"I don't want your broke-ass husband. I have a man."

The woman didn't have a quick enough response and just stood with her mouth open. The neighbors and other people passing by on the street were beginning to tune in to the screaming match.

"Could you lower your voice?" she asked my mom in a whisper. I could tell she was becoming a little embarrassed that all her business was being put out on the street. "Do you think we could finish this conversation inside the house?" Freckle-face asked, her expression nice and friendly now.

"No, I don't want to come in your house. Tell your husband to come back to this door before he gets a big problem."

Raymond came back to the door and leaned against the doorframe. My mom walked up on him and pointed her finger at the side of his head. Poking him in the temple, she said, "Raymond, one thing you ain't going to do is tell my daughter that I'm a liar." She gripped me by the arm. "This is your daughter and you know it. Now, you asked me to stay away and I did. I don't give a goddamn about you. But you don't ever in your life tell my child that I'm a liar." My mom took a few moments to catch her breath. "Are you her father?" she asked, staring him down.

Freckle-face shot him a dirty look. "*Are* you her father?"

Raymond looked at his wife and then at me. He dropped his head in defeat and then looked up at my mother. "Yes, I am her father," he said with a sigh. "Now leave, Lois, and stop causing a scene in front of my family."

His wife looked like she wanted to faint. The two little children were peeking out the window, their eyes wide with shock. Freckle-face wasn't trying to hear what Raymond had just admitted. She sucked her teeth and shook her head. "Raymond, you know damn well you ain't got no other daughter. Your family is right here in this house." She turned evil eyes on my mom. "I hope you don't think you're going to be getting any of our money. My husband ain't never going to take care of that child of yours."

My mom looked like she was about to go off on Raymond's wife. I could tell she wished she had brought that baseball bat out of the car so she could smash some windows and bash Freckle-face upside her head.

"You ain't got no damn money," my mom exploded.

"My daughter is very well taken care of. She don't need y'all for shit. And it will be a cold day in hell before she ever contacts you for anything."

And that was the last I saw of Raymond Hawk. No birthdays, no Christmases, no graduations. I never spoke about that day. I knew it was a touchy subject, something I wasn't supposed to discuss ever again.

Over the years, I have had countless vivid dreams about my father. Sometimes I would be so mad when I awoke because it seemed so real. Now, he was dead. I took a long sigh. I just couldn't believe it. I really wasn't ever going to get to know him.

I knew he wasn't a part of my life growing up, but for some reason I always thought that our paths would cross again. I had hoped we would get a chance to talk. I imagined, actually I prayed, that one day he would come to his senses and claim me as his daughter. If he'd only taken the time to get to known me, he would have liked me and seen how good I am. But that day will never happen. I will never know him and he will never know me.

Chapter 1

I sat at my desk, motionless for a few minutes, still in shock. Then I grabbed a tissue and wiped the falling tears. I cried so hard, the collar of my teal-blue jacket was becoming soaked. Needing someone to talk to, I reached for the phone and called my best friend to tell her the news.

"Tia, my mom just called me and said that my dad died."

"You okay?"

"Yeah." Sniffling, I stood up and closed my office door.

"You want me to go to the funeral with you?"

"No, I'm not going," I said as a few more tears trickled down my cheek. A tap on my office door signaled me to pull it together. I was still at work and had to keep it professional.

"Nicole, a guest would like to speak to you," Maritza said.

I sighed. I really didn't feel like talking to anyone.

"Get Ryan, I'm in the middle of something."

"He told me to get you." Maritza sounded frustrated.

"Okay, give me the room number and tell the guest I'll call in a few minutes." *I hate hotel guests!* I thought. They got on my damn nerves. I didn't have time for that shit today.

Maritza said she'd relay my message. She left, but a few minutes later she was right back in my office. "He said it is very important and needs to speak with you now," Maritza said, sounding distressed.

"I'll call you back, Tia." I hung up the phone and then walked down the hall to my manager, Ryan Greene's, office. He was online, playing poker. Ryan's from the West Coast and is very laid back—too laid back to be a manager of a hotel. With curly brown hair and light ocean-blue eyes, Ryan was cute, but being that he was such an asshole, he might as well have been ugly.

"Why do you try to make me deal with all the crazy, disgruntled guests? It's your turn," I yelled.

"Because you are better at it than I am. Plus, all the time and effort it took you to come in here, you could already have solved the guest problem. Right?" He turned back to playing poker.

At that moment, Maritza rushed into Ryan's office. "Please, will one of you come out and deal with this? They are really angry."

"Okay, I'll be right there," I said with a sigh. I walked back to my office and got some more tissues and blew my nose.

As I went to the lobby and approached the front desk, an upset Pakistani man asked with a heavy accent, "Are you the manager?"

"I'm the assistant manager. What seems to be the problem, sir?"

"I just checked into room 309 and the room . . . Never mind, just explain something, please. I can't quite understand why there is a used condom in my bed."

I was just as shocked as he was. "A used condom?" I repeated, dumbfounded. I shook my head. I really didn't have an answer for him, so I just jumped on the computer and began searching for another room.

He continued to ramble on, saying, "Very disgusting, no one cleaned my room. My wife and my child can't sleep in a dirty bed."

I looked over at his wife, who had a gold earring in her nose. Her hair was parted on the side and pulled back into a bun. She was wearing traditional blue-and-gold garb and had a baby hoisted on her hip. Seeing her and the baby made me feel even worse. I kept trying to see if there were any other rooms available, but every room in the hotel was filled.

The Pakistani man and his wife started going back and forth, speaking in their language. I couldn't understand a word they were saying, but judging by the tone of their conversation, I could tell they were becoming very upset.

"Sir! Listen, just give me one more moment," I said, hoping to calm them down. Finally, I found a room and quickly made a key. I came from behind the desk, apologized, and offered to walk the couple upstairs to inspect their room.

"Has this room been cleaned? I don't want another dirty room."

"Yes, sir. It's clean and I upgraded you to a suite," I said and apologized again.

He spoke again with his wife in their native language, and then began to pick up their luggage, indicating that they would accept their new room. With a walkie-talkie in hand, I escorted the couple to the room and we inspected it together.

He was a little calmer and thanked me. After I exited his room, I got on the walkie-talkie and asked the head of housekeeping to meet me in the laundry room.

This was a normal day at Choice Springs Hotel. I'm

the operations manager and have been on the verge of quitting for the last two years. The hotel is located at the Philadelphia International Airport and we got a lot of convention traffic as well as people coming into town for business meetings.

Choice Springs is a franchise that's owned by a mega-rich family from Dallas, Texas. We don't report to a corporate headquarters, and most problems are handled internally, which means we don't handle anything. Most days are easy, but boring at the same time. I like to keep my door half-closed so I can play around online, forwarding e-mails to my friends, watching YouTube clips and Googling anything and everything that pops into my mind.

I do work from time to time. Every now and then I respond to a complaint or two. I come to work every day, but I do as little as possible. I don't get paid enough to work myself into a sweat. On the flip side, there are not many jobs at places that are open twenty-four hours a day, seven days a week, and even open on holidays. I kind of want to find a better job, but I don't know anyone who would quit a job that's as easy as mine.

I entered the laundry room in the housekeeping department. Rows and rows of white sheets and towels were everywhere and the loud dryer was making the entire room hot. Ms. Annette was on the phone as I entered her cramped office. I waited as she gave me the *one-minute* sign with her big chunky finger. After she completed her call, she turned and said, "What's the dilmo?"

I held back from correcting her and saying dilemma, because she would just shrug and say *Whatever . . . you know what I mean.* She was the kind of person that would argue you down even when she was wrong.

"Ms. Annette, who cleaned room 309 yesterday?"

"I have to check. Why? What's wrong?"

"I just had a guest complain about finding a used condom in the bed."

Ms. Annette looked down at her clipboard and said, "Oh, Crystal cleaned that room. She needs to get fired because this is the third time she didn't properly clean one of her rooms. Plus, she smokes weed during her break with her purple-lipped self."

"I need you to pull Crystal's file," I said, before Ms. Annette went on any further about Crystal. "And tell Crystal to come to the front desk."

There was no union at the hotel. We were at-will property and Crystal was about to be fired. But first I had to hear what she had to say. She was called down from the third floor.

I told Ryan what happened. He didn't like doing any other work, but when it was time to fire somebody he was ready and willing. He clapped his hands twice. "I'll handle Crystal," he said. I handed him her record and watched him swiveling back and forth in his chair as he practiced how he was going to fire her. Firing someone was the worst part of my job, and Ryan's favorite.

Crystal strolled into Ryan's office. Her hair was in long braids and she was swinging her hair off her neck. She had various colored tattoos from her neck to her fingertips. Her eyes were going from my face to Ryan's, and I could tell she was trying to read our expressions to see what we were going to say.

"Crystal, you cleaned room 309 yesterday and it wasn't up to the hotel's standards and—" Before I could complete my sentence she stuttered, "I wanted to say I like this hotel, it is nice and I want to stay here and I shouldn't be fired because I'm not the only one popping sheets. Everybody is doing it."

"What exactly is popping sheets?" I asked.

"You know, like you take the ends of the sheet and hold it up and flip twice and everything like hair and stuff falls off the sheet. But everybody is really doing it."

"Well, Crystal, you got caught and everybody else will be warned about following policy in this hotel, but I'm sorry to say, we are going to have to let you go. Today is your last day." Ryan spoke with such authority and conviction, you would have thought he was Donald Trump yelling *You're fired.*

"Okay," Crystal responded and then started crying. I handed her a few tissues. Ryan walked out of the office to hold a meeting with the rest of the housekeeping department. I felt bad as I walked Crystal to the back to empty out her locker, but there was nothing I could do. I felt her pain. I was going through a lot of shit, too.

After that episode I went back to my office and closed the door. My mind started racing again. I swear, when it rains it really pours. That's the only thing that could explain what was going on in my life recently. I wasn't having any luck lately in love, I hated my job, and my family sucked. My last two long-term relationships were with men who were already taken. And neither situation was my fault entirely. I met the first unavailable man on a dating Web site. We'd been dating for a year before I found out about his wife. She worked at night, and one day decided to play detective and followed him to my house. Needless to say, that relationship was over. I don't know why I didn't see the signs. He never took me to his house. I knew where he lived, but he always said he liked it better at my apartment.

I met the second no-good liar at a singles club. He was there with his single friends. I started dating Malcolm Walker, only to find out he was separated. He said he was getting a divorce, but during the course of us falling in love, he went back to his wife because she was pregnant. I was so upset with him, but not angry enough to leave him alone. My selfish side wouldn't allow me to stop loving him. However, three months ago I came to the conclusion that I could no longer be his side piece. I dated him for three of his five years of marriage. Leaving him alone has been one of the hardest things I ever had to do in my life. Just imagine . . . you meet your soul mate . . . you have long talks and walks and you come to the realization that he is the man you want to spend your life with . . . you find out that he is already married.

Yes, he had to go. I was tired of singing Whitney Houston's "Saving All My Love For You." The hell with that. Besides, it wasn't like I was living the mistress life—set up nice and living good. I hate to admit it, but I paid for most of our dates. At one point, I was even putting gas in his car, trying to help him out because he had to pay his car note and his son's day-care bill. Most of the time Malcolm's bank account read *insufficient funds.* It didn't matter though, because I loved him. I would even get us discounted rooms at hotels. Initially, I didn't feel like I was getting used. I thought I was helping out a friend. But with all I was doing for him, he couldn't do the one thing I wanted him to do for me, which was leave his wife and marry me. And things haven't always been this way. When we first met he was so good to me. I think that is part of the reason I was staying around, because I thought one day, when he left her, he would go back to being the man I met and fell in love with.

Since I left Malcolm alone, it seemed like karma was punishing me for messing with another woman's husband for all those years. Because since I have been a "real single girl," I hadn't been able to find anyone. Not one good prospect for a boyfriend. It's hard trying to do the right thing, because at any point I could be vulnerable and go back to Malcolm. He calls me every few days and tells me how much he still loves me, on my answering machine. He says he knows that I deserve better and that he didn't expect me to wait forever. He also said he knows he was being selfish, but he couldn't let me go even though he understands how I feel, and wishes I would be a little more patient with him.

It's sad because I want to be there for him—I want to be his everything, but I just can't take being number two anymore.

On the morning of the funeral, I decided an hour before that I wanted to go. I just felt like I needed to be there. I had to see him one last time and say good-bye. I threw on a black shirt and black jeans, and barely brushed my hair. I put on my big black down coat, hat, gloves and drove straight to the church. I didn't care how I looked, I had to say good-bye. I felt that if I said good-bye, it might heal all the pain and sadness I had trapped inside of me ever since I was a little girl.

The big church sat at the corner of a large intersection. There were several black Town Car limos and a hearse in front of the door. An older man opened the door to the church and handed me an obituary. He told me I could stand in the back because all the seats were filled. There were people of all ages dressed in variations of black. A woman's voice bellowed from the front row. I looked around and saw sad people in every direction. I was crying too, but not for the same reason as the others. My tears were not tears of sorrow. I was crying because I was mad. I was mad as hell because my father had never been here for me. I was mad because he gave me life, but was never a part of my life. *I hate you! I hate you! I hate you!* I screamed internally. If it were possible, I would have brought him back to life just so I could kill him again. But at the age of fifty, he'd had a heart attack before I could get to him.

The preacher read the eulogy and then the funeral was over. Feeling really nervous, I got in line to view the body. I didn't know what I was going to do when I got up there.

The line moved closer to the casket. I had so many thoughts running through my head. I stopped feeling angry and started to feel sad. Very sad. I saw his wife in the front row out of the corner of my eye. She was heavier than I remembered, but still had those freckles. She had on a big black hat over her reddish-brown colored spiral curls. Her chest was heaving up and down as she cried. For a millisecond, I felt sorry for her. Then she looked over at me and stared like she was trying to figure out where she knew me from. She must have figured it out because she suddenly gave me this wicked look and I turned away. Her evil-ass look invoked old memories and fears.

Finally, I was next up to the coffin and I told myself I wasn't going to break down, but the closer I came to the casket, the harder it became to hold back my tears. I approached the white-and-silver casket and saw Raymond Hawk. He was wearing a black suit and a white shirt. I touched his cold hand and began crying harder. I mean real hard. I don't know what it was, but something about that organ playing made me lose it. I was making the line stand still by crying uncontrollably. It was my last glimpse of him and my last conversation with him. I started talking to him, quietly asking, "Why? Why, Dad? Why didn't you love me?" I asked "Why?" so many times, like he could hear me and was going to give me an answer. They patted me to move forward. I got myself together enough to leave his side. I wanted to run, but I couldn't. I had to walk out of that church with dignity. But while I was walking, my legs began wobbling. Luckily, they didn't give out. I made it to the bathroom door and bent over crying by the radiator. I could not stop crying.

An older woman walked over to me and said, "Baby, it's okay." She hugged me close, trying to comfort me. "It's okay," she said again. "He is one of God's angels, now." I almost laughed in her face as I thanked her and ran out of the church.